ON
WINE-DARK
SEAS

"Tad Crawford has excavated literary treasure from the fragments of epics that continued the stories of *The Iliad* and *The Odyssey*. Channeling the voice of Telemachus, son of Odysseus, he conjures up a lost world of gods and heroes in a towering triumph of poetic imagination. He somehow makes the distant past as real and present as the back of your hand, and as entertaining and compelling as the epics were to the Greeks of old."

—Christopher Vogler, author of *The Writer's Journey: Mythic Structure for Writers*

"The Homeric spirit, alive and productive, can reside in a modern author. That author is Tad Crawford, the story he tells is an inspired one narrated by Odysseus's son, Telemachus, to the poet Phemios, not in the language of modern day, but as if mentored by the spirit of Homer in words and images that *sing* as in ancient times, close to nature, alive with gods. I urge you to read this book, but not just with your eyes. Read it aloud, so that it immerses your ears and engages your tongue with sounds uncommonly heard these days but sounds that carry a clarion call to what we have lost from the past but sorely need for the future. Bravo!"

—Russell Lockhart, author of *Psyche Speaks and Words as Eggs*

ON WINE-DARK SEAS

A NOVEL OF ODYSSEUS AND HIS FATHERLESS SON TELEMACHUS

TAD CRAWFORD

Arcade Publishing
New York

Arcade Publishing books may be purchased in bulk at special discounts for sales promotion, corporate gifts, fund-raising, or educational purposes. Special editions can also be created to specifications. For details, contact the Special Sales Department, Arcade Publishing, 307 West 36th Street, 11th Floor, New York, NY 10018 or arcade@skyhorsepublishing.com.

Arcade Publishing® is a registered trademark of Skyhorse Publishing, Inc.®, a Delaware corporation.

Visit our website at www.arcadepub.com.

10 9 8 7 6 5 4 3 2 1

Library of Congress Cataloging-in-Publication Data is available on file.

Cover design by Mary Belibasakis
Cover image is the painting *Slaughter of the Suitors* by Thomas Degeorge. Dating to 1812, it is in the public domain and was accessed and downloaded on Wikimedia Commons: https://creativecommons.org/licenses/by-sa/3.0/legalcode

Print ISBN: 978-1-5107-7257-1
Ebook ISBN: 978-1-5107-7258-8

Printed in the United States of America

Note to the Reader

The Trojan Cycle is far more extensive than either *The Iliad* or *The Odyssey*. In the centuries following Homer, other authors fashioned six more epics which, unfortunately, survive only in fragments. *On Wine-Dark Seas* scrupulously portrays the little we know from the Trojan Cycle while enlarging the human dramas of characters made famous for all time by Homer's epics. A Glossary of Names and Places begins on page 213, an essay, "*On Wine-Dark Seas*: Sources and Reflections," starts on page 231, and maps of Ithaca and the Mycenean world at the time of Odysseus's return to his home commence on page 255.

CHAPTER 1

Phemios, I have lived my life enduring a hatred and odium that few men suffer. On this stony and barren island to which my father returned from the embraces of divine women and the Underworld itself, I have since manhood known nothing but the evil eye, the muttered calumny, and a sullen obedience that slaves might offer in fear of the overseer's fists. Innumerable times I wished I had followed you on the boundless oceans of the world. I might have traveled to Egypt, where Menelaos himself spent seven years as a merchant on his long return with Helen from Troy. But I would no more abandon Ithaca than leave a child whom I loved.

My famed father, godlike Odysseus, cared little for the odium he and I would suffer for slaying my mother's suitors. He considered those men to be like his enemies at Troy and slew them without even exulting in their deaths. We paid the fortune that Odysseus had hidden to the suitors' families to end the blood feud, but gold and silver cannot bring tranquility or forgetting. My father died at an age when men have lost everything—friends, enemies, the memories of life itself. Twenty years had passed since he returned to Ithaca and enlisted me in his killing of the suitors. Despite this, each of the hundred suitors had relatives who donned black robes for my father's funeral. You might imagine they had come to gloat over his corpse or curse him one final time. But I have never seen such grief, as if the black plume of smoke from my father's pyre carried off the souls of the survivors as well. Soon I realized their grief poured out for the loved ones whom Odysseus and I had slain. I saw the sister of Amphinomos pitch herself among the jagged stones. When another bent to raise her, she pulled her whitened hair and cried her brother's name.

I remember Amphinomos with light in his eyes. He was so fine a man that even Odysseus warned him against his fate. When my spear roosted between his shoulders, he trembled like a sleepwalker trying to wake. He knelt as if before a shrine, as if he might rise again.

All up the skyward-seeking path among the goatherds, the keening of the mourners never ceased. The small clan that grieved for Odysseus seemed lost among these others who longed for loved ones lost on the expedition to Troy or slain by the great tactician on his return. When my father died, I sent my messengers seeking you. You are a poet of both love and war. As a youth I stirred to your account of the heroes who fought at Troy. My father will be known to the future not as the man he was, but as the man of whom you sing. Often at Troy he called himself "the father of Telemachus," so I too have a part to speak in his story. Wealthy men can pay some poets to chant a story first this way, then another. I cannot offer you wealth to hear me, but only the truth I know.

CHAPTER 2

M y earliest memories are of the boats loading by the quay. I would wake before dawn and rush to the harbor to watch the men fill the hoists and loft the supplies into the dark holds. Goats, gourds of wine, dates, amphorae filled with olive oil, fodder— whatever our islands might harvest or earn by trade. Gradually the ships would rest more deeply in the calm harbor, as if their bellies held new life. These supply ships carried the life of our islands to our soldiers fighting in distant Troy. When I was a child, I heard talk only of victory and the pride with which Ithaca and our band of islands had sent Odysseus forth.

The women, including my mother Penelope, would climb the long path up Mount Neriton. Each day they hoped to raise their cries of joy for the sails of the returning fleet. But as the years passed, the women forsook that lookout from which the bay and channel lie bare.

They had chores to do in their homes and few men to help them. Perhaps one woman might be seen there, solitary and staring into the empty distances. I often accompanied my mother. She would point me first in one direction, then another, trusting in my young eyes to see what hers might miss. If I cried out for a sail, she would hold me as if to smother my very life. Of course, these sails were never the fleet from Troy, but perhaps a trader or our own supply ships returning home with more news of the dismal siege.

My mother had her inner vision to comfort her on our long vigils. When her eyes found a waste of empty sea, her heart had already brought her husband home. She cherished him like an inner flame and served her lookout hours in patient dreaming. Often, she would speak to me of my father in such terms that I could only hope someday to be such a man as Odysseus. In our great hall, where later the hundred suitors feasted, I would play with sticks for the walls of Troy and stones for the thousands of Greeks who besieged them. How easily godlike Odysseus in his chariot of gold breached these childish walls. How pitiably did King Priam and Hector and the women of Troy plead for mercy from Odysseus's hands. How often did I imagine that day when he would at last return triumphant to his hearth.

During my father's long absence, I started to hear cruel rumors explaining why Odysseus led our islanders to fight at Troy. I had always believed he fought reluctantly. But some men claimed he feigned insanity when King Agamemnon came to ask him to join the Greeks. That he had so little mettle he wept and could not leave his wife and son.

Only by a clever trick did Palamedes uncover this deception. If you believe these lies, why not believe Odysseus took revenge on Palamedes and murdered him cold-bloodedly at Troy?

The very men who cursed him for being slow to join the alliance of the Greeks cursed him as well for his motives in going. They claimed he left a rich kingdom to seek for plunder he did not need. Or he envied his father, Laertes, for having stormed the walled city of Nerikos and wanted to surpass that feat. Or Odysseus, as a losing suitor for Helen, fought only because of the vow taken by all the suitors to defend her marriage.

I would have sworn to you these rumors and more that I heard were calumnies. I believed my father cared nothing for glory or plunder. He had the respect of every man on this island and a wealthy farm to meet his needs. Nor did he compete with Laertes, who had long since given the kingdom to Odysseus and retired to his own farm to command his herders. When Agamemnon pled with my father to go to Troy, my mother told me Odysseus wanted our islands to stand in their rightful place among the kingdoms of Greece. In this Greek alliance he saw a hope for peace enduring many years after the fall of Troy.

I remember one battle of which you sang, when Hector's greatness let Trojans breach the Grecian earthworks and drive the Greeks in panic toward their ships. Achilles sat in his tent and cared nothing for the ships burning on the beachhead. Great Agamemnon let the Trojans see his noble back as he ran to launch his plunder-filled ships for home. Quaking, he cried to his allies to save their skins and abandon the battle. Your songs were an education to me in the follies of men.

Only my father Odysseus turned the Greeks again to the battle. Only Odysseus cared for the shame that would forever follow the Greek armies in their rout. Only Odysseus remembered the alliance and the cause that would be lost. As the men-at-arms turned their backs to the Trojans, he exhorted and rallied them to face the enemy. Is this the act of a weakling or a man who cares only for plunder?

By the time Troy fell, it seemed Ithaca had been besieged for ten years. Our wealth and the harvests of each year had gone to our armies overseas. If the name of Troy passed a woman's lips, it would be spoken like a curse. The pride for Ithaca's standing in the alliance had long been forgotten. Each day desire haunted us. We no longer wanted one gift or the realization of a single hope. It would not be enough to bring home the father of this one or the husband of another. We craved a far greater reward to quiet these years of needing. If you felt a divine compulsion to sing and yet had no words for your saga, then you can imagine what our lives had become.

Those first ten years were terrible, yet worse followed. Poseidon refused our armies a passage home. Despair filled us all, for when has a victorious army been so vanquished? Only the gods could multiply the suffering we had already endured. If our men-at-arms had died and the burial rites been spoken, we might have learned to accept our lives. But we no longer knew what to hope. Ten years we had longed for the war to end. Now it had ended, but hope itself seemed to vanish with our armies. Each day might bring the fleet to our sheltered harbor, but we ceased looking to the sea. Why pray any longer when Zeus certainly had turned a deaf ear to our entreaties?

After seven years like these, the suitors began to gather in our hall. First came Antinoös, who had escaped service in Troy by the wealth of his father, Eupeithes. My mother refused his offers to wed, but others joined him—Eurymakhos, Agelaos, Ktesippos, and a hundred more. Soon the hall where I had played as a child echoed with the laughter of strangers feasting on the stores Odysseus had kept in our large cellars. My mother worked calmly at her loom while the suitors caroused and hoped to supplant Odysseus in his home and in her heart.

I came to know the suitors and I shall speak more of that later. You might imagine these princes had better tasks to achieve. But they seemed as lost as our fleet and yearned for any new hope. I admit I too fell under their sway, for I was a youth and longed for the company of men. They brought you to the island to sing, Phemios, and I had never heard such wonders as those of which you told. If they stayed against the will of my mother, and kept you against your own will, at least they showed a love for her beauty and your songs. In their contests and trials of arms, I enjoyed a fellowship I had never hoped to have. I felt the great hall filled with my elder brothers who included me in their pranks, feasts, and competitions. We could fatten what remained of my father's herds and forget the laden ships launched for Troy. If our feasting offended against my absent father or the gods to whom we seldom made offerings, I paid a price for my joy.

At last, Antinoös, who led the suitors in their revels, insisted my mother finish her weaving and select her new husband. You remember how Melantho, the maidservant, had told him Penelope unwove her tapestry each evening with the same patience she wove it each day. Seeing my mother's wedding day approach, I fled to the courts of Nestor and Menelaos to seek word of my father. But I had no hope he lived. If a ship with a fair wind can sail from Ithaca to Troy in ten days, how could it have taken my father ten years to return? Only I could defend my mother and my patrimony against these suitors.

I sought King Menelaos as an ally. Seated on my lesser throne near his great one, I exclaimed in amazement at the silver, the gold, the rich-woven tapestries, and the slave girls of every exotic race. The red-haired king wore a crown of gold and jewels peaked by four enormous bull's horns. Necklaces of gold bedecked his huge chest and diamonds covered the thick belt clasped about his immense girth. He liked reclining in his cushioned throne, which could have served as a lovers' bower for a man and a woman of normal size. When he struggled to his feet, his scarlet jowls rippling and his breath racing in his throat, his slaves would cover him with the black pelt of a bear. A great hunter—certainly not Menelaos—must have guided home the arrow that killed such a prize. So Menelaos

7

in gold and diamonds, horned as a bull and pelted as a bear, presided over the rich court of Argos. When I told him he dressed like a god, he modestly denied his luxuries could compare to theirs. Being a youth and naive, I lived in Menelaos's glorious deeds at Troy and imagined him still to be the heroic lord of the war cry who had driven Paris from the field.

How strange I find those brother kings, Agamemnon and Menelaos. Agamemnon besieged Troy for ten years because Helen had been stolen from his brother. Yet Agamemnon took beautiful Briseis when she belonged to Achilles. No man should lose a bride as Menelaos lost Helen, or lose not only a bride but also his life as did Agamemnon. But these men saw right only when it suited them. Were my pleas to Menelaos different from those that made Odysseus seek to bring Helen back from Troy? Just as my father had been lost fighting for Menelaos's stolen bride, I expected Menelaos to offer me men and arms to defend the bride of Odysseus. I spoke of the shame of our hall besieged by suitors and my certainty that my mother would be forced to marry against her will. If Menelaos's beaked warships merely appeared in our harbor, I knew the suitors would slink away. Menelaos reclined on his opulent throne and measured each grape in his thick fingers before dropping it on his palate.

I never imagined he would send me home empty-handed to the murderous suitors. If he had forgotten my father's name, I would have been no more surprised. He wept for Odysseus, whom he swore to have loved and cherished above all others. My heart felt buoyant to hear him. He spoke of giving Odysseus a domain to rule in Argos, if my father had not been lost at sea. Sizing me up like a common merchant in the market square, he offered me a chariot, three of his finest horses, and a golden cup so I would remember him in the reveries of wine. I knew he gave these gifts in place of sending soldiers home with me. I refused them, but at length accepted a small cup of silver from fear he would insist I remain another twelve days in Argos and leave my mother to her fate.

Then Helen remembered my father as a beggar sneaking within the walls of Troy. She claimed to have bathed, anointed, and protected Odysseus. Brazenly she dared say my father told her the plans and disposition of the Greek armies. Not even Menelaos believed this story, and he mildly recalled how Helen tried to betray the Greek soldiers concealed in the wooden horse. Walking outside the horse, she used her gift of mimicry to call to each man in the voice of his wife. She acted as a faithful wife to all those heroes when she could not be a faithful wife to one.

Helen brought out a wedding gown, perhaps like the one she had once worn and later dishonored. Not content with saying it was for my bride and my joyful wedding days, she implored me to have my mother Penelope guard this gown in her bedroom. How Helen must have despised me. She should simply have called me a suitor and sent me home to marry my own mother! She hated all the Greeks for rescuing her from the raptures of Deïphobos's scented bed and returning her to brutish Menelaos. Especially she wanted revenge on Odysseus for the wily trick by which he enticed Troy to dismantle her walls. Smiling, she wished me a speedy journey home to where the suitors waited to slaughter me. And each night she mixed a potion of forgetting in our wine, so that I might not remember the terror in my hall and my rightful claims as heir of Odysseus.

Then I raged against my father and cursed him for a fool. Of all the causes for which he might have struggled, the return of this glutton's queen struck me as madness. I thanked the royal couple for their gifts. When Helen divined that my father lived and would in fury reclaim his patrimony, I swore to remember her as a goddess. For I turned homeward in despair and cared little for the niceties of truth. You mixed with the suitors and heard their plans to kill me. I

9

hoped only to spare my mother from marrying Antinoös, the worst of them. If I could slay him, I would go happily into the gloom of the Underworld and embrace my famed father at last.

CHAPTER 3

Everyone knows how I evaded Antinoös and his gang as they waited by the islet of Asteris, but you couldn't know the turmoil in my heart. As a child, the mere idea my father might have died brought tears to my eyes. For hours I would imagine the many ways death might have found him—pricked by Paris's devious arrow or crushed by the boulders tumbled down from the high Trojan walls. At the same time, within a moment of my most fearful thoughts, I would imagine my father stepping lightly from his warship. From his helmet of golden bronze would rise a vermillion plume. A great scarlet cape, silver-threaded, would flow in layers over his silken tunic to his leggings and sandals of finely worked leather. From the wide sash of blue about his waist would hang the sheathed blade by which he had lived. Since I had never known him, I would recognize him not by his face or the hard-muscled body that had been husband so long to war and dangerous journeys, but by the light within. When I would speak the name "Odysseus," to which no one had ever replied, he would embrace me, and we would weep together at last.

The winds billowed in my sails as I bore down the running waves toward Ithaca. At moments fear overcame me, and I doubted my resolve. Whether I lived or died, my mother would marry. Her ruses and refusals had merely given the suitors a pretext to feast on the estate that should be mine. Perhaps I should have remained a guest of Menelaos or Nestor and returned after the wedding day. After all, isn't it natural for a widow to be courted? If the suitors slept with the maidservants and feasted too long on the cattle and wine, should I add the sacrifice of my life to this shame?

I imagine all men feel these torments. Hector, the finest of the Trojans, ran from Achilles in fear. How quickly I might regret my courage and flee from Antinoös. Or fling my arms about his knees and beg him to remember when Odysseus saved his piratical father from the rage of the Thesprotians. That long night I studied the map of the stars overhead, thinking I should sail on toward the rimless edge of the world and forget this home of sorrow.

Instead, I formed a plan. Among the suitors were far better men than Antinoös, men like Amphinomos, Agelaos, and Leodes, who merely sought a bride. If I could provoke Antinoös to try to kill me in front of the suitors, Amphinomos and the others might come to my aid or, by the gods' glory, I might slay Antinoös in my father's hall. Then I would bring my case before the assembly of all the Greek allies who fought at Troy. If they owed any man a debt for his allegiance, it was Odysseus. I would demand the death of Antinoös and restitution from the rest of the suitors for what they had consumed in their revels. By the time I had sailed wide of Asteris and secretly set foot again on Ithaca, I cursed the poverty of my cunning and thought only of the means to kill Antinoös.

I wonder what might have happened with this plan of mine. Would I have gone early to my death or lived a hero in my land? If I had lived, might I have been beloved and admired by my neighbors? These possibilities I tossed in a beggar's cup.

I had gone directly to the cottage of our shepherd, Eumaios, a fine servant who had belonged to our family since long before my birth. It was there I met a man who reminded me at once of the beggar Helen had described meeting in Troy. Eumaios with his kind heart had believed a bit of this crafty beggar's story and sketched it for me quickly enough. The man claimed to have only recently escaped from the Thesprotians, the very same allies who had once wished to hang Antinoös's father. This story alone should have turned me against the man, but I thought of Helen and my heart went out to him. What reversals of fortune can afflict us all. Even my father Odysseus might once have pretended to be one of the earth's outcasts. And, although I wore a fine cloak, how did my suffering and my exile from my own hall differ from what this man might have undergone?

The beggar had tossed himself on a pallet of straw near the torch. He wore such soiled wrappings about his waist that even a slave would have disdained them. His tunic was also filthy and in tatters, but the most repulsive aspect of his wardrobe was the reindeer pelt he wore as a cloak. Mange had rotted the skin, so it hung threadbare and discolored. I can't imagine it offered any warmth or even a shield against the cold wind. His bare chest had hollowed with illness and a terrible scar spread from nipple to nipple. Dirt clotted on the gray hair covering his chest and shoulders. About his long and furtive face fell sparse, matted locks. The lean cheeks gave him a look of hunger, even after he had feasted on roast pork, bread, and a beaker of our hearty wine. When he spoke, his yellow teeth looked broken, like the ravaged jaw of some dying dog. A horrible disproportion had made the trunk of his body far longer than his legs. He might have been a dwarf had he been very much shorter. His eyes moved constantly, as if he expected to be struck by friends and enemies alike. Never for a moment did he look directly at either me or the shepherd. And from the way he constantly scratched himself and the pungence I smelled off him despite the mist of smoke in Eumaios's cottage, I knew the meanness of his life.

Like so many others, he claimed to have fought beside Odysseus at Troy. The sword scars on his shield shoulder and the jagged tears on his chest and above his left knee showed me he had no doubt been a soldier or a pirate. What tales wheezed from his lungs! On patrol with Odysseus, he left his cloak in the camp and in the early morning hours feared he would die of the cold. Eumaios had already heard this story, but the fellow must have prized it highly and repeated it again. I knew he would make his way to our hall and tell it yet another time for my mother, who would reward him with a hot meal and a night's shelter as she had blessed so many other vagabonds. In any case, with teeth chattering he told my father he could not survive the night without a cloak. To help this careless fellow, Odysseus lied to his men and told them that in a dreadful dream he had seen their small patrol slaughtered to the last man. He asked for a volunteer to run to the beachhead for reinforcements. A noble youth, Thoas, tossed down his cape and raced for the ships. This beggar wrapped himself in the youth's warm cloak and slumbered close by Odysseus through the night.

My blood ran hot to hear the fellow. I felt my father would no more have lied about a dream than he would have insulted a shrine of Athena. Aren't dreams the vessel of our divinity? Many men accused my father of lying, but this beggar's story showed my father lying merely for the sake of the lie. Why should he have done that? Or lied to harm his family, his friends, or his allies? He lied to defeat his enemies; he lied in service to his own honor and his allegiances. What, they say, was the Trojan horse but a lie? In truth, they could have stormed the Trojan walls for eternity and never breached them, except that my father deceived the Trojans. I have even heard men shame Odysseus for his disguise when he returned to his own hall. In truth, of course, the men who utter such remarks never saw the walls of Troy and never returned to face the suitors in their halls.

That night in Eumaios's cottage, I felt a bottomless revulsion for this stinking beggar. Much as I despised his appearance, I hated his stories about my father far more. I didn't believe such a fantastical liar could have known my father or served with him in the war. If Odysseus had a man to spare from the patrol, he could have simply sent this beggar back to the ships on some errand. Through all of these wild imaginings, I believed the beggar merely wanted a fresh cloth for his waist, or at most a tunic and a woolen cloak. Willingly would I have given these to him and more—a sword and sandals—if he would only have continued his wandering and left me to brood. I dispatched Eumaios to tell my mother of my safe return. Her servant Eurykleia could carry this news to Grandfather Laertes, who had been ill with fear for my safety.

The beggar trailed after Eumaios to the gate and watched him vanish on the dark path. In the forest a wolf howled while nearby a sheepdog whimpered. When the beggar turned to me again, he looked larger and far fiercer. I trembled to see the wildness in his eyes and wished I could call Eumaios back. Had the suitors hired him for their ugly work? He came quickly toward me—his bearing and stride like a soldier's—and I cried out to him:

"Remember my offerings of food, shelter, and a cloak of wool. Be merciful, stranger."

"Fear nothing from me," he answered and embraced me roughly. "I am your father."

"You filthy beggar, let go of me!" If I could have freed myself from his grasp, I'd have killed him on the spot. "I believe you were once a soldier by the look of violence on you. But you'll never be my father in this world."

Odysseus stepped away from me and searched in my eyes. "I am the only father you shall ever know, the only father who shall ever return to you. My anguish and wandering will soon end. Act like a prince and not one of those cowardly suitors who tremble at the thought of my return. Accept me as I am."

I wept with humiliation. I put my arms around him. He held me to his unknown body and wept with me. But I couldn't forget my fine dreams of an upright warrior who shone like a god. He spoke of the pain of our separation, but I felt my pain far greater than his. As I listened longer, I marveled to think this was the man who had in truth performed such prodigious deeds at Troy. Except for this man, Helen would have never returned to Argos. Except for Odysseus, the Greek armies would have been routed and the walls of Troy would have stood forever. What was my complaint, I asked myself. That he didn't look like a hero? He had conceived the wooden horse and sprung from its womb in a new and violent birth. I felt ashamed of wanting the image of another man, the man who shone with spirit.

When the gods shake us, they don't stop with half measures. I hadn't dried my tears before my father began planning to kill the suitors, to the last man. Madness is sometimes divine, but not this rage. He had hidden treasure in a cave and feared the suitors would plunder this as they had his home. Why didn't I suggest my own plan to Odysseus? He could have taken my place in slaying Antinoös. But if I had truly planned such a feat, every thought of it had vanished from my mind.

"Great fighter that you are," I pleaded with him, "two of us are no match for more than a hundred. We'll die without benefit to my mother or ourselves."

What a look he gave me, as if he might want a different son to replace one who had lived so long with the suitors.

"I fought with Poseidon on my right side and Athena on my left," he answered. "Our road home lay burning on the beaches and Hector speared men from his chariot like a god of war. After Troy fell, Athena abandoned me in fury. Nine years I wandered suffering before she forgave me. I haven't survived so much to be merciful to cowards who stayed home and feasted in my hall."

I had cursed the suitors, but I couldn't imagine killing them all.

"Tell no one I've returned," he commanded. "Can I trust you not to? Not the shepherd, nor your old nurse, nor any of the slaves, and certainly not your mother." He smiled grimly at my surprise. "Agamemnon never saw his children as I see you now. His wife and her lover murdered him for his homecoming surprise. It won't be that way with me. When the last suitor has choked on blood, I'll cry Agamemnon's name in my heart. Who can count a woman's secret lovers? How easily she can conceal them from a son or a few servants faithful to an absent lord. Wives learn from their sisters and cousins how to cuckold and murder heroes. Find me a single wife faithful to an absent husband and I'll spare a suitor in her name."

"My mother, Penelope," I answered to calm him.

He shuddered like a man in a fit. Where the beggar's flesh had hung slackly on his legs and arms, I could see his writhing muscles.

"Then I shall give one suitor a warning," he said. "Which man has never coveted my possessions or my throne, has never spoken contemptuously of me in my absence, and has never sought to corrupt my wife or any of my maidservants? Is there such a man among the suitors?"

"Amphinomos," I replied.

He seized my cloak like the scruff of a dog's neck.

"Is Amphinomos the one with whom she laughs? He's charmed you too, I see it. He'll be warned, this friend of yours. And if I die,

17

it will be a death men remember—not the slow bleeding of a stuck swine."

"I'll stand beside you," I promised like the youth I was.

He loosened his grip and rested a hand on my shoulder. "I have returned here as Nobody—a truer name for me than Odysseus. When Nobody knocks on your door, Zeus himself promises hospitality. So Nobody will make a list of the maidservants who've whored with the suitors. And the suitors will remember Nobody when they reach the gloomy kingdom where Achilles rules. In that world a man would willingly take a thousand blows to feel the sun's warmth for a fleeting instant. And you, if you are true to me, shall be Nobody's son."

CHAPTER 4

I swear the island of Ithaca changed when my father returned. As if birds became fish, the moon rose at daybreak, and the tides flowed forever away from the shore, the natural laws men obey vanished from our kingdom. You witnessed the deaths of the suitors, Phemios, and I blame you not at all for leaving the island in such haste. Those bodies stacked in the sun had a scent neither burning nor the burial box have purified in my memory. My father bid you play a wedding tune to deceive the families of the suitors. With what spirit you plucked the strings and sang the nuptial chants. At last, I felt myself believing a wedding feast had reached its consummation. As my mother promised, the man whose arrow pierced through its targets won her for a bride.

I made one terrible mistake that day when I forgot to lock the arms room in the confusion of the battle. This scar on my wrist marks me for that mistake. I wouldn't have thought a man could reach the small window in the great hall and slip through into the passageway beyond. With swords and spears suddenly in the hands of Eurynomos, Polybos, Agelaos, and two dozen more, I saw my father tremble. I had never imagined I would live so late in the day, but I saw my own death in the crouching men who circled the four of us—Odysseus, Philoitios, Eumaios, and myself. They balanced their spears, shifting and feinting to watch the movement of our shields. Agelaos, who had never harmed me, broke that panting silence and cried to the others to cast their spears in unison at Odysseus. If I threw myself on Agelaos's knees and swore I had left the arms room unlocked to help the suitors, might he not spare my life and accept my mother as his bride?

How quick the mind can be! For no sooner had my courage receded than it surged forward again. I offered a prayer to Athena and accepted the fate no man can alter. The spears sailed toward Odysseus and I gave a cry of rage and rushed forward to kill Euryades. But you know all this. The point is that my father survived. He didn't rebuke me for my mistake, so why have I wondered so often about leaving that door open?

My father claimed he could see the gods. After we had returned to Ithaca, he built a shrine to Athena and spent hours staring toward the sea with dreams in his heart. Each meal with him brought an invocation of thanksgiving. My father swore Athena and Zeus would fight beside us. You've traveled the world and heard the boasts men make. Did you ever hear another man claim such vision? All men feel the gods at one time or another. I've felt Athena like a spirit within, but I never saw her raise a spear against the suitors. I say this to prepare you for one of the many inexplicable parts of my father's story. Perhaps your song will make more sense of it than I have.

My father, the great tactician, had no plan at all to deal with the vengeance of the suitors' relatives. He spent the night of their slaughter in my mother's arms. No doubt the raptures stolen by Paris and Helen hardly compared to this reunion in the great bed hewn by Odysseus for his wife. At dawn, my gray-haired mother bid him a wordless farewell. Did it remind her of his departure for Troy—a beggar, an old shepherd, and a youth slipping into the safety of the forest? We hiked the pastures toward the ridge where Grandfather Laertes kept his hovel. One moment I felt amazed to be alive with the sun lifting from the ocean's girth and the ceaseless wind at our backs. The next moment I knew this would certainly be my last day on the earth. Like a sentimental fool I longed for all that passed before my eyes; life seemed a memory and I swelled with nostalgia. If we had killed a hundred men, then a thousand would rise in arms against us. For each miracle we had performed a day earlier, we would need far greater feats today. I had never imagined we might kill all the suitors. But Odysseus planned that battle with cunning and courage. Certainly, I saw in him the leader who deceived the Trojans and rode the fantastical horse of Epeios to glory. Now, as the suitors' relatives and friends gathered in assembly to plan their vengeance, Odysseus lacked any plan except to hope. Nor did he rush to his father for Laertes's leadership, but rather to relieve himself of the burden of pain a son feels for so many years of separation from his father.

But does one test the father who has worn the goatskin cowl of grief and chosen to waste in a hovel longing for his son's return? Odysseus couldn't simply tell old Laertes that he had returned. He had to deceive his father with yet another history of his origins and travels. He called himself Strife, son of King Allwoes. Even so, it surprised me Laertes didn't recognize the sword and cuirass Odysseus wore—for this sword and armor had been Laertes's when he besieged Nerikos.

Odysseus left us at the farmhouse and went alone to the orchards to find his father. Eumaios began to regale me with the fables by which Odysseus had deceived him.

"I didn't believe half of his lies. Every beggar has a bagful, though few so splendid as that uncouth fellow's. I marked him in my heart for his craft—a man to be watched. He claimed to be a son of Crete, his father a wealthy man and his mother a slave. He married well, a rich lady, but cared neither for the farmer's life nor fathering a brood of children to tie him down. As a warrior he excelled, and his countrymen convinced him to lead the Cretan ships to Troy. Only after ten years of war, when Athena's sacred image had been captured and the city sacked, did his deepest trials begin." Eumaios grinned with a peasant's appreciation for cunning. "How cleverly he weaves truth and lies together. Then, on the homeward journey, he turned coward in battle and spent seven years in slavery in Egypt. But even as a slave he made a fortune! These riches Poseidon stole from him by sinking his treasure ship bound home for Crete. Yet the king of the Thesprotians nursed him back to life and launched him homeward again. Only to have his crew turn on him with the plan of selling him into slavery, as I myself was once sold by my faithless nurse. He escaped in the rags with which he arrived at my door—or so he claimed. And I believed him more or less—except for the part where he swore to have met Odysseus." Eumaios could have continued this proud recitation of Odysseus's ingenuity, but we saw my father and grandfather coming slowly across the empty fields. As I watched them, I wished Eumaios had spared me his stories. What could have persuaded my father to leave a young wife and a newborn son? Paris hadn't violated his hospitality or stolen his bride. What debt did he owe Agamemnon or Menelaos? Could it be, I wondered, that he had preferred the trials of the world to the quiet life of husbandry he would have lived at home? But if that were true, why had he returned at all?

My father supported my grandfather as they neared us. I realized how far my grandfather's health had been spent since he moved from Odysseus's hall in shame at the suitors' revels. He wore his goatskin hood, his clothes tattered and patched time and again by his own awkward stitch. He had been mulching saplings and grime covered him. He might have been a beggar put to work for the reward of a meal. More than anyone else, he reminded me of the way Odysseus had appeared when I first saw him cloaked in reindeer hide with all his belongings in one battered knapsack. I recalled the pelts of ferocious beasts that had decorated the court of Menelaos, who himself had worn the horns of a bull and the fur of a bear. Why should my father have dressed in the skin of a deer and my grandfather in that of a goat, one lost in the wilds of the world and the other weary with the unyielding chores of his farm?

Laertes's thin voice cried for joy. "My son has returned!" With that he pulled the goatskin cowl from his head and cast it down. He spat on it and scuffed the dirt as if to bury it from sight. "We'll feast to a life regained, a thanksgiving to Athena."

Soon after we banished our hunger and thirst, the lookout cried a warning. Laertes clapped on old armor, and the farmhands—big, sturdy men—grabbed pitchforks and an odd spear or bow. We rushed to form our ranks by the roadside.

Facing us stood Eupeithes, the father of Antinoös, dressed from toe to head in golden armor. He led men armed for war, many more than in our small group. What a handsome leader he made—more as you might imagine the great leaders who fought at Troy than the humble men who lived thereafter.

Eupeithes cursed Laertes and yelled to him: "Goat-griever, isn't it enough your son took a generation of men to die at Troy? Now he's back and slain another generation. If you want to die with him, so much the better. We'll rid Ithaca of your line. That's my promise to you."

Grandfather Laertes cursed back in a voice regained from his youth. "Eupeithes, pirate and slaver, you saved your son from Troy while mine had ten years of war and ten years of wandering. I can't count the times I cursed you. I lost all heart for the joys of this world, knowing my son lived no more. I watched his wife age, his son grow to manhood fatherless, and his mother die early from grief. At times I doubted I ever had a son or a life that was other than endlessly sorrowful. If you lost a hundred sons like Antinoös, even if they had been the best of men instead of the vilest, my suffering would remain unimaginable to you. If your treasures can buy you back life, raise Antinoös up and let him stand here among us. But if men's wealth means nothing to the gods, then I beg Athena give me strength to heave this spear to its home."

His withered arm balanced the long war spear and he cast it with the war cry of the warrior who had broken Nerikos's high walls. The bronzed point pierced the visor of Eupeithes's helmet and ground through the eye socket to the skull's secret heart. He toppled as if no man had ever lived within that armor. Panic seized his followers. I raised my sword and followed my father to cut them down before their prowess returned. How quickly the hunger for killing rose in me.

But Mentor, my father's old friend and keeper of his hall, stepped calmly to the center of the road between our groups. He lifted his hands to still their retreat and our pursuit. Like a priest of Athena, a goatskin covered his shoulders and back. The goat's head dangled on his chest, its horns, eyes, jowls, and teeth all twisted and transformed to the terrifying face of a Gorgon. Athena herself might have worn this miraculous and horrible pelt to serve as her aegis. In my childhood, Mentor had given me a bow, a sword, and the other gifts a son expects from the hands of his father. For his fair dealing and wisdom, he had long been loved by all. His quiet voice brought us to our senses.

"My friends," he said, "when Odysseus ruled, he was a gentle king and virtuous, whose benefaction all enjoyed. Did any of you leash your princely sons who consumed his belongings and demanded his bride? He cannot change the retribution decreed by the gods. He cannot make young men whole again to succor your old age and meet your wants. He can only give you what this world provides to men. He can pay you in equal measure the gold, silver, and fire-hardened bronze he has brought home. Accept your share of this and the air you freely breathe. If you demand vengeance, you shall have only the wealth of slaughter."

I saw the fight go out of them and turned with joy to my father. Who cared for the treasure he had hidden? Even after the suitors had bled us for three bitter years, his estate far exceeded our needs. Odysseus left for Troy with his herds of cattle, sheep, swine, and goats numbering a dozen each. In his deep cellar rested row upon row of wine-filled casks and other stores he had husbanded by hard work and careful exchanges. When the suitors finished with their visit and their lives, we had at most a quarter of what we had possessed twenty years earlier. But I cared nothing for that. Why measure more or less, when what we had would feed us and our servants until the harvests replenished stores and livestock?

My father stared at Mentor like a man betrayed. I couldn't say why this should have been. When we fought the suitors, Mentor appeared late in the battle and heartened us by his presence. But only the day before, Odysseus had listened to no one's counsel when he wished to kill the suitors. Perhaps he couldn't deny the wisdom in his old friend's words. The sword and shield fell from my father's hands and he sat on his haunches in the red dust. His hands tore the plumed war helmet from his head, and he flung it clattering end over end to rest at Mentor's feet. Tears drenched his cheeks, and he lifted his arms in supplication to Mentor. But what more could Odysseus have desired than peace? Or if it pained him so greatly to surrender this treasure, what made him quit the battle? At last, my father collapsed and writhed on the dust.

A kinsman put a foot on the chin of Eupeithes's corpse and twisted free the glistening point of the spear. Four men seized the carcass by its limbs and heaved it on a cart. The helmet rolled free, a golden cup spilling Eupeithes's warm blood. Quickly it was upended and tossed alongside the rest of the handsome armor. They dispersed, most returning to town and the rest to the great hall. Laertes draped the right arm of Odysseus over his shoulders, and I did likewise with the left. Without thought we followed Mentor down to the ocean. Odysseus woke to the crescendo of the waves leaping on the rocky shore. He shrugged us away, his right hand on the hilt of his sword as if to strike the seaborne mist.

In this mist I could still hear the waves and the faint crying of gulls, but I saw nothing. Mentor's strength surprised me, for he glided easily before us. My grandfather leaned against me and Odysseus followed with his hand always on his sword.

Mentor halted by a tall olive tree growing beneath the cliffs. Like a far younger man, he rolled aside a large rock to reveal the opening of a cave and beckoned Odysseus come forward and enter the blackness after him. My father did as he was bidden and, in a moment, vanished beneath the low ledge of rock. I had no heart to follow and rested beside my grandfather.

Laertes raised his hands to entreat the gray-eyed goddess.

"Athena, allow my son Odysseus to descend beneath the roots of your sacred olive tree and return alive to us. Make him a king as once he was before the voyage to Troy. He ruled far more wisely than I did before him. So many despised me for sacking rebellious Nerikos that

I welcomed the chance to have my son rule in my stead. Hear my pleas for Odysseus, and for Telemachus too, whose time will come to rule these islands."

After this I slept for a long while. When I woke, the mist had burned away, and the sunlight glowed on a treasure that lay in a hundred piles before me. These riches belonged in the court of wealthy Mycenae, not on the stony island of Ithaca. I saw gold and silver worked masterfully into goblets, plates, jewelry, and seal-stones. Vases glazed by a craft surpassing any I have seen since depicted the histories of our gods and heroes. Bronze swords and armor lay heaped before me. The clothing surprised me, a king's wardrobe woven by some magic into tunics and robes that might have suited the gods themselves. Tapestries and the skins of exotic beasts with enormous tusks and fangs had all been carefully parceled to one pile or another.

I saw this treasure once only, so perhaps I've embellished it in my recollection. Often, I've marveled that Odysseus might have returned with such wealth and yet had the cunning to wear rags to Eumaios's cottage. But what king has such wealth that he could give a stranger these treasures as Odysseus claimed? The wardrobe, for example, seemed more like plunder than a gift. But if it was plunder, who had plundered it? My father had no men-at-arms when he returned home. I wondered if he had hidden this treasure on Ithaca before he left for Troy. I can't explain why he might have done this, except for a premonition that suitors would enter his hall. Of course, if he had such fears, I wonder why he left at all. So much of his story is as difficult to believe as to explain another way.

We left the treasure on the beach at twilight. As we three sons of the line of Arkeisios trudged toward our hall, I imagined a beggar stumbling on this unguarded treasure. He would think himself in a dream, drunk by the moonlight or the spell of a sea nymph. Perhaps this spirit seized my father as well, for he laughed heartily to leave that treasure behind. Throwing his arms around his father and son, he made us stumble back and forth across the road like dancers to your dulcet plucking.

Each portion of the treasure was distributed by Mentor according to the terms of the peace to which all had agreed. I knew the families of the suitors would despise us, but I looked forward to peace and the richness of my father and mother reunited. I said my prayers to the ever-near Athena in thanks for these miracles and my life.

Such thanksgiving as I made, however, hardly sufficed for my father. His way of offering thanks to the gods was soon to be revealed to me.

CHAPTER 5

The dolphins danced as we cleared the white cliffs of Leucas bound for the mainland. Could it have been only a single day since Laertes killed Eupeithes? And two days since Odysseus and I faced the hundred suitors?

The wind blossomed in our sails and the uncountable dolphins surrounded us. My regret at leaving Ithaca vanished for the moments I watched this life-filled ocean. Off bow and stern, port and starboard, their silver bodies leapt skyward. Perhaps Poseidon sent them in a gesture of forgiveness for my father, who had seen the ocean devour his men and his plunder from Troy. Odysseus put an arm around my waist and pointed to the dolphins.

"When I first went to Troy," he said, "my shield had been emblazoned with a boar for my triumph in the hunt with my grandfather Autolykos." He touched the jagged scar above his knee. "This scar

29

showed my courage to never despair. My second thrust hit the boar's heart and saved my life. So I felt it would be at Troy. Whatever injuries I might suffer, my courage would bring me through. But I saw too much slaughter to believe this year after year. Longingly I looked to the sea and thought of you and your mother at home. Often, I called myself the father of Telemachus, tears within me for the life I would never live. From our beachhead I watched the dolphins ride the waves. I dreamt I might be like the dolphins, made of spirit only and free to follow my heart. When innumerable blows wore down my boar's shield, I asked the master Epeios to craft me a new shield with two dolphins silver on its front. Those dolphins shielded me from harm at Troy."

Like my father, I love the dolphins. They have men's eyes, although I doubt they have men's souls as some have said. When Antinoös died, he didn't become a dolphin leaping in the sunlit seas. He passed to the Underworld and the grayness of forever. But I feel the dolphins share a common divinity with men. That-which-is-not-to-be-named lives in both.

"Why did Poseidon curse you?"

I had asked him this and many other questions the night before, but he refused to answer me. He would only say a prophecy required he travel inland to where neither shrines nor sacrifices had ever been given to Poseidon. In this place he must plant an oar; sacrifice a boar, a bull, and a ram; and appease Poseidon by his prayers.

Odysseus urged me to borrow Noëmon's ship, which I did, although I felt the strangeness of this journey. In our time prophecy is in ill repute. Men like Teiresias are myths and those like Halitherses are memories shared by few. Prophecy remains easy enough, but there are no men so excellent as to fulfill the visions of the prophets. Halitherses saw the deaths of the suitors in the fury of eagles, but no suitor listened to his warning. Isn't it better to be pious like my father and seek harmony with the divine?

My mother tried to dissuade Odysseus from this journey. After we left the treasure on the beach, we returned to find her waiting in the great hall. She knew of our triumph over Eupeithes and no longer looked like a weaver of shrouds. She wore the necklace of golden links given to her by my grandmother. Tall as Helen, she had the spirit that beautiful Helen would never have. If my mother's mouth was overwide as she drank in joy, or her nose prominent and her eyebrows thick and dark, what poet of the human heart will ever care? For those who sing to Helen, if any do, will sing to themselves and their dreams of women.

My father poured cups of wine. Black grime from the cave caked his skin and clothes. The wine that spilled from his lips streaked the filth on his chin.

Laertes placed his helmet on the table. Resting in his armchair, he gazed at this helmet like a treasure unearthed. His cup he lifted overhead.

"Athena, protectress of soldiers, accept my thanks that I lived to see my son reunited with his family. If any pleasure surpassed this, it could only be my joy to see Eupeithes die."

We drank in thanksgiving. In a few moments Laertes's head lolled, his white beard against his cuirass as he slept.

My mother spoke, gently at first. "My lord, let me bathe you now and keep you by me. Plunder and the gods can wait a month or a season. In twenty years, I heard so many lies from footloose men who claimed to have known you. If I had believed their tales, you traveled east of Egypt and west of the pillars of Herakles. You alone know the truths of your travels, and I don't ask you for that. I only implore you to remain here. When I believe you always yearned to return to me, then make your journeys."

My father answered simply. "Poseidon will not wait. I have told you of my life since Troy. I have no other truths than those."

Tears wet my mother's cheeks. She reached across the table. Her pale hands nested in his dark ones. "My wandering husband, I beg you to stay. Here is the hearth for which you longed. Here are the fields which knew your plow, the great bed hewn by your own hand, and the son whose life sprang from your own."

Slowly he shook his head from side to side.

"I don't ask for your love, stranger that you are." My mother spoke more sharply. "How could you love me like the youth who fathered our child? I don't ask you for promises of what may become of us in a year or forever. But stay long enough for us to know one another. When you left for Troy, I felt in a few months we'd return to each other's arms. But I'd curse Agamemnon if he came again to beg you to accompany him. Now you say it's a god demands you go. Stay with me, Odysseus."

My father wept too. "No man who ever lived could make me leave you. My life has cracked beneath the demands of others. But I must honor that divinity which calls me. To survive, to be your husband and Telemachus's father, I cannot do less."

She flung down his hands and stood above him.

"Will you return to another house filled with suitors?" Her tears fell on the darkened man over whom she bent. "Must I weave another shroud for your father? Shall Telemachus never take his rightful place in this hall?" Receiving no response, she walked to the hearth and raised trembling hands to touch the cold stone of the fireplace in which many an ewe had roasted on the spit for the feasting suitors. "So many beggars sat where you sit and told me of the exploits of the Ithacan Odysseus. From that hero all the world knew of Ithaca, but Ithaca knew neither its hero nor itself. I should be joyous. Of all the wives who waited, only my husband will ever return. But I never felt abandoned or forgotten until I heard of the life you claimed to have led. On our first night together, shy as virgins, you spoke already of expeditions to plunder the herds of weaker men. Does nothing move you but war and wealth? When you left for Troy, you told me of the dangers there. You asked that I wait for you until Telemachus became a man. I waited longer than that, but no more."

"It's a short journey," my father answered, "a matter of ten days or twenty at most. I'll take armed men, but only to protect our lives and the sacrifices we bring Poseidon." He looked up at her. "If I had returned and found you married to a suitor, I would have loved you nonetheless. If you had been happy as the wife of Amphinomos or some other man, I would have silently traveled on to the farthest reaches men know. Your love kept me here. If I bragged last night of riches or adventure, forgive me. Ten years have passed since I vied with Achilles, Aias, and Diomedes for what glory one can gain in battle. Your love—and the sight of my son and this island for which I had yearned so many years—gave me courage to face the suitors. If I can't love you as did the youthful Odysseus, I'll love you as best I can."

My mother came to my arms. With her head on my shoulder and her arms clinging to me, I could hardly believe her the woman who had always scolded me by conjuring an image of my heroic father. In my father's eyes I saw no plans, no ruses, no hint of the saving war cry by which he might meet this heroic measure.

Gently I helped my mother into their bedchamber. Dressed in her fine gown, she slept the moment her head rested on the pillow. In the hall, my father bundled together a pile of furs for his bed. Having done this, he stared at the doorway where my mother had exited as once he must have gazed at the walls of Troy. The man of many thoughts shook old Laertes awake. And later Laertes slept on that pile of skins, for Odysseus had chosen to spend another night beside my mother.

CHAPTER 6

Our overland march lasted nearly a month, an exhausting trek through the lands of Callidice, queen of the Thesprotians. Two dozen men joined us—Eumaios the swineherd, Philoitios the master of bulls, Dolios the farmer with his many sons, Medon the herald, and another dozen who welcomed the return of Odysseus. Great bonds joined these men with my father. For fighting with us against the suitors, my father freed Eumaios and Philoitios from slavery, found brides for each, built houses for them close to our own hall, provided them with herds for their livelihood, and honored them as my brothers. Old Dolios praised us for killing his son and daughter, Melanthios and Melantho, whom he cursed for their fawning service to the suitors. Because Melanthios armed the suitors in the great hall and insulted my father, I fed his puny genitals to the curs. After that I slashed off his nose and ears, his feet and hands, and let him howl as the blood streamed from him. From my life before and after that killing, I would never have imagined myself capable of such cruelty. But Melanthios's death was not one that later disturbed me. Age kept Laertes and Mentor at home with my mother. But my father's loyal friend Halitherses came with us, despite his age. When I was a baby, Halitherses had prophesied that Odysseus would be gone nineteen years if he led our army to Troy. Not only had Halitherses forecast the death of the suitors, but he had also pled with the townsmen not to fight on the side of Eupeithes. Shrunken and bald-skulled, his gait a hobble, he had been a captain to Laertes when they ended the rebellion at Nerikos.

The hulking beasts Odysseus had chosen to sacrifice gave us endless trouble. The boar hated walking and had to be coaxed—no doubt he had spent his life mounting sows and gorging at the trough. This boar had an odious smell and squealed constantly, as if in anticipation of the knife. If the ram were loosened it charged the nearest man. Only the bull marched with a stolid and kingly step toward its death. Annoying as they were, we practically fed these bucks by hand to keep them sleek for Poseidon. Their fodder weighed down a dozen donkeys—far more than carried our own supplies as we lived from hand to mouth.

If all this weren't enough to make men laugh at us, my father walked to our front and carried an upright oar. The base of the oar fit in a leather cup held on my father's waist by a makeshift harness around his shoulders. So we progressed slowly, and on the first night camped in view of the ocean. What distances the realm of Poseidon stretched toward the far edges of the world. The next day, when the ocean vanished from our sight, Odysseus beat the earth three times with the butt of the oar.

The day after this began with a rainfall blown in by the ocean breeze. Perhaps this was Poseidon's reminder of how far men like us must travel to escape his element. We reached a broad plain where the fields had been sown carefully by long labors. Ithaca offered no lands as fine as these. Day followed day and we neared the distant blue-gray peaks rising toward the bluer sky. Wheat flowed about us like the rippling waves from which the dolphins had leapt. At last Odysseus stopped a passerby, a slender farm boy younger than I was. He had curls of dark hair, shining gray eyes, and a fair skin that few who toil in the fields can keep. The boy glanced wonderingly from face to face. He petted the nose of his donkey to quiet it and looked up and down the length of the oar.

"My friend," my father called courteously to the boy, "You can see by our clothing that we are strangers here. We know little of the crafts by which men husband crops and livestock as fine as those we've seen. This implement I'm carrying"—here he gestured to the oar—"we found not far from here. Is it used for harvesting?"

"Don't you know, sir," the boy questioned politely, "what it is?"

"If I knew," my father replied, "I would have fields as fine as these."

Looking in the direction from which we had come, the boy frowned and tried to make us out.

"Have you ever seen the ocean?" he asked us. "What you're carrying is an oar. It's used to make ships move through the waves as if Poseidon himself had willed it."

Odysseus handed me the oar and embraced the startled boy.

"I thank you for your answer. If ever I go to sea, I'll always remember you first told me of this."

So we parted from the youth, Odysseus laughing for his own folly. I complained to myself about this foolish journey. If my father had to be so pious, why couldn't he have made his sacrifices on Ithaca? But if not there, couldn't we have done so in Thesprotia in sight of the ocean where Poseidon rules?

After provoking the laughter of these farmers many times, Odysseus kept silent as he labored beneath the oar. Only when we had climbed into the mountains whose peaks vanished in the clouds did we leave Poseidon behind us. Looking down on the yellow fields, we seemed to rule a kingdom of air. Ithaca is a stony island, but here stone excelled itself in shapes that tumbled, twisted, and soared. Waterfalls dropped endlessly to valleys bottomed by mist. We searched for the easiest paths, but the upward ascent left us gasping and we rested frequently. Perhaps Odysseus hoped to find some landlocked tribe that lived in caves and eked out its sustenance by eating roots and wild berries. However, we met no one. The full moon hung pale in the twilit sky, growing ever brighter as the sun vanished back of the mountains.

Out of this bright darkness, a woman stepped quietly forward to stand by our fire. In daylight, in any town or even a court like that of Crete or Mycenae, this woman would have been striking. But at night, arriving unheard and unannounced in such a place of desolation, she amazed us. In robes of black fringed by skins and heads of vipers, bearing a black shield and wearing a black-crested helmet, only her face and arms reflected the moonlight. I recognized her as Queen Callidice, who had greeted Odysseus warmly when we arrived in Thesprotia. He had been her father's friend and had amused her with his storytelling when she had been a child. She might have aroused rapture in countless men had she not guarded her spirit and her kingdom with a manlike ferocity. No suitors feasted in her court after her husband's death. She could have had as many men war for her as Helen, but she preferred to rule.

"Most men use oars at sea, Odysseus."

In this way she greeted my father, a smile on her lips and her wise eyes shining.

"So everyone in your country has told me," my father replied, smiling easily at her jibe. He gestured for a chair and Philoitios brought a wooden box. On this rough stool the queen sat, her shield, helmet, and bronze-tipped spear on the ground beside her.

38

"Did you miss my storytelling so much?" my father asked, as if she remained a child on his knee.

Callidice smiled in response. "Any child would miss such tales."

"Bring out the mixing bowl," Odysseus ordered, and Medon hurried to comply. We had brought the amber wine that sings to the divinities. When we sacrificed to Poseidon, we would need wine such as this. Odysseus mixed it with water.

"Athena, shield us by your strength and give us wisdom as we journey." Odysseus spilled a good portion of wine as his offering and poured the rest from cup to cup.

"Why don't you pray to Poseidon?" Callidice asked when we had drunk. "Didn't he bring you here?"

"He has brought me here, but Athena is close by me." My father eyed her like a merchant wary of too good a bargain, "What made you follow me such a great distance?" he asked.

The amber wine leapt to my limbs and my head reeled. The presence of Callidice made me feel that deep emotion a minstrel arouses when singing of passion.

"You've wandered through my country as you've wandered through the world. In every town men spoke of you, the navigator of the wheat fields. But you've traveled too far. If you go farther, you'll find no men at all. Sacrifice here to Poseidon and go home."

We filled our cups again. I wished my father would agree with this delightful woman, so we could return to Ithaca. How I longed for my bed in the tower that lofts itself above our courtyard. I wanted the cooing of the sparrows in the eaves above my window, the fragrance of the cooking from the kitchens below, and the banter with my old nurse who cared only for my comforts.

My father stared into the fire, his misshapen head seeming to flicker. The bull lowed, a deep-chested hungering sound that echoed to silence.

"How far will you go to escape Poseidon?" Callidice asked. "When you find such men as those you seek—men who never saw the sea, nor heard from any wanderer about it, nor dreamt of its incessant motion in the caves of their dreams—will you have escaped at last from the violence of Poseidon? Will you search ten years for such a land? Twenty? For in Thesprotia you'll find no such men, nor do I think you'll find them anywhere. Prophecy is so easy for the prophets. Only we have to live with their imaginings."

"But I must meet men who never saw the sea," Odysseus protested.

Callidice stood, her long hair tumbling among the vipers curling on her robes. She opened her arms to the cliffs and the night. "Here are no men who have seen the sea or eaten salted meat." Her clarion voice convinced far beyond her words. "I've come from Dodona, where Zeus speaks in the rustling of the oaks. I made offerings in the sacred square and the priests spoke of you. In your heart you'd rather wander than make peace with Poseidon. Plant your oar, Odysseus. You've fulfilled the prophet's wish, now honor the god. Show me the bull for Poseidon."

Philoitios brought forward the bull. Lit by moon and fire, it no longer looked like a beast bred and raised on Ithaca. It had grown with its shadow into some deity of marvelous Crete. If any bull might pacify the fury of Poseidon, here it stood.

"Offer the bull first," she urged. "After that, the ram. From the bull, give burnt thighbones as offerings, but leave the carcass of the boar untouched. Slay it for Poseidon, but offer him no flesh, nor eat of it yourselves."

My father slowly stood and lifted the oar. Beside the fire he slipped its stem into a hollow in the stone. I tumbled rocks into the hollow until a small pyramid supported the oar in front of the flames.

Callidice signaled for more wine. Medon poured first for her, then my father, and finally the rest of us. Next Medon unwrapped the knife and chalice. Philoitios garlanded the bull with woven dried flowers from Ithaca. Dolios and Eumaios did likewise with the ram and boar. Standing beside the oar, my father sprinkled water and handfuls of Ithacan barley on the ground. Screwing up his face and staring at his feet, he finally spoke with fervor.

"Hear me, Poseidon, great spirit of the moving sea and the trembling earth, you who are both savior of ships and master of horses with flowing manes. In this place beyond your power, I offer sacrifices to you. Here is a bull as fine as men might ever breed. Accept this as my gift to you."

Philoitios lifted the bull's halter. As its head raised up, a white spot of fur showed on the bull's black neck. With a graceful sweep of his arm, Odysseus slashed the throat from tendon to tendon. The bull's breath hissed in its throat. White slobber spilled from its lips and blood poured through its nose. Odysseus held the chalice beneath the blood welling from the wound. In a moment, the bull's knees buckled. My father raised the chalice aloft.

"Hear me, dark-haired shaker of the earth, and for once hold me safe from the tempest. Remember in Troy when I fought beside you. Let us both forget what happened thereafter. Allow me a tranquil life and a peaceful death. Look with kindness on me, my son, and all who are sailors. Help us in our voyaging."

Philoitios and Eumaios butchered the bull while the others stoked the fires. Soon the blood of the ram and boar had filled the offering chalice. The boar's carcass we dragged by its heels to one side. What a feast we made of the bull and ram! Again and again we filled our cups with wine. One of Dolios's sons plucked his stringed instrument. The others danced arm in arm, side to side and forward and back with the leaping fires for their elemental partners. If some of the men had expected a dramatic sign—a lightning flash or a tremor in the earth— I felt the dancing and the amber wine lift our spirits toward that frenzy in which one feels the gods within. Odysseus careened among us. Spattered by blood and wine, his mood changed with the steps of the dances. He did everything to extremes—twisting, whirling, and leaping until our rough celebration seemed gentle in comparison with his. Callidice sat to one side, but Odysseus no longer looked to her. He had become like the sea in a storm, violence rising from his depths. His wild laughter echoed up the cliffsides. At last, I feared he might have a seizure as he had after Eupeithes's death. I tried to hold him in my arms and calm him, but it was like holding motion itself. He shoved me aside and rushed headlong against each of the dancers in turn. They took this for a game and butted heads with his until he pummeled and kicked them. When he had caused the dancing to cease, he rained handfuls of ash over his sweat-streaked body. In this makeshift sackcloth, he cried out to the oceanic god.

"Poseidon, do you remember Odysseus? If you don't, surely your giant son Polyphemos does. I fought at Troy for the peaceful joys men cherish. I fought to make Ithaca safe from marauders like Paris who care nothing for hospitality and the rules by which men live. I suffered as much as any man should. When I washed the blood from my hands and packed my sword and shield in my sea chest, why shouldn't I have had a good wind and a storm-free passage home?

"You killed my crew, men who had been my friends on Ithaca and valiant comrades at Troy. You stole the treasures with which I might have made Ithaca a proud and beautiful land like Crete or Mycenae. You took the years of my life, stranding me in the abyss of your seedless ocean."

Tears streamed from my father's eyes. I looked for Callidice, but she no longer sat near our fires.

"Before I blinded your son, I trusted him as any stranger trusts another man. I believed he would welcome me and share his mutton and cheese. Instead, he murdered my men before my eyes and taunted me with death. When I blinded him to escape, you held it against me. Why single me out? Achilles strangled your son Cygnus when we first landed on the Trojan beaches. But you forgot graceful Cygnus and fought as Achilles's ally. Why did you listen to the prayers of your son? Why did you promise him that you'd keep me from my home and condemn me to a life of bitterness and tears? Why did my prayers mean nothing to you?" Odysseus shouted at the sky. Looking again at us, he said more quietly, "Bring me the boar."

Eumaios and several others leapt to his command. The long snout of the boar bounced on the rocks as the men strained to pull its great bulk beside the fires. I wanted to speak with my father, but he lived in past events of which I knew nothing. With the boar at his feet, Odysseus filled his cup to the brim and raised it toward the sky.

"Poseidon, taste this offering of wine from a holy grove of Apollo. As it sings in your gullet, remember I, puny Nobody, fed wine like this to your child Polyphemos. He slept like a baby until we Ithacans drilled out the jelly of his eye. Fathomless, blue-maned monster, where were you when that eye sizzled and your giant cried for his daddy? At my feet is my sacrifice for you—a disgusting beast that lived its life in filth. Gorge yourself and wash down this pig's meat with the wine of blindness. If the prophecy is true, I'll live a long and peaceful life despite your cruelty. So I curse you, Poseidon, as you cursed me."

He lowered the cup to his lips and drank greedily. I had never heard a man speak to a god in this way, especially a pious man like Odysseus who believed the gods move among us. Like Dolios and his superstitious sons, I imagined the earth might shiver beneath us until the world we knew vanished before the rage of the earth-shaking god. But the moon shone steadily down as we looked at one another.

Old Halitherses had drunk so much wine that he barely staggered through the first of the dances. Odysseus mixed this amber wine with twenty parts of water, but Halitherses added four parts or five at most. Whether this brought him closer to the gods, I can hardly say. For most of our celebration, the old captain lay besotted with his back on the rocks and his face to the full moon. But divination is Apollo's art, and this wine flowed from Apollo. Hearing Odysseus, Halitherses rose and tottered to the center of our group.

"It's no gift to prophesy of death," he said. To hear his quaking voice, I wondered how in his youth he had the deep war cry of which Laertes often spoke with admiration.

"All men die," my father said roughly. "Say your piece or go back to sleep."

"When you were gone, I never wavered in my loyalty to you and your wife and son. Many times, I warned the suitors to leave off their siege of your hall. I cared nothing for their threats and curses. I might have told them the hour of their deaths, but none listened. Remember too my service with your father at Nerikos. I would have gone to Troy as well, if I had been younger."

"Nerikos." Odysseus spat the word. "When will you and my father stop telling me of the glory of storming Nerikos? You never saw Troy. Its walls make those of Nerikos look like sand piled up by children. Sleep it off, will you?"

The trembling man stood poised between the world of the gods and that of men. As a man, no doubt he would have kept silent. But as a messenger, he had to speak his prophecy.

"Odysseus will die at the hands of his son."

My father scooped up a supple branch smoldering in the fire. With this scourge he lashed Halitherses's shoulders and shanks until the man fell sobbing on his knees amidst the showering sparks. Eumaios and the others strained to pull my father away.

"Liar," Odysseus yelled. "Teiresias brought me here to placate Poseidon. No man ever saw the future better than he. For me, the great seer predicts a long life and a gentle seaborne death. Predict what you like if it gets you a meal, a bed, or the favors of a maidservant. I am Odysseus whose fate is known."

Consternation seized us all. We stood like speechless shadows.

At last, Eumaios spoke. "My lord, Teiresias is long since dead. Who told you of his prediction?"

Wild-eyed, Odysseus turned on us.

"I met him in the Underworld and fed him the sacrificial blood. Then he foretold all I must do to live at peace in my home."

I trembled within. No man returns from the Underworld, except in fantasies. In the slaughter of Troy or the suffering of his journey home, my father had escaped like any beggar into a world of his own imagining. Only a madman would attempt to kill a hundred suitors or carry an oar overland for twenty days to plant it like a seed in mountains stonier than Ithaca. Wise Callidice stopped us, or we'd have wandered forever in our quest. Only her wisdom might have kept Odysseus from his vengeful tirade against Poseidon. Whether Poseidon's storms are on the tossing sea or within us, I would never address him as my father had.

Odysseus sat with his face in his palms and rocked himself. At last, he rose and took the cloth and salve from Medon's hands. Gently he treated Halitherses's burns. When he had finished, he enfolded his arms around the old man and sobbed on that ancient gleaming skull to have harmed a loyal friend to him and his father Laertes.

I didn't believe the prophecy. Of course, I might kill my father by accident, but how likely would that be? I no longer had the handicap of Oedipus, who never knew his father. I worried far more about what Odysseus might feel toward me. Hadn't I sat comfortably among the suitors in my father's hall? Of all the men who feasted, my mother loved me the best. If Odysseus had gone to such efforts because of a vision in which he heard Teiresias, would he be able to ignore completely the predictions of Halitherses? My father had struck him to silence the voice of a god. It would make as much sense to whip the pythoness of Delphi when she trembles on her tripod in ecstatic revelation. The words aren't hers, but those of Apollo the diviner.

I thought of the dolphins leaping in the waves off the cliffs of Leucas. Our legends say when dolphins die their skins become radiant with the colors of the rainbow. But what hero descended in the deep to return with this story? And if a man as daring as Odysseus witnessed such miracles and survived to tell us, who in our time would believe him?

CHAPTER 7

"Our son looks like a tramp. Good work, Odysseus."
These were my mother's first words when my father and I
returned to the great hall. She didn't ask what dangers we had faced
or if we had succeeded in our sacrifices but looked through us as if
we were drifters cast ashore on Ithaca. Like a child I had expected her
praise for enduring the journey. If it hadn't been for my father beside
me, I might have thrown myself weeping on her lap and blurted out
the sorrows I had suffered. We had fled Callidice's lands like men
cursed by the protecting deity. On an open-armed sea so calm I might
have believed Poseidon had graciously accepted our offerings, we
only imagined the risks ahead. The closer we came to Ithaca, the
more we feared the unknown.

I felt stolen from my home and abused by the rigors of my father's
miserable life. Yet I worried constantly what Halitherses's prophecy

might cause my father to feel toward me. If Odysseus had known me as a child, no doubt he would have always loved me. But isn't it different to meet a grown man who calls you father? How can this stranger be your own flesh? If my father felt a doubt, who would blame him for treating me like any stranger he might meet? Odysseus had lost the humility with which he left Ithaca to make amends to Poseidon. Instead, he had a gleam and a grimness of slaughter. I might have approached him while he stood alone at the rail, but I didn't want to admit my fears that he might not love me.

"Shall I break open more wine casks?" my mother continued, sitting at the head of our long table. "I hear you drank all of the potent wine you took along. I'm sure that pleased Poseidon."

I had hoped to see my mother with a ribbon in her hair to show her joy for our return, but she wore a rough cloak and cowl of black-dyed wool. If I had still been master in the hall, I'd have silenced her quickly enough and sent her to her room to change to brighter garments. But our new master stood with his head bowed like a servant accustomed to beratement.

"Soon Telemachus will know everything you know. How to wander, plunder, beg, and fight. Where is your eloquence? Or are you too tired to answer me?"

"Yes, I am tired," my father answered. "Much lies ahead of me, and a great deal behind. When I see your scorn for what I'm commanded to do, I remember men like Hector who also loved their wives. Where is Hector's wife, Andromache, today? The son of Achilles, Neoptolemus, took her for a prize. She belongs to the man whose father killed her husband. I brought Neoptolemus to Troy after Achilles's death and gave him Achilles's armor. In the wooden horse Neoptolemus silenced each man in turn as Helen called to us in the voices of our wives and lovers. I trembled to hear your voice, Penelope. I would have dropped my sword and shield and wandered from that horse like a man in a dream. Only Neoptolemus stopped me, for he loved nothing but his father's glory. Now he has married Hermione, the daughter of Helen and Menelaos. What a life Andromache must live as a slave in his great hall."

Odysseus straightened to his full height with a dignity that made one forget his short legs and the grime on him. Turning on a heel, he strode from the room. I could feel how my mother wanted me to stay with her, but I followed my father to the baths. The maidservants stoked a fire to boil the buckets of steaming water. I shed my filthy clothes and slipped into the shallow pool beside my father. The women drenched us with water, scrubbing us with soap and kneading our muscles with their agile hands. I could have remained there for hours, but the outer door opened and Philoitios, Eumaios, Dolios, and several others stood before us. My father, a foam of lather on his chest and thighs, stood up and raised a dripping hand in greeting.

"Joy and health to you and your families."

They nodded and shuffled awkwardly. The room was almost too small to hold us.

"I want my flocks and herds from Ithaca, Kephallenia, Doulichion, and the other islands brought to my hall. As you go to each island, invite everyone you meet to a festival, especially the wandering tramps who wear rotting skins and beg from door to door. It's late tonight but start tomorrow at dawn. Our sacrifices shall last for ten days. To each god in turn, I'll offer pure hecatombs as Teiresias warned me to do." So, my father showed again he cared nothing for whether we believed the tale of his journey to the Underworld. As for the other fantastic stories he would later tell, I can only say he alone encountered the magical people and places of which he spoke.

He assigned the islands to the different men and they filed from the room. We settled again in our warm water. I wanted to ask him why he would bring so many animals to our hall. How would we satisfy their hunger and thirst? What possible need could we have for them? He looked cheerful for the first time since our sacrifices in Thesprotia and spoke to me with an eager pleasure.

"It wasn't an accident I met Polyphemos, the son of Poseidon. It had been fated long before that. Even while I fought at Troy and offered burnt thighbones to Zeus and Poseidon, the gods knew of my wandering future. But a wanderer has little to lose, only memories and hopes. If you feared most when the sea was calm and Ithaca close, you're like me. Dangers—storms, battles, or a lover's arms—are easily faced. The excitement of each moment urges you to the next. Only when you have all your joys almost in hand do you fear for yourself."

My father had spoken so little on our homeward trip that I hadn't dared ask what he thought of Halitherses's prophecy. It was enough he spoke to me at all. But lying side by side in the baths, his friendliness encouraged me to ask another question over which I had brooded.

"Why did you curse Poseidon?"

Odysseus lay silent in the steaming waters, prompting me to say something more.

"Menelaos told me," I continued, "of Aias's shipwreck when the Greeks were returning home from Troy. Aias swam to the reefs and defied the gods to kill him. As he raged and waved his fists at the sky, he slipped and was swept drowning away. Why couldn't he have simply been thankful to be alive?"

Odysseus splashed water in his face and wiped it free of his eyes and beard. I could see that my question made him remember, for he sighed, and his eyes looked inward.

"That wouldn't have been Aias," he answered, "whose father was Oileus of Kynos. That Aias could toss a spear farther than any of us. He commanded forty ships. What man wouldn't curse to lose them? His friends, his wealth, the trust with which his countrymen sent him off—all this vanished with his command. Alone on a rock in a storm-swept sea, should he have offered another thighbone to Poseidon? You want him to be wise when he was impetuous. And what of men whose virtues are loved by the gods? Sarpedon was one of the finest of the Trojans, a son of Zeus himself. But Patroklus speared him like a boar. If we burned the thighbones of all the oxen in Greece, it wouldn't placate the least of the gods."

"If that's true, why did we sacrifice to Poseidon at all?"

"To make us better men," he answered without hesitation.

I might have asked him so many questions, but my perplexity must have shown. If he sacrificed to show himself a better man, why had he cursed Poseidon? If he believed in obeying a prophet like Teiresias, how could he not think I might someday kill him?

He laughed and seized me in a wrestling hold. Quickly his hard body slipped across mine and I felt my head pulled beneath the water. I struggled, but he held me like Poseidon himself. Once he let me up for air, but then plunged me down again and held me until I thought the water would rush into me. At that moment I felt he intended to kill me and save himself from Halitherses's prediction. Then he thrust me into the air like a dolphin leaping skyward to his laughter.

"Who described Aias's death to Menelaos?" he asked as the maids dried us and handed us our fresh clothing.

Menelaos had told me a fanciful story about how he learned of Aias's death and my father's survival.

"Menelaos said he wrestled a demon of the sea. When this ever-changing monster assumed a single shape and called Menelaos his master, the great warrior asked which of his friends had made a safe return from Troy." This sounded so incredible to my own ears that I added, "Of course, he might have simply heard it from a trader in Egypt."

My father smiled to hear that. He tousled my damp hair and boxed my shoulder. "Rise early tomorrow, we've work to do."

He left me at my tower in the outer courtyard. I trudged up the winding stairs to my circular room. Setting my torch in its holder, I flung open the wooden shutters to breathe the sea breeze. On my bed, I felt this room had changed since the suitors' deaths. Had it become smaller? Or did the air no longer move as freely? The sword, shield, and spear with which I practiced with the suitors hung on the wall where I had left them. The wooden sticks that had been the walls of Troy and the tiny ships that Dolios had carved for me still rested in my wooden chest. In this circular room I had always felt a full world at my command. If that world had been largely one of women until the suitors arrived, it had nonetheless offered me many delights. Recollecting the sea voyages and overland march with Odysseus, I wondered what kind of man he might have been if he had stayed at home with me. Instead of learning from the suitors, my father might have taught me to use the sword, discus, spear, and bow. I imagined him sleeping so near to me—only a short walk through the courtyard and the vaulted hall would bring me to his hewn bed. So many nights I had wondered where he might be sleeping, if he lived at all.

Yet those dreams lacked any relationship to this Odysseus. When I imagined all our flocks and herds crowded into our courtyard, I felt him like a trickster who wanted to amaze us. If you sacrifice more than you can eat, everyone knows you'll attract a crowd of beggars. How quickly they become supplicants of Zeus when their nostrils quiver from the aroma of a succulent roast. As if doubtful their hunger would guide them to our tables, my father had to summon them from the islands for his feast. And what feast was this, anyway? What festival did our calendar mark? It was Odysseus's devising. With these thoughts and many others, I smothered the torch and fell into a deep and dreamless sleep from which Odysseus roused me before the dawn.

CHAPTER 8

In the darkness I matched him stride for stride on the familiar path where I had climbed to the lookout as a child. Light rimmed the sea, a violet that gained substance as we climbed. The birds roused in their rocky nests. When we reached the shelf of rock that overlooks the island's approaches, Odysseus stopped and opened his hands to the dawn. Silently he bowed his head. I could hardly know his thoughts, but I felt the awe of this light unfolding across sky and sea. Around the irregular coastline I watched the cresting white breakers sweep forward. The sky paled with yellows and greens rising toward the bluer heights. At last, my father sighed and spoke to me.

"The greater Aias, son of Telemon of Salamis, died on a dawn like this one. Next to Achilles, he was the finest of the Greeks. Why list the Trojans he slaughtered or the comrades he saved? His triumphs never touched me, but rather his guileless heart. After Paris"—here my father hawked in his throat with contempt—"killed Achilles with his arrow, we fought for hours to save the body of Achilles and give it proper honors. Aias and I drove back the Trojans time and again. At last, Aias heaved the body of Achilles on his shoulders. I defended his back as he carried corpse and armor to our camp."

My father fell silent, thinking over the rest of this story to give it form for me.

"At the funeral games for Patroklus, Aias fought Diomedes for the armor of Sarpedon. Fearing for their lives, we cried for Achilles to call them both victors. Instead, Achilles awarded the beautiful armor to my friend Diomedes. Later, at the funeral games for Achilles, some said Aias should have Achilles's armor for saving his body from the Trojans. Others said I should receive it for guarding Aias as he retreated.

"Agamemnon urged us to battle for it. For one night I hesitated, knowing Aias had lived in Achilles's shadow and longed to be acclaimed the first among us. What man should hope for less? I felt Achilles's armor belonged to his son. Agamemnon disagreed. Could he have wanted to test me after all those years? Or rouse the spirit of our armies? Reluctantly I agreed to pit my strength and desire against that of Aias.

"When Aias's first blow resounded on my shield, I knew he would kill me for this armor. He attacked, his sword blue with motion. I parried, but no man could have outfought him that day. In a lull I feigned that my shield strap had broken and took a new shield, which I averted from him. On its face I had had Epeios secretly paint the image of Aias himself. Within range of him, I lifted the shield and saw the surprise in his eyes. He froze, for an instant unable to separate this image of himself from the breathing man. Quickly my sword leapt above his shield and touched his naked throat. How the ranks of our soldiers applauded my victory. Agamemnon himself handed me the sacred armor of Achilles. But Aias despised me for my trick and brooded in his tent.

"The next morning at dawn Aias filled his mixing bowl with the wine that brings forgetting. Then, as if he were no more than the painting on my shield, Aias braced his sword handle and rushed on the blade. His great strength drove the point through his chest and out his spine. Some said Aias offered himself as a sacrifice to Zeus. He had been named for the eagles which Zeus commands. I took his mixing bowl and poured the wine on his earthen floor. As I did this, I said to the others, 'This wine by death we now withhold from the gods.' I remember those exact words.

"Agamemnon cursed Aias, a dead man who could care nothing for the curses of the living. But I knew only Zeus could be blamed for his death and our years of suffering at Troy. And what good can come of blaming Zeus? In the hope of calming the spirit of Aias, I pled with Agamemnon to burn the corpse on a pyre. Agamemnon swore he wouldn't waste the firewood. Can you imagine—not for a man like Aias? Instead, they curled the handsome body in an ill-made coffin and slipped it upright into a slit dug in the earth. His soldiers from Salamis covered the dirt with a pyramid of stones to keep the wild dogs from pawing at the corpse. Not long after this I sailed to Scyros to bring Neoptolemus the avenger to Troy. I almost think I brought him not to sack Troy, but to rid myself of his father's armor. After Aias's death, I wished I had never fought to own it."

For a moment, my father's eyes glistened. My heart opened to his sorrow, but I remembered another part of the story of Aias. When you sang of Aias's suicide, Phemios, you told how his madness came at twilight. He prowled through the encampment grunting like a beast as he sought Agamemnon to kill. In the darkness he could no longer tell man from beast, and he rampaged among the herds of the Greeks. The bulls he castrated and the cows he slaughtered to starve the suckling calves. At dawn he saw the beeves maimed, dying, and dead. Only then did he go to his own tent and offer himself as a sacrifice to the gods.

If Odysseus knew your version, as he must have, why didn't he tell me the story in its entirety? Could he have hoped to make me a better man by touting the excellence of Aias? Or did he no longer recall the true violence at Troy? Perhaps he cared for Aias's name or thought to spare me part of the horror of this story. Love my father as I might, I never knew exactly his experiences and whether his tales for me were truths, half-truths, or less than that.

In any case, we began our work of lifting the scattered flat stones to build an altar for his shrine to Athena. We strained and often joined together to carry a heavy stone to its place. I didn't argue that a barren shelf of rock could never be a shrine. I had stood here so many hours as a child that the lookout had a special meaning for me. As I glanced toward the horizon, I recalled how often I had hoped to see the fleet returning from Troy. I knew the light, dawn and twilight and all the variations between. If I had chosen a place for a shrine, this would be my choice as well. At last, we had built the altar chest high and rested awhile in the midday warmth. Now my father rose and spoke to the light itself.

"Many-spirited Athena, accept this as my shrine of stone. Receive the many sacrifices of beast and spirit that I will make to you in this sacred place. Give me the far-ranging vision to see the light by which you move. Allow my son the excellent spirit to make him equal among the finest of men. Give him sons by which his name and mine and those of our fathers shall be known in the future. Illuminating Goddess, whose wisdom has shown me the infinite possibilities of the world and my own soul, let this shrine be the place where I remember the great-souled men who died at Troy and on our voyage home. If I live in pain and grieving, accept what little I or any man may offer an immortal, you who know our truest natures."

So Odysseus initiated this shrine where much of his later life would be passed in contemplation and prayer. What he sought may have been far less tangible than what I longed for as a child when I looked to the distant reaches of the sea, but nonetheless I felt how much we shared by our quests.

Chaos greeted us on our return home later that afternoon. Our courtyard overflowed with livestock and beggars ready to feast. That huge, slack-bellied buffoon, Iros, had set himself a lean-to for shade in one corner of the yard. The fellow didn't have any muscle, since he only loafed, begged, and feasted on the sacrifices of pious men. He glowed with appetite for Odysseus's feast. His puffy white cheeks were tinged with a healthy flush, his dark eyes gleaming like a birthday child's. When Odysseus drubbed Iros in front of the suitors, I thought we'd seen the last of him. Of course his father, a potter named Arnaios, had followed my father as a soldier to Troy. Iros's mother had been a gentle woman who gave what little she owned and earned—along with all her affection—to her only son. He stood on a rock and addressed his fellow scavengers like a captain preparing his troops for a daring campaign.

"If the gods favor you with a good portion, seize it without hesitation," he said, the broken teeth visible on the left side of his jaw where Odysseus's punch had caught him. "A squirt of wine, half a mouthful, is excellent to moisten the flesh and may save you a bite or two. If you speed down your first and second portions, your reward will be extra trips to the laden serving tables."

You remember Iros, so you can imagine how much more he had to say. Amusement at his fanciful speeches earned him as many handouts as his begging. But from his blubbery flesh that Odysseus had quickly pummeled to submission, I wondered what man might have stepped forth if his father Arnaios had returned to him from one of those twelve ships we sent to Troy. I questioned the misfortune of each of these beggars—legless, blind, or their sense vanished. What family brought them into the world and what fate cast them down? Each had a painful story. For Iros, I admit, I felt a fondness. Of all the men who ate our victuals, only he took bones and scraps to feed the hound, Argos, I had loved as a child. Bred to hunt, Argos made as fine a companion as any boy could have. When his muzzle grayed and his eyes glazed—for he had lived more than twenty years—the suitors whipped him like a cur and flung him out on the dung heap to die. If I brought him into the hall or courtyard, the suitors taunted me and abused him as soon as I left. Argos died about the time Odysseus returned, and I gave the hound a better burial than many of the suitors received. But Iros, a beggar who couldn't even justify his gluttony by pretending to be a suitor, fed Argos with a gentle hand as if transported to find any creature as miserable as himself. If a beggar had to feast on my patrimony, I would as soon have had Iros as another.

A single day had filled the courtyard and surrounding fields with livestock. Goats, pigs, sheep, and beeves stood crowded together, their filth slippery underfoot. What a cacophony rose from the unfed, thirsting animals. And these herds came only from Ithaca and Kephallenia, while those from the other islands would be again as large.

Odysseus paused at the edge of the rough group that listened to Iros. They would have listened to any speaker on the most improbable subjects, their main interest being to jibe and interrupt when the spirit moved them.

So Odysseus fit easily into this group, calling to Iros: "My well-padded friend, have you returned already from visiting the court of King Ekhetos in Epirus? Antinoös promised you a visit there, don't you recall? And said the king would make a thinner man of you by far—flaying off whatever flesh he found excessive."

Iros blanched when he heard that voice, his hands and knees trembling. But he had always been quick-witted and replied: "Praise

Zeus, I say, the patron of beggars, who demands all men treat them as supplicants."

"Praise the thunderbolt," my father answered menacingly, advancing through the throng.

Iros stepped off the rock, his eyes darting from side to side for a way of egress. My father caught him by the nape of the neck.

"Welcome to my hall, Iros, and to my festival. Ten days I'll feed you, so loosen that rope around your ample girth. In future years, when you compare this feast to any other, you'll feel surfeited with the memory of my generosity. You're not a fighter, but you may yet be our champion of feasting. With a stomach like yours—trained for long and strenuous meals—I think you'll outshine our expectations. And if you have more friends as fine as these, please invite them to join us. You're renowned as a messenger—even if you're not quite as swift as Hermes—so bring the good news to everyone in town." Thumping Iros's shoulders and giving several pats to the horizon of his stomach, Odysseus freed the messenger to bear his tidings.

CHAPTER 9

In the great hall my mother sat at the head of the table. She glared when she saw us but surprised me by speaking quietly to Odysseus.

"Is this necessary?" she asked. "The livestock in the courtyard, the stench, the filth? Couldn't you pen them elsewhere until your sacrifices?"

"They'll be gone soon enough."

"Into the bellies of those vagrants," she countered.

"Men like I was," Odysseus answered, "and may be again."

"If I return to my father, you'll be poor quickly enough."

Odysseus waved an arm to clear the servants from the room.

"If you return to Ikarios, you'll go with nothing."

"I'll take my dowry."

"You'll have no right to your dowry."

I wanted to intervene between my bristling parents, but what could I say? Nothing had prepared me for their quarrels or their reconciliations. For all I knew, they had acted this way from the day of their sacred marriage vows.

"The wealth of a hundred Ithacas would vanish in my father's country. When you waste our son's patrimony on your sacrifices, remember the bronze tripods and armor, the bars of gold and platters and goblets of silver that my father gave you to celebrate our marriage. Those are my belongings."

"If you were a faithful wife, certainly I'd agree. But when you wove Laertes's shroud, didn't you want to frighten him from my hall? You succeeded and freed yourself to enjoy the suitors. Didn't you hope to hear of my death as well? Isn't that why you let our son go to Nestor and Menelaos for news of me?

"Desire is so fragile, but you preserved it in a hundred men. Why didn't you lock yourself in your room and never come out? Or, if you couldn't resist seeing so many young men compete for you, why didn't you serve them meals that burned their gullets? Why didn't you sing in a strident voice? Or tell stories of your girlhood until they wept from boredom? Why didn't you hire ruffians and have them murdered? Or pay them each a share of my wealth to leave you alone? Or rub the dung of goats in your hair and let spittle run from your lips? You'd love to go home. How quickly you'd find another hundred suitors."

My mother smiled and raised a slender hand to quiet my father's ranting.

"If you call me unfaithful," she said to him, "you're a liar. And were you faithful to me?"

"They were divine," he answered with surprise.

"That's what men always say about women. You couldn't wait to tell me about your adventures. Transformed men into swine, indeed! It wouldn't be a great transformation. When your Circe and Calypso tucked you into their beds, did you have the faintest recollection of your own wife, your son, or the island of Ithaca? You've cursed Klytaimnestra, but how many women did Agamemnon enjoy— Briseis, Cassandra, how many others? At least they were slaves, not free women like your magical nymphs."

"I told you the truth about that," he replied and parried, "Admit you prayed for our son's beard to darken so you'd be free of me."

"I prayed for him to reach manhood. Whether I hoped he'd drive the suitors from our hall or free me to marry one of them, I honestly can't say," my mother answered calmly and added, "You're the one who never came back from Troy. For seven years, everyone waited. Even after I let the suitors court me, I couldn't decide if I wanted another man. My feelings changed. I felt such confusion. If I laughed with Amphinomos, I might dream for the daylight hours of a new life. But at night, alone in our bed, my thoughts returned to you."

Odysseus sighed and shook his head. "Twenty years is so long. Only the memory flees by in a moment."

"After twenty years apart, what's left to call marriage?" I felt shocked to hear my mother say this and continue, "I ask nothing of you. If you wish to live with me, then stay. If you prefer to travel, then go. I had always thought Athena your guiding spirit. Of course, according to you, she fought at Troy—as warlike as Ares. But why would you worship Poseidon unless you plan to sail again? You dream of a world filled with cities to sack and bronze to plunder."

"I'm done with war," Odysseus answered. "Sieges are for young men with years to squander. Let the gates of strange cities stand."

"If life with me is a shroud," my mother said, her eyes piercing as if to see the sources from which his erratic dreams quickened, "go elsewhere."

They looked like the immobile figures in a mural. Soon they might run or dance or sing, but now they gazed inward. I imagined them like young lovers unknown and fantastical to each other. As a mural captures the expressions of a moment and elongates them in time, I saw how enduring their perplexity might be. Each had carried an image within for so many years, but would they love one another again? Or despise the other for killing cherished dreams of what might have been? I had imagined them fitting into a perfect whole, so my fantasy vanished with theirs. Only time could unravel what their lives together, or apart, might be.

My father broke this tableau by saying, "I'll rid the courtyard of the animals as soon as I can."

So, Odysseus restored the word *hecatomb* to its true meaning. When you sang in our hall, we should have offered sacrifices to the gods more often. Nonetheless we quartered many a goat as an offering. On a festival day—perhaps to greet the new moon's birth from the sun's bright head—we might slaughter an ewe or a bull and fill our cups with Ithacan wine. My grandfather Laertes gave hecatombs such as these, and I doubt his father Arkeisios offered more. To me, a hecatomb meant merely an offering, nothing more.

That night we drove one hundred oxen from our courtyard to the olive tree where Odysseus had hidden his treasure. What a crowd came with us, their torches bobbing along the length of the shore. One hundred oxen would barely stuff the stomachs of the scavengers his invitation had drawn. Our islanders came too. On Ithaca where nothing ever happens, godlike Odysseus in his piety would give them tales to tell on long evenings. As the relatives of the suitors despised my father and me, so these men of the islands remembered loved ones who had followed Odysseus to Troy. Forgetting my father's years of suffering on their behalf, they asked: What folly made Odysseus take Ithacans to fight at Troy? And what leader returns from war alone? No one remembered how they had greeted Agamemnon with open arms and made passionate pleas to share in the glory of his battles.

Of course, many were sons of the men who had sat in the assemblies when Agamemnon came to Ithaca. Their fathers had been dazzled to receive a king of Mycenae on stony Ithaca. Odysseus told me how they resisted his advice to send an embassy of peace to Priam. At last Agamemnon agreed, dispatching Menelaos and Odysseus to Troy to negotiate for the return of Helen. Having forgot all this and come to feast at my father's expense, these men gloated to see Odysseus waste his oxen on sacrifices fit for those ancient times when men lived close to their gods.

I hardly heard my father offer these hundred oxen to Zeus. Nor did the waves crashing in the cavern of the night deafen me. If the suitors—and I—had failed to make generous sacrifices, Odysseus raised the sacrificial knife time and again until blood caked and dripped from his head to his feet. I could have wept to see each ox slaughtered. A man who owns an ox has the respect of his neighbors. It can be yoked for plowing, haul trees to build a fence or cottage, or carry vegetables and fruits to the market for barter. To own five oxen is prosperity, and to own one hundred is a marvelous wealth.

Of all men, certainly my father knew how little attention the gods pay to our sacrifices. One fine bull would have been an ample offering for Zeus. According to Odysseus, it took only a few sips of blood from a ram and an ewe to make famed Teiresias sing of the future. What lavish praise Odysseus had for each god and goddess in turn— Zeus, Hera, Athena, Apollo, Aphrodite, Artemis, Poseidon, Demeter, Hades, Ares, Hephaistos, Hermes, Iris, and many more. To Athena he sacrificed one hundred black bulls. To Poseidon he sacrificed one hundred goats and humbly thanked the earth-girdling god for our tranquil voyage home. Unpredictable as he was, I welcomed that sacrifice for reasons I'll tell you soon enough.

Why should my father destroy my patrimony? That question obsessed me during this impromptu festival. I had no appetite to join the loafers in their drunken revelry. I heard Odysseus's affirmations to the gods, but the words meant nothing to me. When my parents quarreled and my mother withdrew to the women's quarters and wept more tears than she had before Odysseus's return, I no longer cared. She saw in his destructiveness the hard life that faced us. My father took ritual baths each morning and evening and spent his days in prayer at his humble shrine.

The extravagance of these sacrifices could only be explained by Halitherses's prophecy. I believe Odysseus killed his herds to punish me. He denied me my patrimony because I had sat among the suitors and eased my mother's grief for his absence. He punished me for the fantasy that any man might usurp his father's place. He never discussed this, so I can only glimpse and surmise why he withheld from me the pleasures of life that the gods had denied to him. My punishment would be to live as hard a life as his. If I slaved a lifetime, I could never restore to our family what Odysseus had destroyed.

By the eleventh day, the dawn showed only scorched earth and heaps of carcasses stretching away from the olive tree. So, my father fulfilled the prophecy of Teiresias and settled again on Ithaca to live his old age in peace.

CHAPTER 10

Twelve ships sailed to Troy, nearly a thousand soldiers under the command of my father. He returned, the sole witness to the deaths of so many men who had been husbands, fathers, sons, and brothers. Once he resumed his place in our hall, each relative came to make inquiries and left grieving. For weeks these mourners flowed ceaselessly. But what good is it for a mother to learn that her beloved Leukos was speared by Antiphos, a son of Priam? Is it better to be killed by a prince? If they pressed my father, as they did, was it soothing to learn the spear had penetrated through the groin and emasculated him at death? The pain of unknown losses became the certainty of how a man had died and whether the Trojans stripped his armor or the Greeks carried him back to a pyre by the beached ships. So deeply did they yearn for news of these missing loved ones, no gruesome detail could be held back from them. They had to know that Leukos fell writhing and biting the dust as if this added to their memory of the smiling youth who sailed to glory so many years before. Unable to cease their questioning, they learned the spear tossed by Antiphos had been aimed at the greater Aias and struck Leukos by chance. Could this succor them? Or the fact Agamemnon killed Antiphos with a blow of the sword behind the prince's right ear?

At least Leukos died in the war. But what if you learned your beloved had fallen in a drunken stupor from the roof of some enchanted villa where Odysseus brought his men on the voyage home? That was Elpenor's fate. Of course, I knew none of these men. They had embarked with my father too soon after my birth for me to recollect them. In Elpenor's case, Odysseus recounted how he saw the ghost of Elpenor in the Underworld and fulfilled all the pitiable ghost's requests. That is, he returned to Aiaia Island and torched Elpenor's body and armor, piling a pyramid of stones above the foaming breakers to mark this sailor who would otherwise be unknown to future men. Elpenor's kin left muttering, enraged Odysseus would tell them fairy tales believable only by children.

Yarn followed yarn—or so it seemed to the grieving visitors. According to Odysseus, the giant Polyphemos took heavy-shouldered Eurybates in one massive hand and devoured him feetfirst. The herald's screams echoed from the cavernous mouth until his bloody carcass vanished in a single swallow. The most loyal and popular of the officers, Polites, ate of the ambrosial lotus and raved and wept for weeks when deprived of its strange visions. So avidly did he crave pleasures beyond those ordinary men enjoy that he pulled the wax from his ears to hear the Sirens' forbidden singing. In an instant of desire, he dove into the billowing waves and vanished while Odysseus strained to free himself from the mast. Eurylokos, the kinsman of Odysseus, persuaded the crew to feast on the beeves belonging to the Sun despite my father's warning against this. By some magic, the flayed skins writhed on the earth and the roasting meat lowed on the spits. To exonerate Eurylokos, Odysseus explained to his family how the winds had kept them landbound and starving. When the winds started the ship homeward again, a sudden gale broke open the hull and spilled the crew drowning into the waves. Only Odysseus survived.

If my father wanted to anger these relatives, he couldn't have told more provocative stories. When Odysseus fought at Troy, I often imagined a messenger might bring me word of his death. But it would be a death that completed a life, a source of pride as well as grief. In these deaths on the home voyage, men found nothing familiar. If I had been told Odysseus died by such magic, I would have cursed the messenger for a liar. Here the relatives cursed Odysseus doubly, for he had been entrusted with the lives of the men who followed him. Who wouldn't imagine my father's improbable tales hid some shameful failure that had caused the deaths of so many men?

Soon the local wits ridiculed Odysseus. Behind my back they called me the little sacker of cities. Rumors of my father's cursing Poseidon had spread over the islands after our return. Quickly the suitors' relatives forgot the promises of peace given in return for the treasure of Odysseus. Polybos, whose shame was to have been father of the suitor Eurymakhos, accused Odysseus of impiety. He claimed the treasure had saved Odysseus from vengeance for the suitors' deaths, but that no man can curse the gods with impunity. So Polybos and his gang raised a clamor across our islands. At last, another assembly was called, as if assembling fools together might make for wise counsel. When the hundred suitors sat in assembly, what man would have freely given them respect? Did they have honor, wisdom, or generosity? And when Eupeithes stirred up the islanders' foolhardy valor, didn't wiser voices speak for moderation and go ignored? Why didn't they listen to Halitherses, who pled for understanding? In my lifetime, no assembly voted for peace when violence was possible. If Polybos carried the assembly, my father would be stoned to death and his carcass left exposed for the gulls and dogs to devour.

Had your father Terkias sacrificed his herds to the gods and lied to his countrymen so they would despise him, what would you have felt? I understood my father's life had been filled with experiences unimaginable to me. If he wished to sacrifice to the gods, I could hardly tell him not to. If he believed in the truth of his adventures and the deaths of his comrades, as he swore to my mother and me, how could I order him to tell more pleasing stories? But I ached, approving of nothing he did and loving him nonetheless. Why should I have trembled when Polybos stirred our neighbors against my father? Wouldn't it have been better for me to pray for the worst for Odysseus and hope to save the precious little that remained for my inheritance? Instead, knowing I would find him at his shrine, I rushed skyward to pour out my fears.

Gravely he listened to me. When I finished, he told me of events in the Trojan war of which I never heard you sing.

"Our last assembly at Troy condemned a girl to die. I spoke in favor of killing her." My father shook his head with sorrow at this memory. "You've heard the bards sing of the visit of King Priam to Achilles to beg for the body of his son Hector. The nobility of the old king moved Achilles to offer back the body. Then Priam, weeping not only for Hector but for all the men who had perished in this long war, offered a remarkable gift to Achilles—marriage to his daughter Polyxena and peace between the Greeks and Trojans.

"Achilles first entrusted this story only to me. His mother, the divine Thetis, urged him to accept Polyxena as his wife to ease his grief for his beloved Patroklus. Since so many allies and enemies alike would oppose peace in their lust for victory, I agreed to go alone to arrange this marriage. Dressed as a beggar, I had my own men beat me and pour filth on me. Then I moved through the Trojan lines by stealth in darkness. At the Skaean Gate, I told how the Greeks had abused me. The Trojan guards gave me cuffs and kicks instead of the bits of twisted bronze for which I begged. They dragged me to the palace of Prince Paris for questioning about the Greek armies. Leopard-skinned Paris ordered I be bathed under the watchful eyes of Helen herself. When they brought me to Helen, she sat before her mirrors. The glow of innumerable torches cast a haunting light across that face she studied with utter absorption. I hadn't seen her so closely since before my marriage to your mother. When I courted Helen with the other princes of Greece, she had been much the same. These fire-lit mirrors would serve her for a while, but she loved best the mirrors of men's eyes. Remember you told me how she recognized you as my son when you met her in Sparta? That was faint praise, for she found me the ugliest of men. She preferred beauty to cunning—or charm, as men call it in peacetime."

"Why didn't you kill her?" I asked him, blushing with embarrassment to realize Helen had insulted us when she lavishly praised my resemblance to him.

"She had to be returned to Menelaos. Our only hope for peace rested in her. If not for that, I would have brought Menelaos her severed head as a beggar's gift. Instead, I let her bring Queen Hecuba to set the marriage terms. That night Helen did as she promised. Perhaps she had tired for a moment of the beauty of Paris and longed for the kingdom of Sparta, where she had grown to womanhood a Greek. How Hecuba cursed me for killing her beloved Trojans. She wept with shame to imagine a Greek—especially Achilles who had murdered Hector, Troilius, and many more of her sons—as the husband of her daughter. But Helen soothed Hecuba until the old lady agreed to the marriage day. The Trojans would return Helen and her treasures and allow bronze destined for Greece to pass without

71

tax for ten years. Why hadn't we agreed to such terms when I made my embassies of peace nine years earlier? I can't explain men's follies to you. But when I returned to our armies in that vast camp on the beachhead, Achilles and I persuaded the others to call a wedding truce. Each day of peace made us hope for the joyous times that would follow the marriage of Achilles to Polyxena. Even Menelaos smiled at the fantasy that he would reign with Helen again in Sparta.

"The wedding preparations consumed us. Forsaking the tactics of war, we planned for feasting, games, and gifts fit for such a marriage. We must have been enchanted, Greeks and Trojans alike, for it had been predicted Achilles would die in this war. How could we hope his marriage would save us? At last, the feasting and exchanging of gifts began. I won't digress about the games, except we Greeks outshined the Trojans by far. Finally, when Polyxena and Achilles stood at the wedding altar, Paris became crazed to imagine losing Helen. Drawing his bow, he caught Achilles with an arrow in the back of the ankle. Swords flashed on all sides. Achilles swooned in my arms, our hope for peace vanishing with his death. I found myself fighting to defend his body and armor. The wedding guests danced forward and back over his corpse, this violent consummation a far greater delight than the trembling struggles of lovers. What can you expect when men wear resplendent armor and choose their finest swords and shields for a wedding? My force in a wall of Greeks at last let the greater Aias risk lifting the heavy weight of Achilles. Breath burning in our chests, we defended Aias as he carried Achilles to the black-hulled ships. Seventeen days we mourned for our losses. I felt myself diminished by these years of war and boredom. Although I might often call myself the father of Telemachus, I was no longer the same man who sailed from Ithaca.

"A year later, when we had sacked Troy and clouds of black smoke billowed above its walls, a rumor spread through our armies that the ghost of Achilles demanded Polyxena as his bride. No one claimed to have seen this ghost, but everyone knew the ghost's desire. The Trojan men and boys we had killed on the spot. But in the chaos, I feared our soldiers might seize any provocation to kill the Trojan women. I heard in the demand of Achilles's ghost the desire of our armies for a ritual sacrifice, one girl wed to all our fallen heroes. Then let the rest go unharmed to their miserable lives as slaves. To protect these Trojan lives, I pleaded in our assembly to slay the girl. How the heads of the captains nodded, my eloquence the sleep of reason. Agamemnon spoke against me, but everyone knew his passion for the girl's sister Cassandra.

"Quickly I found myself at the grave of Achilles. The girl gave a silly speech, prattling how she'd prefer death to slavery. Then she bared herself to the waist, her ripening breasts a promise of new life. I saw the hand of Neoptolemus tremble as he raised the sacrificial knife. This was so very different from killing men, this glory of our hard-won peace. She closed her eyes, her head averted to one side. He hesitated with the knife poised above her. He was a finer man than many believed, courageous—not heartless. I brought him from Scyros and knew him well. When I found he deserved to be called the son of Achilles, I gave him his father's armor, sword, and shield. Seeing his hand tremble above this child, I wished the knife were in my own hand. I knew why the girl should be sacrificed and he had no idea. I could have struck her as a savior of her people, while Neoptolemus struck her in honor of the dead."

For the first time I understood why my father had argued in favor of the death of Polyxena. I had always imagined he despised her as a Trojan or wished to pay tribute to the fame of Achilles. Fascinated as I was, he spoke so pensively I wondered if he cared at all for events in the world beyond his shrine. His runtish body and blunt features faded to insignificance compared to his far-seeing eyes that re-created a far more glorious and dangerous world than Ithaca. If he could explain why he had acted as he had in that past world, perhaps he felt no need to fear consequences from men like Polybos. As for the violent Odysseus who killed the suitors heedless of whether they had the worst or best of motives in coming to his hall, he had only a distant kinship to that man. For his own grief, a man can take revenge on a hundred weaker men and call that justice. But what good is his revenge when others are grieving? For years, my father had missed his wife and son, his comrades-at-arms, and his land of Ithaca. Now, for the first time perhaps, he felt the grieving of others who held him responsible for their lost loved ones. So he summoned the past, with all his failures and cruelties, to judge if he should be the vessel for the odium and grief of so many. At that moment accusations of impiety meant nothing to him, much as I worried for his life. And he chose me to hear the misgivings of his heart.

CHAPTER 11

My father and I sat as I sit with you. Side by side at his shrine, we looked far over the sea. He spoke in a deep yet quiet voice, his feelings controlling the pace of his narratives. Often, he paused to marshal his recollections. Occasionally I questioned him. He could hardly tell me everything that happened at Troy, any more than I can give you each detail of his life after his return to Ithaca. But as Polybos gathered allies and planned his strategies to carry the assembly against Odysseus, my father told me the truth of many of the accusations men made against him. As I listened, I hoped I might find his defense to the charge of impiety. I doubted he would defend himself against men such as Polybos, and I had little to say on his behalf that our islanders would find pleasing. No doubt those who despise him will say he lied to me. Since he could hardly deny the acts others had witnessed, they'll say he fabricated motives men would find faultless. I only want his story to be heard with theirs.

"Early in the war," he began, "not long after our first landing near Troy, I recall standing in a grove with Eurylokos, Polites, and a few others. Down the sloping hillside, in the patches of light breaking through those towering trees, I saw a Trojan soldier who staggered like a drunken man. His shield remained strapped to his arm, but his sword had been lost in some skirmish. I don't believe he knew where he was or even that a few hours earlier he had been a soldier. He no longer wore his helmet and blood clotted in the curling hair about his ear. Strange I remember this so well, when in every way it was of no importance.

"Polites nocked an arrow and offered me the bow. But I had no desire to kill the man. Disarmed, defenseless, why should I kill him? What did I have to fear from him? It's true we had a duty to kill Trojans, but in that case I felt the duty onerous. The man's shield had none of the hero's emblems. Before our landing, he might have been a carpenter or mason working in the small towns near Troy. Even if he stumbled back to the Trojan lines and regained his strength, he would never have the skills to harm me. I handed the bow back to Polites, who pulled the waxed string with ease. The first arrow dropped the Trojan and we strolled to the corpse.

"Polites exercised his right to strip the man's meager belongings. In his pouch we found a few bits of bronze and a circular piece of leather imprinted with the silhouettes of a woman and child. We stood silently, forgetting the war for a moment. Remembering my hearth and the hospitality Zeus demands toward strangers, I wished we had left the man unharmed. I believe we shared a dull grief for the bravado that brought us to this distant kingdom. Polites knelt and brushed the black flies from the wounds. With one hand he pressed open the jaws and placed the bronze within the Trojan's mouth.

Although later we would have left such a corpse for the wild dogs to devour, he returned the leather keepsake to the man's pouch and ordered a shallow grave be dug and piled above with stones.

"I killed Demokoon, Pidytes, Charops, Hypeirochos, Chersidamas, Ennomos, Deiopites, and many other nameless men. Let me tell you about Dolon's death—for it came after nine years of war. With our armies driven to the sea, Diomedes and I set out in darkness to spy on the Trojans. Athena favored us for we quickly captured Dolon, a weakling who ran like the wind. Hector had promised him the horses and golden chariot of Achilles if he could spy in the Greek camp. With Achilles alive, that gift was premature at best. What a lavish ransom Dolon offered us in turn if we would spare his life. So we promised not to kill him, and when he had told us all he knew, we killed him nonetheless. Then we slaughtered a dozen Thracian soldiers in their sleep, including King Rhesos, whose chariot horses we stole for our prize. How did killing a captive weakling or slumbering men differ from killing that dazed Trojan we had found wandering in the woods? I could have killed Dolon or Rhesos and his men with my own hands, but again I let my companions do the slaughter. My feelings made the only difference. For I no longer felt sympathy, reluctance, or sadness. In fact, I felt only excitement and a pleasing expectation of the praise of my peers. And if you had said the war changed me, I would have cursed you for a liar."

None of our islanders cared a whit for Trojan dead, so I saw no advantage to my father in these recollections. One defense I had imagined would be to argue he returned from Troy bewildered, even demented. How else could the fantastic stories of his journey home be explained? But if I learned Hector or Aeneas had struck the sense from my father, could I really say this before the assembly? Could I present my father beggared of mind and plead for a magnanimity I knew none of these men possessed? Would I want to live my life as the son of a fool rather than a hero? Worse, it reminded me of the charge against Odysseus that he had feigned madness to save himself from fighting at Troy. Wouldn't Polybos argue he merely pretended once again, his honor nothing compared to his desire to live?

"Why did you go to Troy?" I asked him, "Was it because you had been a suitor of Helen?"

My father smiled wryly.

"All the captains at Troy had been suitors to Helen—Menelaos, Idomeneus, Aias the greater, Menetheus, Diomedes, Protesilaus who died first when we landed on the beaches, and the archer Philoctetes, whom I brought from Lemnos to help us end the war. No doubt you know much of the story—how Helen's father, King Tyndareus of Sparta, forgot to worship Aphrodite. The goddess cursed him, promising his daughters would marry two and three times and desert their husbands. Fearing this, Tyndareus made all the suitors swear to defend the marriage of Helen. Whichever suitor might be chosen, all the rest vowed to fight any man seeking to carry her away. We were young, overbearing, and violent with our desires, so I don't blame Tyndareus. Once the suitors had sworn the vow, he freed Helen to choose whichever man she loved. If Achilles had been among us, I believe she would have chosen him. But Agamemnon had married her sister Klytaimnestra and pushed his brother Menelaos forward. Richest among us, Menelaos showered her with gifts. Personally, I didn't try to compete. Why should I give her gifts when she would never marry me? But to feast and compete in our daily games was such a pleasure that I lingered at the court of Tyndareus. After Helen wed Menelaos for his dazzling wealth, I married your mother and returned home to Ithaca. Soon you were born—my hope through all my hardships.

"I heard of a handsome visitor from the east who came to the court of Menelaos. His name was Paris, a son of Priam and Hecuba. If the well-known story can be believed, he—a mortal man—had been asked to judge whether Athena, Aphrodite, or Hera was the most beautiful of the goddesses. Aphrodite promised him any woman he might desire, a bribe which worked only too well. Bull-headed Menelaos left Helen alone with Paris, their guest, and Aphrodite charmed Helen to love this stranger and flee from her husband and her marriage vows. If you can trust all you hear, Hecuba had had some prophetic insight about Paris and exposed him to die as an infant. Shepherds raised him, kindhearted peasants whose caring ultimately led to the destruction of Troy itself.

"Then Agamemnon and Menelaos convened the princes who had courted Helen. Invoking the vow we had made to Tyndareus, they argued we had no choice but to go to war and recapture Helen for Menelaos.

"I disagreed and refused to join them. Even if you believe goddesses care for what men call beauty or believe a man could judge what is beautiful in the divine, I saw no reason to be bound by my vow. I had promised to protect Helen's marriage against any man who carried her away against her will. What her father had feared was that one of her other suitors, enraged not to be chosen by her, would murder the man she loved and carry her off by brute strength. No one had imagined she might go of her free will—and with a foreigner, not even a Greek. No single prince of Greece could have stood against the armies of the suitors, but we knew little of Priam's strength or the fortifications of Troy."

What joy I felt to hear him! Today, years later, I feel that same joy remembering that he didn't desert me because of his vows for Helen. What a mean abandonment that would have been, a child left fatherless over a faithless woman. Listening, I felt how Helen's suitors had acted much like those who courted my mother. What had Eurymakhos been but another Menelaos? Using the wealth of his father Polybos, his gifts so transcended those of the other suitors that my mother's family urged her to forget Odysseus and marry Eurymakhos. How inexplicable that my father's wanderings began and ended with these unruly bands of suitors.

"You didn't pretend to have lost your mind, did you? Palamedes didn't trap you into going to Troy?" For the moment I too forgot the threat of Polybos. Like the youth who had lived with so many calumnies against my father, I wanted him to clear his name for me. If the twenty days until the assembly slipped away from us, at least I would know my father for the man he truly was.

"After I refused to squander the lives of our islanders, Agamemnon, Menelaos, and Palamedes came to beg and harass me into agreeing with them. They said I owed a debt to the family of Penelope, since Helen was her cousin. Father Ikarios sent a message by Palamedes ordering me to Troy. Our islanders called on me to lead our expeditionary force. But your mother wept each time she saw me and begged me never to fight for Helen.

"I tried working in the fields to ease my anxieties. Strapped to the ox-drawn plow, I ran the furrows back and forth in the heat of the sun. But the aching of my body couldn't transport me from the pain I felt within. Often, I burst into tears and cried aloud to the empty fields.

"If you want to know how contemptible a man can be, listen to what follows. Palamedes spread a rumor through the islands that my work in the fields, my weeping and talking to myself—all these were a pretense to show myself unbalanced. Once he convinced some people such a pretense existed, he claimed he would prove to them I was as sane as any man. He kidnapped you from our home by lying to the maidservant who watched over you. What a procession of men followed him across my fields to where I worked. By the time I realized you were the swaddled bundle he carried, he had dropped you squalling and twisting directly in front of my plow. Of course, I stopped and ran to pick you up again. If I hadn't had to comfort you in my arms, I would have killed Palamedes there.

"How the people began to speak against me. They would curse Laertes for his brutishness in razing Nerikos and curse me for my cowardice in refusing to go to Troy. What a shame, I heard again and again, that Athena hadn't blessed our family with the virtue of moderation. Or, as others put it more bluntly, what a shame to have the father be a butcher and the son a coward. If this campaign had continued very long, I would have been an outcast in my own country. If my beliefs were just, you might ask, why not be such an outcast? Who cares for the respect and admiration of troublesome and foolhardy men? But I was young and newly called as king. I wanted my example to show that my father's zeal in sacking Nerikos had come from patriotism. What had he gained by it, after all? I cared for the opinion of the world. So, I placated everyone by offering to lead an embassy of peace to Troy. There I met Priam, Hector, Aeneas, and all their leaders. Troy governed so many lands and cities that we Greeks—divided into small city-states—seemed laughable and savage to them. If I had been the most skilled negotiator, I doubt if I could have struck a bargain."

"Did you know Aeneas escaped from Troy?" I asked him, eager to add my small story to his.

He sighed as if the very name of Aeneas were a burden to him.

"Two years after the war ended," I told him, "I saw a spot on the horizon, then another and another. I doubted my sight, but ten ships were closing fast on Ithaca. I felt a boundless exultation to see warships with beaked bows and lean hulls. What else could these ships be but the fleet from Troy?

"I raced to the town and cried to everyone that the fleet was returning. Leaping aboard the fishing boats, we left the harbor waving whatever came to hand. We tacked into the wind, trying as best we could to hurry to this fleet bearing down on us with the wind full behind them. But I counted twenty ships, not the twelve with which you left Ithaca. You might have built new ships to carry the spoils from Troy, but these ships flew black foreign pennants. Gaunt with hunger and dressed in full battle gear, the crew looked to have suffered greatly on their journey. Women, children, and livestock huddled on the decks of the ships. They looked despairing, hardly the victors of a great campaign.

"Laertes called across the water to them, 'What land are you from and where are you headed?'

"The cry came back, 'We are survivors of Troy bound to raise a new city. If you are men of Ithaca and Odysseus is your king, take for yourselves and him the curses of Aeneas and his followers.'

"They brandished their spears and the archers on their decks nocked arrows in their bows. But I cared nothing for their threats.

"'Where is Odysseus?' I cried out to them, although I was only a boy. 'Where is my father?'

"The voices of other men drowned mine, for each had a relative who had gone to Troy. Their cries rolled over the waves. 'Where is Perimedes? Arnaios? Leukos?' Laertes beat his forehead in a rage to be weaponless with the Trojans so near. I wept in disappointment. Soon these deep-displacing ships had left our fishing boats in their wake. What rancor I felt the gods must bear toward me. You had triumphed, but these Trojans survived in your place. I felt I despised them as much as you must have during the long years of war."

My father put his arm around me as if to comfort the child who had been so disappointed. Finally, without responding, he continued.

"At Priam's court, Menelaos spoke first and pleaded for the return of his wife. He spoke simply and showed he loved Helen as much as he could love any woman. When I spoke after him, I felt the strangeness of eloquently addressing men who in another week or month might be my enemies in war. For I didn't feel these were men to be despised. I admired Priam and Hector. Even Paris, whom I felt a fool, had beauty and a quick wit. If we had found peace, I might have thought fondly of the Trojans and remembered my embassy to them with pleasure."

"But they refused to return Helen," I said to urge him forward.

My father smiled at my mistake.

"The Trojans would have given Helen back with delight. They cared nothing for her. Paris could have wept like a woman, since his father paid little attention to him. But Troy had been built as a fortress to guard the trade in metals from east to west. No caravan passed without paying tax to Priam.

"We agreed on the return of Helen in the first few days of our negotiations. But what tax would be levied on shipments of bronze for the cities of Greece? After all, bronze made Mycenae and Sparta great. We felt the Trojans demanded too much; they considered our offers far too little. Had we known what the war would cost us, how easily we would have compromised our differences. I wish we had agreed to pay the full tax they demanded. If this caused the courts of Agamemnon and Menelaos to be slightly less opulent, would men on Ithaca or Kephallenia have cared?

"That embassy of peace proved my great mistake. If a man refuses to go to war, what duty has he violated? But when I placated Agamemnon and the rest by going to Troy, I committed myself to the cause of the Greeks. If I won the peace, I would be wise and revered. But if I lost the peace, how could I disassociate myself from the alliance I had represented? Without admitting to myself that I made any choice, I had become a leader of the Greeks.

"More than that, what I had seen at Troy disturbed me. The power of Priam, the arms of Troy, made me fear someday he or one of his fifty sons might dream of expanding westward and enveloping Greece

83

in the empire of Troy. I began to see the Greek alliance as a bulwark against this. Since I admired Agamemnon, I imagined him our savior from future wars. If you feel these reasons that finally led me to Troy amount to nothing, I can only say again how great my pain was to leave you and your mother. I fantasized a short war and a glorious return. But having seen the ramparts and armies of Troy, I knew in my heart we would pay beyond our means for this war."

What closeness I felt to my father when he finished speaking. In everything connected with the origins of the war, he had been blameless. If the rest of his revelations were like these, what could possibly distress him? But my feeling of closeness—of love—only increased my worry over the approaching assembly. He had said nothing I might use in his defense. If I argued from this history that he had been a fine citizen and a loyal captain, others might call him a liar in any case. I needed more forceful proofs and wondered who on our islands might help me.

CHAPTER 12

What shall I say of the witnesses Polybos might have called to testify against Odysseus? They were the men who had traveled through Thesprotia with us, friends and servants loyal to the memory of my father. No doubt my father's curse of Poseidon upset some and outraged others, but what man had never cursed a deity? Also, my father made that journey to offer sacrifices to Poseidon, so who could know what to make of his erratic speeches of praise and condemnation? As the days passed, I visited these men who had accompanied us. One of Dolios's rugged sons swore he had seen, in shining lights above Odysseus's head, the blue trident of Poseidon clash against the golden aegis of Athena. Our herald, Medon, had drunk less of the amber wine, but claimed he never heard Odysseus curse any god. After nearly losing his life with the suitors, he became fearful when Odysseus ranted and spent much of that night hidden beneath a pile of skins. But Eumaios, now a free man, recalled the words of Odysseus exactly as I did: "So I curse you, Poseidon, as you cursed me." I didn't know who spread the story of our adventures—the appearance of Queen Callidice, the planting of the oar, the flow of amber wine splattering our faces and gullets, the words with which Odysseus made his sacrifices—so I could only surmise what rumors Polybos had heard and how he would present his accusations to the assembly.

I visited Halitherses last. His house in town was as mean a hovel as that of my grandfather Laertes. I don't know why these old heroes chose such surroundings. Laertes could have lived comfortably in our hall, but he refused because of the suitors. Even after Odysseus's return, Laertes preferred to live in his rough farmhouse. And Halitherses once had the plunder that lets a man buy slaves, oxen, and fields. I never heard he wasted what he won. But he lived with a single servant, a woman with crippled hands who was as old as my nurse Eurykleia. No trophies from Nerikos or his other campaigns decorated his walls. In fact, the house had been built into a hillside and only a few chinks in the stone allowed light and air to enter. No firewood stood stacked on his hearth, nor did I smell the aromas of cooking from his kitchen.

Halitherses sat bundled on a high-backed chair, his legs drawn up beneath him and his arms wrapped about his chest. The light of the sea had left his blue eyes. In Thesprotia he had looked a vigorous veteran of many campaigns, but in this gray light he appeared fragile and pained to glimpse what would come.

He gestured me to a bench before him. The maidservant brought a beaker of wine and cups. Praising Athena, he splashed a generous portion of the wine on the earthen floor.

"I hear the men call you Poliporthis, destroyer of cities," he said once we had drunk, "When your grandfather and I were young men, that was a name for praise, not jesting. In those days I had strength and anger like your father's. Now I have the seer's imperfect vision."

"But do you believe I'll kill my father?"

Halitherses raised an open hand.

"The words I spoke were beyond dreams or drunkenness. I don't pretend to know their meaning. For the most part, the gods keep the future to themselves. They want it that way. No seer—not even Teiresias who lived seven generations—sees the fullness of the future."

I would have asked him more, but how could he ease my fears?

"Do you know anything of Polyphemos, the son of Poseidon?" Even as I asked, I felt the absurdity of my question. I had asked everyone—sailors, beggars, traders—and no one had heard of such a man, or a giant race called Cyclopes.

"There was a man named Polyphemos," Halitherses replied, "a captain of King Pirithoös of Thessaly. He won renown fighting in the north against savages who were such skilled horsemen that rider and mount seemed one creature. Theseus of Athens fought beside him, as did Nestor of Pylos when a youth. But of his ancestry, or his life after his campaigns, I know nothing."

"But he couldn't have been the Polyphemos whom Odysseus blinded."

"No." Halitherses shook his head. "This Polyphemos was a man of our size and possessed two eyes."

"Had my father heard of him?"

"If he didn't hear from us, I'm sure Nestor spoke of him at Troy."

Why should Odysseus claim to have blinded a giant with the name of a hero of Laertes's generation? Perhaps he had truly met such a monster, a son of Poseidon, and by coincidence the monster shared the hero's name. Or could this be an example of the eccentric humor that made Odysseus introduce himself as Strife, the only son of King Allwoes, when at last he met Laertes? This mystery, like so many others about my father, I could never solve.

"If you believe Poseidon cursed him, could it have been for another reason? Not that he blinded a cruel monster, but that he killed a grandson of Poseidon—Palamedes of Euboea?" I asked Halitherses this without any hope he might answer. But in my father's grotesque stories, there lingered some shape of the truth. I had heard my father accused of killing Palamedes on the voyage to Troy, of drowning him during the war, or of falsely proving he aided the Trojans so Agamemnon put him to death. My father could hardly have committed this crime so many ways. Might Odysseus have felt compelled to sacrifice to Poseidon, but refused to admit the true reason? Instead of saying he killed a hero of the Greeks, might he have invented a monstrous contemporary of his father to blind and escape from?

To my surprise, Halitherses chuckled. "You're confused over names today. What was the name of Palamedes's father?"

"Nauplius," I replied.

"And there's the city of Nauplia named for Nauplius, but not the father of Palamedes. The city of Nauplia is named for the son of Poseidon and Amymone, but Palamedes's father came from men as mortal as you and I. Let me tell you something about him. As king of Euboea, this Nauplius made murder an instrument of his rule. If he had craft and skill, it was in finding more shameful uses for his violence. This quality—if you call it that—he raised to an art when he lured the Greek fleet onto the rocks of Euboea to revenge his son's death. After the trials and losses at Troy, this monster with his false beacons killed more of our sons. Palamedes inherited his father's vices. Traitor to the Greeks, he deserved death—whether Odysseus killed him by stealth or Agamemnon condemned him before the assembly."

Phemios, I don't know why you never sang of Palamedes. None of our other heroes escaped your praise—Achilles, Diomedes, Philoctetes and the rest. Were you embarrassed to include him as a Greek? Or perhaps he proved of so little significance in the fighting at Troy that you omitted him. If so, his greatest feat was to trick my father into going to the war. Unfortunately, I had learned nothing from Halitherses that would help me defend my father before the assembly. Feeling how quickly the hours passed, I thanked the old man.

"My father owed you respect as a man and a friend of our family. If I could have stopped him that night in Thesprotia, I would have. When he salved your wounds, he wept with regret for what he had done."

Halitherses answered me gently. "What he did, he did because he loved you."

He didn't rise but waved me toward the door. The maidservant fumbled with the latch, her arthritic hands curled in fists. But something she saw in me made her smile, and that smile carried me into the daylight with a firm step.

Soon I sat with my father, listening to the last of his story of Troy. From his aerie, we watched a mist rolling toward Ithaca from the edges of the sea. Again, my father's voice carried me far from my fears of the assembly that would convene at dawn the following morning.

"I designed the wooden horse," he continued, "but Epeios built it. What mastery he had in crafting a shield or the hull of a ship. As a boxer, no one matched him. He was a free man, of course, but hardly a noble—certainly, no hero. In fact, he made a mediocre swordsman and for his own good I often assigned him to carry water to the men fighting.

"This horse had to be as large as a ship. One hundred of our finest soldiers would be concealed within it. To entice the Trojans to pull it inside their gates, we made the horse a gift to Athena. Our inscription asked the goddess to guard us on our voyage home to Greece. But I never imagined what it would truly mean to hide within this horse. Our last glimpse of light showed our encampment in flames as our armies burned everything and boarded the ships as if to sail home. Then came a night and day of utter darkness. For ventilation Epeios had drilled holes winding down from the horse's nostrils and ears, but this hardly met our needs. At first, I smelled the breath and perspiration of the other men. If I wanted to turn or stretch, another body always pressed on mine. Since the wound to my chest, I had felt pain there and my muscles cramped without movement. Sounds filled the darkness—breathing, sighing, shifting—but no words, none at all. I knew in the darkness where each man rested. From time to time, we passed the water skin, but soon we had exhausted that and lay stunned in the heat with our tongues parched. I had ordered Epeios to build boxes for excrement, but in the darkness and the close quarters a horrible smell permeated the air we breathed repeatedly.

"I heard the cries of the Trojans outside. Occasionally a blow resounded on the outer casement of the horse. For a breath of the fresh air they breathed, I felt I would give a year of my life. How long would they deliberate? Days? A week? Death by fire would seem merciful compared to this slow suffocation. What if our fleet, hidden behind the island of Tenedos, were scattered by a storm? How could they return to save us? What if the Trojans never brought the horse to the altar of Athena but simply guarded it on the beachhead? Agamemnon would never betray me, but should he lose innumerable men in a futile attempt to rescue us?

"But our worst trial remained ahead. After the ropes had whispered over the wooden skin and the horse had rocked slowly forward to we knew not what destination, Helen came and called to us. Only then did we know the horse rested within Troy. Muffled by the walls of pine, she sounded like women we had loved so long ago in Greece. I could have sworn I heard the voice of my mother, Anticlea. But would my mother have begged me to open the trapdoor and meet certain death? My sister Ktimene called, weeping for the years she had lived apart from me. All the while, the other men heard Helen call them as well. What made her voice magical that day? Beside me Diomedes shivered with longing. Why not sing back and run to the arms of these fantasies we loved? Diomedes whispered again and again the name of his wife Aigialeia. I struggled against Helen's spell, resting my hands on the men nearest me to calm them. I heard Antiklos begin to speak, muttering at first in his pain, and I clapped my hand to his lips to muzzle him.

"Then I heard your mother's voice. So close to triumph, I felt my courage desert me. I only wanted to be home with my wife and the baby I had cradled. Often on the field I had seen men routed by brute force, but I had never felt such fear as this loss of my own heart. I wanted the world left long behind, the world of my hearth, my family and my fields. I wanted the island of Ithaca, more beautiful to me than others, vaster and more fertile.

"What possessed Helen to act as she did? Was she a wanton for destruction? Or had she glimpsed the horrors we would bring to Troy? I must have risen in the darkness and readied myself to return a tender shout. Neoptolemus saved us, holding me in his arms until the fullness of my heart subsided.

"Then I realized every man in that horse had been a suitor of Helen, except for Neoptolemus. Nor had heroic Achilles courted Helen, but rather served at Troy for the glory heroes find in battle. Hadn't we suitors continued our rivalry for Helen those ten years— each vying on the battlefield to be first among us? We fought as we had competed—our feasts, our games, our striving. By our vow, we had all married ourselves to Helen. What had we become but one hundred arms of Menelaos, the outraged husband? Or such were my wild imaginings in the arms of Neoptolemus.

"Some men say Paris never carried Helen to Troy but seduced only an illusion of Helen. The real woman was spirited to Egypt in a mist and lives in a shrine of Aphrodite. How can you or I refute this? I saw Helen at Troy and you saw her recently in the court of Menelaos. In that horse I remember Helen's laughter lilting through our darkness. She spoke, but I only heard the name Deiphobus. As if the shame of marrying Paris hadn't been enough, after his death—within a few months—she married his younger brother. Had she chosen him long before, imagining that Paris would someday die? Did she have another son of Priam waiting for her after Deiphobus? Her spell vanished and I raged against her in my heart.

"Then I heard music—flutes and lyres and a wonderful chanting that made me feel the singers' joy. Peace, the Trojans celebrated! Or should I call it victory, for the sweetness soon left the singing and what sounded like drunken revelry began. At last, we heard nothing at all. We opened the spy hole Epeios had crafted for this moment. I saw only darkness—it was night, not even a torch burning.

"Too long I had lain in the darkness, confined, my senses revolted by all around me. I couldn't go forward into that night. What daring, what bravado to imagine a hundred men could open a city like Troy to our armies. I trembled, although no man could have seen me. But I felt the gentle touch that had sustained me through my longing for Penelope. A clean-shaven cheek brushed close to my ear and Neoptolemus whispered only two words: 'Remember Achilles.'

"What kind of war lasts so long that another generation comes to fight it? Would you have to follow me there, Telemachus? Would your sons follow you? I felt deranged, longing for my home, longing to remain in the black emptiness of that terrible horse, longing to slaughter until Troy vanished from the earth and the memories of men.

"I eased open the trapdoor in the belly. The horse stood in a moonlit square in front of the temple of Athena. First among my men, I took the long rope in hand and descended knot by knot into the city of Troy."

CHAPTER 13

Odysseus rose, stretched, and stared at the billowing mist that approached our island gently from every direction. The mist often rises this way from the sea, lambent and pervasive. Bowing his head, he stood before the altar we had built and spoke a prayer I couldn't hear. Why shouldn't he pause at this moment? Every storyteller knows how to increase the listener's desire to hear. But I knew that wasn't why he stopped. I imagine he wondered if he dared tell even me the truth. What if I, his only son, should cease to love and respect him? Why had he needed to confide in me the truth of his experiences? Nonetheless, we settled on our stony bench and he continued his narrative.

"That night the strongest force followed Menelaos and me to overpower the guards at the Skaean Gate. Neoptolemus led the rest toward Priam's great hall, burning everything that could be burned.

As we moved through the moonlit night, I heard cries behind us and knew Neoptolemus's diversion was succeeding. How poorly the city was guarded! Their soldiers staggered from drinking. The few men we met died without a sound. Quickly we reached the gate and fell with fury on the guards. At last, I stood on the ramparts where Priam, Hecuba, and Helen had watched us so many years in the fields below. We gave the signal with our torches. The drawbar raised and the gates swung inward. From the darkness a vast multitude approached, whispering in many voices. I imagined our dead had risen from those fields, so many dim shapes moved into the city. Leaving Diomedes to command the gate, Menelaos and I took a picked squad and rushed up the terraced streets toward the hall of Deiphobus to capture Helen before she could be taken from the city. Fires lit the far side of the city and cries of alarm filled the night.

"Fighting men guarded the doors of Deïphobos's house. But we knew the Greek armies were within the city, victory close by us. The Trojans knew only the chaos of fires, cries, and armed intruders. Courageously as they fought, we killed the guards and leapt up the stairs to where Helen and Deiphobus slept.

"Can you imagine who met us at the door? Helen. She wore an embroidered robe with royal fluting and held the gold-handled sword of Deiphobus in her hands. But she wasn't defending him. Hardly! She offered the sword's handle to Menelaos. When he refused it and grabbed her by a handful of that rich red hair, she fell and grappled for his knees while raising one hand to his chin. Like a conquered warrior she clung there until Menelaos kicked her aside in his lust for vengeance.

"We burst through the bedroom door and found Deiphobus sleeping. He woke—quick-witted—and reached by his bed for his sword. Poor man, I knew what Menelaos intended for him. After Paris died, Menelaos mutilated his body as we struggled to win it from the Trojans. I would have liked to thrust my sword quickly into Deiphobus's chest, but instead I held him on the bed. Menelaos cursed and drew a short knife from his belt. Speaking constantly of Helen, he carved the face of handsome Deiphobus. How the man screamed! His two ears were hacked off, his cheeks slit, his nose split top to bottom, his eyes impaled. This wasn't war. Imagine a world without rules—not even the rules of war. Nothing restrained us. That night we could be as cruel as we secretly desired and no one would ever speak against us—the victors. When Menelaos carved free the genitals and cursed the sons Deiphobus would never have, I gently broke the man's windpipe and let him die.

"Menelaos ordered Helen brought before him. She hardly glanced at the outraged body of her husband Deiphobus. That marriage—and her love for Deiphobus—had vanished from her mind. Again, she flung herself on the knees of Menelaos, her face burning with fear.

"Menelaos took the genitals like a cup and gloatingly dripped the blood over Helen. I believe he would have killed her, but she recoiled and fell back on the floor. Blood ran from her hair to her face. Cunningly—for her skills in love were certainly equal to mine in war—her robe had opened. She wore nothing beneath. If you think she slept unclothed, I can only say I doubt that. She had heard the alarm and sensed the end of Troy. She had prepared for Menelaos. Even as she cried, 'Spare me, I gave you his sword,' she used her wiles to charm him. Her breasts gleamed in the torchlight. Menelaos, who could withstand the rage of innumerable men, groaned in his chest with desire. It filled me with shame! He forgot his soldiers were present, he forgot the battle for the city. Gently he caressed her with the genitals of Deiphobus, his rough hands streaking her body with blood. Like Priapus he panted over her, justice and vengeance forgotten. I pitied him. He had saved my life and had always been an honorable man, but Helen possessed him. I ordered our soldiers from that room and left them guarding the door to these lovers.

"Outside the flames rose around me. Buildings toppled in storms of cinders. I cared for nothing. No world existed beyond this one. Trojans fell to my left and right, writhing and pleading for a mercy I would not give. I fought to Priam's palace where I had been received on my embassies of peace. By the splintered door rose mounds of dead and wounded men, the wordless cries of Greeks and Trojans indistinguishable. In the wide courtyard Neoptolemus held the dying king.

"Priam's lips moved and I heard Neoptolemus reply, 'Great Priam, soon you'll see my father Achilles. Tell him I won glory for him and his father Peleus within the high walls of Troy. Fear not for your funeral fires or those of your sons, for I promise to honor you as if you were not only great-hearted but Greek as well.'"

Odysseus had wrapped his arms about himself and rocked to and fro with grief for these recollections.

"Why should I catalog so much slaughter? Do a hundred deaths sound more pitiable than a single corpse stiffening in its blood? Alliances, vengeance, prophecies—who can name all the reasons we give for what we do?"

I wanted to put my arms around his shoulders. If I did, would he shake free in irritation or give any notice to my comforting? Pained to feel unable to touch him, I asked questions to encourage him to finish his narrative.

"Was Palamedes in the horse with you?"

"Surely you know he died." My father's eyes challenged me to question him further.

"When did he die?"

"A month or so before the quarrel between Agamemnon and Achilles. Our assembly condemned him—death by stoning. Of all the Greeks, only he, I, and Diomedes dared steal within the walls of Troy. The first time I disguised myself to enter Troy, I was spying on Palamedes. Unerring, he made his way through the darkened streets to visit Helen. Why do you think I dared go to Helen later? I had already seen she didn't turn Palamedes over to the Trojans. I heard her tell him how Troy bored her. She had tired of war. Palamedes confessed he loved her. He swore that each night she appeared in his tent—conjured by some magic. Breaking our suitors' vow to defend her marriage, he begged her to go with him. She agreed and promised to approach Priam as if Palamedes were the Greeks' secret emissary of peace. If the Trojans would give her to his custody to be returned to Menelaos, the Greeks would sail home. Had they given her up, Palamedes would have vanished like a phantom. He would have taken her beyond the boundaries of the world we know, questing for what his own heart could not give him. Then the war could never end—the Trojans having no Helen to return, the Greeks unable to leave without her."

"What proof convinced the assembly?" I asked, hoping to learn some tactic that might help me the next morning.

"His tent filled with the gold I put there."

"His family ruled Euboea," I said, not wanting my father to have done this. "They had wealth beyond any man's desire. Who would believe he betrayed the Greeks for gold?"

"There was a forged note as well." My father made this sound like both an admission and a boast for his own cunning. "If I had accused him, it would be my word against his. Men like Aias might laugh at the idea I had entered Troy in disguise. But gold is irrefutable— especially when Palamedes had denied possessing it. We met in a secret assembly. To confuse the Trojans, we agreed to tell various stories of the death of Palamedes—never comforting them by calling him a traitor. Menelaos threw the first stone."

My father needed no more urging to unfold his story.

"I helped Agamemnon kill his daughter Iphigenia when we needed a wind for Troy to begin our glorious war. I carried a note to Klytaimnestra telling her the girl would be Achilles's bride. But I hoped Agamemnon would see the brutality of the war that faced us. I never imagined he would simply slaughter the child. If you care to listen, men will tell you Aphrodite spirited the girl away in a mist to live in a shrine—just like the story of Helen. I wish we had only sacrificed a doe, as those storytellers would like you to believe.

"I killed Astyanax, the young son of Hector and Andromache. I took him by the ankles and swung him high to crack his skull on stone. Then I tossed him down the ramparts to lie unburied on the field below. Why was this merciful? Because no boy in Troy survived; we spitted them on our swords through the genitals and intestines. I would have been a fool to kill the fathers and let the sons live. Of course, I could have let Neoptolemus kill the boy. But I knew he would take Andromache home with him. If she could bear her life at all, wasn't it better I be the murderer of her child? And I gave him a quick death, painless compared to shrieking boys impaled on swords.

"You wondered if I knew Aeneas escaped from Troy. In the Underworld I met a beautiful spirit named Dido, queen of Carthage. When she learned I had fought at Troy, she approached and asked if I had known Aeneas. I told her how I saw Aeneas the night Troy vanished from the earth. Dressed in Greek armor, he fought like a man who loved slaughter. I pursued him through the flames, never able to corner him in the maze of narrow streets. Dido told me she had welcomed him and his sea-tossed band of refugees from Troy. She offered these Trojans every hospitality, much as Menelaos had been generous with Paris years before. At last Dido loved Aeneas and dreamt he would build Carthage with her and reign as king. But he cared only for building a new Troy. He longed for an empire of obedient men to worship him and his sons as gods. In this empire that he dreamt would span the world, poets would sing him slavish praise and philosophers prove his divinity. How could love compare to that? Not even his promises to Dido, the nights of joy shared by them, kept him from sneaking out to sea. So she cut her wrists, and I found her with Achilles and Aias and so many more.

"Priam's wife, Hecuba, I took as my slave. Of all the Trojan women, why did I choose the eldest, least attractive, and most spiteful? I appreciated her nobility as Achilles and Neoptolemus had admired the kingliness of Priam. If she had to die a slave in a foreign land, at least your mother would be a gentle mistress. But Hecuba robbed me of my property. We had hardly embarked when she began raving. I didn't try to explain to her what I'm telling you. To her I had ruthlessly killed Astyanax and swayed the assembly to condemn Polyxena. Near the rocks called dog's point, she leapt into the waves. The crew laughed at her antics and waited for her to surface, but she never rose from those waters that washed the beaches of Troy.

"Will another tale help you defend me at dawn? Perhaps you wonder why I'm not like my old comrade Menelaos, who basks in his wealth and his memories of our feats. Let me tell you what happened after I lost the trail of Aeneas and started slowly back toward Priam's palace. Suddenly I heard a woman calling Aeneas. I peered through the smoke and darkness in the hope of glimpsing this woman whose voice in a single name could convey such love and longing. When I saw nothing, I wondered if some goddess sought him. At last, I thought I should let this spirit wander and go to guard the growing piles of treasure in the palace that had been Priam's. Then she appeared before me—Creusa, the wife of Aeneas.

"I had covered my nose and mouth with my cape. She stopped when she saw me with my drawn sword and the blood and filth covering me from head to feet. She wore white, this daughter of Aphrodite.

Seeing her—and knowing she had raised a small child by her husband's side through the long siege—I wept within for the ten years I had been deprived of my own wife and son. Ten years Aphrodite had fought against the Greeks, Athena, and Hera. I could understand that Aphrodite charmed Helen, but had she bewitched all the Trojans? Hadn't I offered them peace?

"What would you have done? I could have let her go free— perhaps she might have found Aeneas. Then she could have more children—fifty or a hundred—who would despise the Greeks. And when Aeneas or his sons had built a new Troy, they would revenge Priam, Hector, Deiphobus, and the innumerable others.

"Should I have taken her to the palace to be chained to the other Trojan women? After spending that never-ending night as a plaything for our soldiers, she could ride in the darkness of a rat-infested hold to slavery.

"I dropped my cape. Recognizing me, she knew her fate. Neither tears nor pleading demeaned her. I killed her as gently as I had learned to kill."

Phemios, you recoil. How much more of this tale can there be, you're wondering? So, I felt revulsion and my father saw that too. For my own sake I wanted him to stop. What had become of that shining hero I conjured as a child? Could this voice be all that remained of godlike Odysseus? But would it have been better for him to lie to me, or me to lie to you? My father might easily have killed you for entertaining the suitors, but he praised you as a singer of many voices.

"What kind of mercy did I show her?" he demanded. "It was the mercy of war. It was the best I or any man could have done that night.

"Carrying her body through the streets, I felt bereaved for what I had lost. O mirage of Troy! The flames leapt skyward, a funeral pyre for a dream. I prayed for Creusa and let the flames devour her."

My father rose, a hand on my shoulder restraining me from rising with him.

"If Aphrodite had never charmed Helen, I would never have seen Troy. I would never have outraged Athena. After Troy fell, years passed before Athena forgave my transgressions. If she hadn't abandoned me, I would never have blundered into the cave of Polyphemos. If mine had been a different fate, I might have prospered on Ithaca and had no story to tell you."

With those words, he lifted his staff and began a solitary hike on the stony path twisting downward to our hall.

CHAPTER 14

That long staff reminded me of the scepter each speaker would grasp when he spoke to the assembly. First Polybos would take it firmly in hand. Then Laertes, Odysseus, and I would speak while the sun lifted free of the swelling waves. Holding the scepter invested each man with authority and protected him so he might express himself fearlessly.

Once more my thoughts returned to that day we killed the suitors. Because I believed we had trapped them in the great hall, I didn't lock the door to the arms room. It seemed to me the suitors could reach that door only by killing the four of us who blocked their escape. Afterward I often wondered whether I had purposely left open the door. Hadn't I felt myself as much a suitor as a son? When my mother agreed to the archery contest in which the winner would take her as a bride, I asked to be first to string Odysseus's great bow. If my arrow pierced that narrow passage through the sockets of the twelve axe heads, what could I have won? I might have strung that bow—I know I could have—if Odysseus hadn't glared at me with such fury that I put the bow aside for another to try. Of the men in that crowded hall, my mother far preferred me to any of the others. I had enjoyed the feasting and games, the male companionship of men like Amphinomos and Agelaos who filled a small part of my longing for my father. No wonder I had pled for the life of my friend Amphinomos.

If I left the door open from some faint hope that Odysseus would be slain, why hadn't I refused to help him kill the suitors? I had never seen men die. In so many ways I was like that youthful Odysseus who courted Helen. I wanted my peaceful life to continue without the trials my father had suffered. Certainly I questioned, if only to myself, the extremity of his vengeance. But did I resist him or question my own actions? Did I consider joining or warning the suitors? If I hadn't forgotten my affection for Amphinomos, how could I have tossed that long spear between his shoulders?

Why should my father love me? How many boys like sons had served under him at Troy? What of the avenger of Achilles, Neoptolemus, whom my father obviously loved? Odysseus had lived with dreams for a son, boys as fine as any hero I might have imagined. If he decided I had wasted his wealth and slackly spent my days with the suitors, why shouldn't he have treated me as he treated them? I armed the suitors. I let Melanthios slip through that window on a ladder of desperate hands. After he handed down spears, swords, and shields to our enemies, I had to redeem myself in my father's eyes. What could change the fact I left open that door?

In our hall the suitors lay strewn across the vast floor. Blood coated my father and me. Joined by the herdsmen, we struck each body another lethal blow so no mimicry of death would let a suitor escape us. While you and the herald sat in our courtyard by the sacred altar of Zeus, Odysseus sent my nurse Eurykleia to bring the maidservants who had taken lovers among the suitors.

"Have those women who worshipped Aphrodite scrub clean my hall," Odysseus ordered us. "Make them carry their lovers' bodies to the courtyard. When this hall with its holy hearth is as I so often remembered, take the women out beside their lovers. Kill them cleanly with your fine-honed swords."

Although Philoitios and Eumaios stood to my right and left, I felt my father spoke to me alone. We began to drag the bodies into the sunlight where you and Medon sat. I found Amphinomos pitched forward, a length of the spear keeping his chest from touching the earthen floor. I pressed a foot to his spine and pulled the shaft of the spear, but the barbed point ground on his breastbone and wouldn't return through the thickness of his body. Each time I yanked his body flopped like a slaughtered animal. Why didn't he take my father's warning and flee? If I had heard he died far from my hall, what pain I would have suffered. At last, I axed the bronze tip from the shaft.

The women came in twos and threes—a dozen in all. When they saw the lifeless suitors, they keened and wept and trembled. My father directed them, but he said nothing about what he planned. Perhaps they imagined this purification of our hall would be their only punishment. After all, slaves like these are worth five oxen apiece, hardly a trifling amount.

Melantho, whose lover had been Eurymakhos, dared to glance at me from the corner of her insolent eyes. Eurymakhos gave my mother more and finer gifts than any of the other suitors. If he had carried his suit, he would have gone from the arms of this maidservant to the bed of my mother. Knowing him, he would have kept Melantho for occasional indulgences. How ironic that Polybos, the father who provided Eurymakhos with the wealth to make his gifts, dared bring charges against Odysseus for impiety.

We finished in the hall. The women were relieved to be done with their grisly work. You've mentioned to me more than once how the sight of those women being herded by Philoitios and Eumaios past their dead lovers remains vivid in your mind. We walked them behind that round tower where I had my room to the alley closed by the meeting of the courtyard wall with the tower.

Did I want to kill them? Of course, they had abused my mother and me. But they lived as slaves. Didn't the suitors offer them a glimpse of freedom? Was it wrong to dream one of these princes might buy his love and release her from servitude? In his own land Eumaios had been a prince. So might these women have been noble once. When the amorous suitors competed for Helen, didn't my father ultimately win my mother for his bride? The disappointed suitors might seek other loves to share their hearths. If these women had hopes, weren't they like you or me or anyone? And if they were wise and hoped for nothing, at least they found a brief freedom in the pleasures of Aphrodite.

Who could forget Melantho's undulant hips, the desire of her indolent walk? I saw the beauty in her slanting eyes, the promise. I admit I desired her and others of these women too. My youth saved me—aided by the example of Amphinomos, who cared only for Penelope. If Odysseus had waited another year to return, no doubt one of these girls would have been sneaking out to meet me on those long evenings. Innumerable times my nurse Eurykleia told me how Grandfather Laertes desired her. How could she have disobeyed him? Only the intervention of my grandmother, Anticlea, made Laertes forget that passion and devote himself to farming and war. But you don't think he paid twenty oxen intending to use Eurykleia as a common servant? As I made these twelve women stand side by side in a line, I knew that what they had done was shameful only because they were owned by Odysseus rather than the suitors with whom they slept.

Should I have shown them mercy because of this? Isn't death too harsh a punishment, even if they cursed my father in his own hall? After all, he came disguised as a beggar and let these women delight in imagining him to be less fortunate than they.

I had another fantasy as the herdsmen looped the long rope from neck to neck. I imagined my father pulling me roughly aside. As many suitors as I had killed, he would berate me for leaving open the arms room and say, "See if you can do better fighting with whores."

That fantasy kept me from pleading with my father for those women. In my zeal, the quick death by the sword that he had ordered hardly struck me as sufficient. While my father never accused me for my failure to lock that door, he never praised me for the slow, cruel death I gave the maidservants. Later I wondered if I had pleaded with him to spare their lives, would he have embraced me with admiration for my mercy?

Philoitios tied one end of this thick sea rope to the top of a high column on the courtyard wall. Then he and Eumaios mounted to the window on the first story of the tower. I handed up the other end of the rope and they slowly pulled it taut. At first the women pleaded with me, their voices shrill with sorrows and recollections of kindnesses done for me. When the rope tightened, their hands spoke with an eloquence beyond their words. But the herdsmen pulled until their feet kicked the air. When we had certainly killed them, the herdsmen dropped the rope and let them tumble. We carried the bodies around to where you and the herald sat dazed and stacked the maidservants beside their suitors.

You witnessed the death of Melanthios in the courtyard. Why should he and his sister Melantho have blackened the reputation of their father Dolios? Why did Melanthios climb that wall to arm the suitors instead of fighting on our side as his father and brothers did against Eupeithes? I might have killed Melanthios simply for betraying us. But would I have slashed off his ears and nose, emasculated him, and hacked off his hands and feet? I had played with him as a child. His father carved miniature soldiers, ships, and rampart walls to amuse us. For those memories I might have been merciful. But I had to banish any doubt from my own mind as to my loyalty. I had to show Odysseus this man could never have been my accomplice—or, if he had been, that I repudiated him. So I tossed his genitals outside our courtyard gate for our hounds to devour.

Odysseus explained his justifications to me, but what were my justifications? Could I tell my story as truthfully as he had told his to me? He would have preferred not to do so much that he had done. But his life had followed a course he had only imperfectly been able to affect. What I understood most clearly was that he had brought me close to his own experience of life. Before each act he had considered and tried to make the best of his choices. If he had been a god, he might have refused to choose. But how could I dare accuse him? He had examined the actions he was called to do. He considered whether to go to Troy and decided he would not go. If later he changed his mind, nonetheless he had lived both possibilities. But I never made choices. When the suitors feasted, I feasted with them. When my father swore to kill the suitors, I vowed to follow him. Courageous? Of course, but isn't that courage paltry compared to a fearless knowledge? When my father killed, he had a reason. Whatever my father's accusers might say, they would never make me believe Odysseus lacked the life of the soul that discriminates between the better and lesser courses of action.

I had so many thoughts as the imperceptible sinking of the sun brought nearer the assembly at dawn. How many times that night and over the years I wondered why Odysseus had ordered me to kill the maidservants when he might easily have done so himself. If Athena helped him kill the suitors, why did he need me beside him?

110

I believe he wanted me to share what he had experienced at Troy. If this were so, I can hardly say whether he was a wise or a cruel father. But wasn't our slaying of the suitors like the killing of Trojans? Amphimedon, Leokritos, Euryades, and many more—I can list the men I killed like Odysseus named his Trojan dead. Our great hall piled with heaps of the dead must have taken my father back to the soldiers dying by Priam's gate.

No one need ever have known that he slew Creusa, the daughter of Aphrodite. But I remember his curse of the maidservants for worshipping Aphrodite. When I slaughtered them, wasn't it as if I joined Odysseus in the killing of Creusa? Why didn't he let her live a slave? He could have taken her with Hecuba to work in our hall—as I might have let these maidservants live. Didn't I slaughter Polyxena when I killed the maidservants who once hoped to be brides? In the mutilation of Melanthios, what was I but the loyal captain who held handsome Deiphobus while Menelaos disfigured and castrated him?

For so many years I longed to help Odysseus from afar. In turn he carried the war within him and brought it home to me. He made me his ally to finish that endless war. Had he done less, he would have left me among the suitors imagining that wine, victuals, and the endearing warmth of women are the only realties in this world. I felt as reluctant to fight beside Odysseus as he had felt to board the black-hulled ships for Troy. I knew other men would condemn my father for his violence and cruelty at Troy and on his homecoming to Ithaca. So much of my life has been spent pondering all this. Should I have condemned Odysseus for what he had done, for not being the man I imagined him to be? I believed myself unworthy to judge him. When he let Polites send a streaking arrow to down that wounded soldier in the Trojan forest, was he an evil man? Whatever he might have been, was I better than he? No, I neither condemned nor praised him. Instead, I felt the need to prepare my own defense, the story I would tell as he told his of Troy. If Odysseus judged himself and cared nothing for assemblies, I would do the same. Nor would I defend myself against the accusations of men like Polybos, but rather against accusations as yet unknown to me.

The sun had run far to the dark quadrant, casting long shadows over the fissured path I would have to follow. But with the intensity of my feelings, I hardly remember my walk down that mountainside. It was as if I woke on the steps winding up to my lookout in our tower. My door stood open, the light of a torch flickering into the hallway. So late on this of all nights, who patiently waited for my return?

CHAPTER 15

"Twenty years you spent with me. But when your father came it was as if I taught you nothing. It was as if I never knew you. Is killing so glorious, so much finer than love?"

My mother sat in the low chair Ikmalios crafted for me as a child. Her coarse black dress made her look already a widow in mourning. She wore no jewelry, her eyes swollen from weeping. But why did she weep? For the death that might come to Odysseus the next morning? Or for her admirers whom he and I had killed?

"What made you so ready to take arms? Phemios with his songs of war? Or those rough sports with the suitors? Why wouldn't you speak with me?"

The pained timbre of her voice didn't invite me to answer. I sat opposite her on my bed.

"Am I nothing to you? Are you so much like your father? With every supply ship that went to Troy, I made the captain or one of the crew my messenger. I begged Odysseus to return home. Let Helen live in Troy—she chose to go there. At last, I offered to go to Troy myself and bring you with me. He refused. He chose to live without me."

Her tears flowed freshly to remember Odysseus need not have left her alone so many years. I shared her pain, knowing he had abandoned me as well.

"But he returned," I said. "He always wanted to return."

She masked her face with her hands as if to press back the tears in her eyes.

"Tonight, he lingered in our room. From his chests he took first one garment, then another. What craft, I thought, to prepare in every detail for this cursed assembly. But when I saw what he would wear tomorrow, I grieved with a pain made greater by his presence. He chose a soft and woolly cloak of purple and a tight-fitting chiton of the finest silk. From the golden brooches he loved as a young man, he selected one with a handsome hound like Argos in pursuit of a stag that seemed to fly with fear. Just such a cloak, chiton, and brooch he chose for his departure to Troy. Where does he plan to voyage? What places are left for him to go? While he stormed Troy and adventured homeward, I waited patiently. But does he care for what you or I suffered?

"I've begged him to live in exile, but he refuses. If he prefers dying, why did he ever come back? Why should he have cared whether I married another man or not? One day I had my husband and son miraculously restored to me. But what can I expect? Having dreamt to see you and him together, tomorrow I'll lose you both. If he dies, they'll come for you—promises or not. Make him go. He knows the sea. He knows how to live as a wanderer."

She leaned forward and pressed my hands in hers.

"Let him leave us as we were. No one will dare harm you for fear he'd come back. How much more useful he'd be to us away. After they kill him and you, they'll plunder our hall and herds and sell me to slavers. Shall I live like a Trojan woman, a slave mourning loved ones who died vainly? Did only Helen triumph in that war?"

As she spoke, I wondered whether another hundred suitors would fill our home if Odysseus departed. Or would I have her to myself, mother and son aging together in our great hall? Would she return to sleeping alone in that hewn bed while I lived unmarried in my soaring tower?

"How could I make him go?" I said.

"If you speak to him, he'll listen."

"Neither to me nor you."

"Odysseus's mother died grieving for him," my mother said. "Do you want that for me? Or do you simply not care? Have I become a woman of air, nothing to you? Will you tell your drinking friends you met me in the Underworld and three times tried to embrace me? Why don't you speak? Why don't you tell me whether you and your father will be alive at twilight tomorrow? I have a shroud for old Laertes, but none for my husband and my son."

I wanted to defend myself, but that wouldn't have calmed her. Instead, I looked at the small ships that had decorated my room since my childhood. On these high-prowed toys, Dolios had built masts and sails.

My mother smiled craftily.

"Are you hoping to inherit his estate tomorrow—what's left of it? Do you think you can overcome the assassins Polybos will hire to murder you? If you did, what pleasure would you find in this hall and the possessions of Odysseus? Knowing you could have saved his life by persuading him to flee—and enjoyed your inheritance while he lived."

Amazed my mother might imagine this, I simply shook my head to deny what she said.

"Why didn't you ask my permission to go to the courts of Nestor and Menelaos?" How quickly she found a new quarrel with me. "And what did you learn on your little adventure? Do you think I'm happy Odysseus lived with this Calypso—a so-called nymph? How quickly you blurted it out to me. You must have amused Menelaos and Helen. She dared give you a wedding dress to entrust to me for safekeeping. How she would have loved to see me marry with Odysseus still alive. She pushed my father to make me marry again. Remember how the suitors strutted and smiled when one of their fellows failed to string your father's bow? Helen wanted me to fail. She wanted the pleasure of my being as unfaithful as she had been. How could you go to them for news of Odysseus?

"And did Nestor help you? I'm sure you heard a lot of windy stories. Did he tell you about the marriage of his friend King Pirithoös when Nestor and Theseus fought the Centaurs? I'll bet he did."

I recalled the joy of my visit to the court of Nestor. If I could have chosen a brother and a younger sister, I would have wanted Nestor's son Peisistratos and silent slender daughter Polykaste who bathed me. In a family of single sons, I often longed for a brother.

My mother rose and walked to the window facing the town.

"What help will these great kings give you tomorrow when the stones are flying?" she asked, gazing at the faint outlines of the roofs in moonlight. Turning her back to the town, she spoke forcefully to me. "Take the wedding dress to Odysseus, master of disguises. He can wear it through the town to Noëmon's ship. Give him my gifts from the suitors to wear as well. That golden necklace of the sun that Eurymakhos gave me, its amber rays filled by light. Give him the pendant earrings in threefold clusters Eurydamas hoped might please me. And that silver band with emeralds Peisandros offered for my throat. Over these jewels and Helen's fine gown, let him wear Antinoös's gift—that embroidered robe with its twelve clasps of gold. Have him embark in the darkness, a fear for our enemies long after death claims him."

"Whose bride do you want him to be?" I asked, imagining bearded Odysseus sneaking through the streets in a bridal gown, jewelry, and a woman's cape.

"Let him marry Athena," my mother snapped. "She cursed the returning fleet of the Greeks and started his wandering, but he burns thighbones to her nonetheless. He lives with her already, so let him sail with her. Plead with him to go."

"It won't do any good."

"You have to try. Please go to him."

In exile Odysseus might live the long life promised him by Teiresias. But I remembered how you sang of Patroklus's pleas to wear Achilles's armor when the Greeks had been routed to their ships. Of his comrades, Achilles loved Patroklus more than any other. He could have refused to lend that armor. Certainly, he knew the danger to his friend. Why didn't he keep Patroklus in the tents? Why let him out on a field where Hector reigned unrivaled?

I didn't want Odysseus to flee. But even if I had, I would have nonetheless honored his desire to face his accusers. So I answered my mother as best I could.

"Neither you nor I can know what will happen in the morning. Remember how often Odysseus has risked death. If you had pled with me the night before the suitors died, I might have fled Ithaca myself. What hope did we have against one hundred? Love made Odysseus return, even if he's not the man of whom you and I dreamt."

"Child, am I such a fool? Don't you understand? He has returned exactly as I remember him. When a beggar in Troy claimed to be Odysseus, Helen recognized him. Do you imagine she could recognize him and I couldn't? When he came in a beggar's rags to our hall, I asked Eumaios to bring him to me at once. We'd have been reunited then, if it hadn't been for the enemies in our home. Would I have dared to let the suitors compete for me, if Odysseus hadn't been among them? Yes, I doubted, but in the way one doubts a miracle. Again and again I had to see him to reassure myself this was my husband."

I replied with the boldness of youth.

"I hope to be remembered with honor. If Odysseus flees, what will men say of him? What rumors and lies will ill-bred men carry to us from all parts of the world? If he goes, we'll never see him again. No man could make his journey twice. What reason would he have to return to us and the death sentence of the assembly? The choice must be his."

From my father's narrative of Troy, I felt his wish for judgment. If the gods chose to punish him, he no longer cared to escape them. So why should he flee from this assembly?

My mother seated herself beside me again and spoke with quiet conviction.

"Go for yourself, if not for him. When they kill the father, they'll certainly kill the son. Hasn't your father said that to you? Will Polybos sleep soundly while you live? If you were a weakling, he'd fear you. But you're the true son and avenger of Odysseus. What can you hope for but a painless death?"

Hearing her words, I admit a weakness overcame me. For a moment I shared my mother's fears and I yearned to flee with Odysseus. What adventures I might find with him beyond the boundaries of the lands we know.

My mother felt this hesitation in my heart. She quickly knelt beside me, her cheeks glistening with new tears. Her hands sought mine again.

"Who cares for the opinion of the world? If men think Odysseus a coward, will it make him more or less than he truly is?"

Her pain moved in me; tears rolled on my eyes. Encouraged by the grip of her child's hands, she continued:

"I've pled with him to forget me and Ithaca. For the man he is, for the miracle that made him. What is my claim on him compared with the claim of life itself? He must live, he must be what he is to be. My love as a wife I yield despite my pain. But help me save him. Let him seek his life elsewhere. I would follow him still. Or, if he finds the loves of other women, I begrudge him nothing."

Her head fell to our hands, while her shoulders trembled with the spasms of her weeping. How I admired what she had said. I had often felt she encouraged the suitors to come to our hall. Princely by birth, they acted like beggars—worse, because beggars take only what is offered. Was her weakness for a husband so great that she could enjoy the presence of men such as these? Amphinomos was surely better than the others and Antinoös certainly worse, but none of these men belonged in our hall. Now she would surrender Odysseus as a husband simply to know he would live the fullness of his own life.

I raised her to her feet. Embracing her, I tried to calm the tremors that came with her fitful tears.

"He doesn't stay here for me," she said. "That's why you must go to him."

Gently I encompassed her waist with my arm. Supporting her down the winding stairs, I walked with her across the courtyard and into the great hall. We halted by the door to my parents' chamber. My mother entered, but I remained. When she turned to me, I raised a hand to silence her.

"He doesn't stay here for me," I said, "but for himself."

Having spoken those words, I let her go alone to her husband.

CHAPTER 16

That dawn came pink, glowing over long ridges of clouds in the eastern sky. Shoulder to shoulder, the men of our islands filled the assembly field with its rock-strewn knolls and hollows. Lord Aigyptos, the aged master of the assembly, stood with his herald Peisenor and the other speakers on the higher ground. From where I stood near Aigyptos, I could see the town and the island of Asteris beyond in the channel.

Aigyptos raised the snake-headed staff.

"Men of Ithaca," he called, silencing the men in the field. "Odysseus stands before us accused of impiety. Listen well to those who speak today. The life of Odysseus depends on your vote."

Aigyptos called Polybos forward. A short, bony man, Polybos would often frown and shake his head as he walked the streets, his eyes dark with unspoken rage.

Polybos took the staff and stepped forward hesitantly, like a man who had lived apart from those whose aid he would invoke.

"Hear me, islanders, I will not keep you long.

"I haven't called you here to demand justice against the man who slew my son. Had I done that, I might have touched your hearts with pity. I might have said I am childless, who once had a son named Eurymakhos. My boy courted a seeming widow, an older woman who charmed him and his innocent friends to give her endless gifts in hope of marriage. I might have aroused your anger by telling you what kind of man killed him. I might have said, 'Odysseus, the great liar, killed him by trickery. Odysseus who lost our sons at Troy in his lust for Helen. Odysseus whose shame kept him wandering ten years in fear of facing the fathers and brothers of the men entrusted to his command.'

"Forget Odysseus's crimes against us. This assembly has no interest in avenging personal injuries. Bitter as it is to a loving father, I accepted a bloodless peace. I never asked you to avenge my son.

"But Odysseus is a reckless man. By his own admission, he taunted a son of Poseidon and risked the life of his crew. Not once, but twice he had to brag that he, Odysseus, had burned out the large man's eye. His crew pled with him to stop, as they had pled with him not to enter this man's well-stocked cave. But Odysseus gladly risked the tossed rocks and surging waves to crow for his triumph. No doubt he'd battle with the gods themselves if men could."

Polybos pointed to my father.

"What happened in Thesprotia, Odysseus? Deny to me, if you dare, that you cursed Poseidon."

Of course, my father said nothing, since Polybos held the speaker's staff. Men's heads turned from side to side as they murmured their approval of Polybos.

"Impiety is a crime against us all, against our well-being," Polybos continued. "Who can know what Poseidon may do? Will gales wreck the fleets of our fishermen and traders? Will our fresh water turn briny, or our islands vanish in the fathomless sea? Must we risk plagues, failed harvests, and childless generations?

"If we wished to have a choice, Odysseus has left us none. The gods must abhor us while he lives."

With these words Polybos threw down the staff and stalked off the promontory to join his supporters in the crowd. I won't repeat the speeches of the others who called for Odysseus's death. They dwelt on the ways in which Odysseus had wronged them, although they were hardly gods. The old calumnies sprang from their lips. How ambitious they found my father! Hadn't he angled to go to Troy, pretending madness until the Greeks made him a leader among them? What I feared was the number of men who nodded in agreement with Polybos and these others. Our friends like Eumaios, Philoitios, and Halitherses were far outnumbered by those who cherished some grievance against Odysseus. At last, Peisenor handed the staff to Laertes.

My grandfather raised the staff like a spear and thrust its point toward the ranks of Polybos's supporters.

"Curs, scoundrels, liars, thieves—I salute you. I know you're brave men, since our cowards all died at Troy.

"You're probably wondering why I speak on behalf of Odysseus. I know you call him a bastard and me a cuckold. But let the man step forward who calls Sisyphus the father of my son. Step forward."

No man took this challenge, since Laertes looked ready to use the staff mercilessly. If his warlike tone didn't suit this assembly, it heartened me nonetheless.

"You've forgotten your own glory. Amazing, isn't it, how modest you've become. Didn't this assembly ask Odysseus to go to Troy? I can tell you he never wanted to go. If any man doubts this, I call on Lord Aigyptos to bear me out.

"It must have been your fathers or their fathers who sent me against Nerikos. What calm and wise opinions were voiced in this very place! When our fleet dropped anchor off the white cliffs and our expeditionary force landed, why had only I imagined they'd wall themselves in the city?

"Years earlier I warned against building those fortifications. But wiser men said the trade routes between east and west needed such a stronghold. I bowed to their judgment.

"Does this sound familiar? Go farther east and you'll see the ruined walls of Troy.

"Did you want me to raze Nerikos peacefully? To storm the city without swords, spears, and our great siege engines?

"You gave me my orders. When I obeyed and undermined the fortifications we had built ourselves, you commanded me to spare even the men. I did this. Then you received a delegation of their leaders. How sympathetically you listened to their stories of my violence. How quickly they made a fine bargain with your fathers, that generation of merchants.

"At last men said I should never have attacked Nerikos. If I had held my temper, I could have taken the city without loss of life."

Laertes turned and shook the staff at the master of the assembly.

"Aigyptos, you lived when I sacked Nerikos. Is truth like wind, invisible, ever vanishing?"

Aigyptos raised a hand and nodded his long-bearded head. He looked contemplative, so this gesture might have been agreement or simply a signal that he heard my grandfather. I had always wondered at Lord Aigyptos, his face wrinkled with so many years before my own. No man, not even Laertes, could remember a time before Aigyptos.

Laertes turned to face the crowded field again.

"Calumnies, rumors, lies—these made me surrender my kingship. If I had known of Troy, I would never have let Odysseus follow me as king. I could have told my boy what gratitude you'd give him.

"Do you blame Odysseus for the men he lost at war? Should he have fought with magic, and not with swords and spears? Is there any warrior among you homebodies that could have bettered my son?

"You aren't fit to sit here in assembly. Honorable men obey you and you repudiate them. Honorable men give up the precious years of their lives and you forget what you commanded.

"I besieged Nerikos three months. We angled our trenches closer and closer to their walls. We knew when the city would fall, inevitable and cataclysmic. How easily you could have called me home.

"If you kill my boy, kill me with him. I have no desire to live in a world where he is no more."

Tears ran on my cheeks to hear Laertes. Athena must have given him the strength to speak, for he settled weakly on a stone with his shoulders trembling beneath my hand. I embraced him, the strength of his words bringing warmth to his aged body. But I wondered why he hadn't spoken of the piety of Odysseus. What did these men care about Nerikos?

Peisenor took the staff from Laertes and carried it to Odysseus. He wore the purple robe of which my mother warned me. He looked resplendent, his graying hair curling over the fine woven collar. Beneath the cloak his chiton clung to the muscled contours of his torso. Many men stood a head taller than my father, but none showed his strength. Closing his eyes, he embraced the staff with his face pressed close to the head of the life-giving snake. He might have been mute or a fool, until he looked at the men assembled before him and spoke with that same voice heard long ago at Troy.

"What can we say of men who nourish other men?" he asked, staring directly at Polybos, who lowered his eyes. "Are they always beloved of the gods? What of men who nourish ill manners? Men who nourish the theft of others' property? Men who nourish cowardice? Isn't there more to honor and life than mere nourishment?

"I rode to Troy. In your service I nourished myself on wounds—not only the wounds of memory."

Unbuckling his cape, he raised his chiton overhead and handed it to Medon. Naked, he stood at ease. From waist to shoulders, he looked an athlete, a godlike man. But from waist to feet, his thighs and calves were thick and short with power like the haunches of a beast. His white-scarred chest made me wonder how he survived that wound.

"Polybos calls me a liar. How few are the tales men can prove. What have we but words, fancies? This scar is my proof. Here Sokos struck me. I saw the world waver in a mist. If not for Aias and Menelaos, I would have died that day. Ask King Meges of Doulichion how I suffered this wound. Ask Menelaos of Sparta or Nestor of Pylos. What man here carries such scars?

"If I were merely a liar, why didn't I lie when you asked what became of your loved ones? Why didn't I invent glorious deaths to make your hearts sing? Why tell you fantastical tales that no man could believe unless he had lived as I have in unknown seas and lands?"

He turned to Medon, who quickly slipped the chiton over his body and clasped the purple cape across his chest.

"This same Polybos who accuses me of impiety tried to buy my service at Troy. He, Eupeithes, and Melaneus, Agamemnon's good friend, offered me wealth to lead our forces. But I had no quarrel with the Trojans. If I lacked the riches of these men, I led a fruitful life. My herds grew, my fields gave harvests. I saw no reason to bring Helen back from Troy.

"Polybos claims my lust for Helen made me pursue her to Troy. Are cowards always forgetful? Or has his wealth made him so godlike men should believe his lies? Many of you are too young to have sat in assembly twenty years ago. But Polybos spoke here and urged me to go to Troy. I regret his lies injure me. But far more I regret that his lies injure this assembly. How many of you are wise enough to care that he acts from self-interest? How many has he already corrupted to think as he does, whether by his example or the promise of rewards?

"My father, Laertes, chided you. I will not do that, if I can help myself. After all, I am the accused. Your virtues are hardly the issue.

"Ithaca nourished me. It bred me and brought me to manhood. My father and his father lived long lives before me on Ithaca. I hope Telemachus and his sons shall live here after me.

"I might have fled instead of appearing unarmed before you. How easily a captain with a sleek ship can evade the eyes of our young men. But enough of that. As I said to Amphinomos, 'No man should flout the laws.' I lived twenty years in exile. It's no life for a man like me. Do you wonder what kind of man I am?

"I learned war at my father's knee. As a youth I watched him bring Nerikos down. Years later, when he could no longer bear to rule over you, he entrusted his duties to me. I needn't list all he taught me—honor, love of family, piety. If you had known me, you would have known I worshipped with a humble heart. I observed our rituals, our feast days. Good sacrifices I made to our gods, including great Zeus and his warrior daughter Athena. Nor did I simply make a show of my observances. For what are sacrifices and festivals but the outer symbols of the spirit?

"If this is true, you may say, why did I suffer at Troy and on my journey home? If I honored the gods, why didn't I have the easy life men desire?

"I had a friend—Prince Philoctetes, the son of Poias—who joined us on our expedition to Troy. When we stopped at a shrine to worship, mindful of our duties, a snake struck Philoctetes on the foot. Within a day his wound gave off an unbearable stench. Nor could the best of our physicians cure him. He howled incessantly in his pain. At last, despite his bow of Herakles that would have aided us at Troy, Agamemnon ordered he be left behind. Years passed before I rescued him to be healed and fight at Troy. Why, when we knelt in worship, did the snake make Philoctetes its target? Shouldn't the gods have shielded him?"

Odysseus paused, his eyes gazing at the snake's head on the staff in his hand. When he resumed, he spoke more quietly.

"Why didn't my piety save me from suffering? Ingenious men imagine they know the gods' desires. I say no man knows what pleases the gods. No man knows when he may transgress and face their wrath. How else can we understand the suffering of Prince Philoctetes? Or my own suffering on the long return from Troy?

"Why didn't I flee Ithaca? Because, unlike Polybos, I respect this assembly. It is the source of law in the community of men. As a younger man, I stood where you stand and voted as you will vote. To flee would say I never believed in this assembly, I never believed in the laws by which I seemed to live. If I am a pious man and go free, you will have vindicated the spirit that brings us together. But if you find me guilty and I die, even if my death is unjust, I will have honored my obligation to these islands and to you. By the sacrifice of my life, I will regain for you what Polybos has taken.

"Nor am I eager to die. I have a wife, a son, a life to resume after twenty years of absence. If you wish to glimpse into my heart, imagine this your last day with your loved ones in this loved land.

"Teiresias sent me to Thesprotia to make sacrifices to Poseidon. I made those sacrifices as best I was able. When I returned, I sacrificed again to Poseidon and the other gods as well."

"Billy goats," yelled a derisive voice from the midst of the crowd.

"One hundred of them," my father answered, "flesh-heavy. Who among you failed to join our feasting when I offered those goats to Poseidon?"

No one answered, perhaps not wanting to let him best them with his rejoinders.

"Teiresias promised me a long life. But if I am meant to die today, I am ready to live that death. My heart is full. Home I am, yet my journey continues. I hear the great currents rushing toward distant shores. How shall I go where I must? I've sailed all manner of ship and raft, but none can carry me farther. If I'm to be swept away by death, then death must be the manner of my journey. No ending is in sight, no landfall even as I plan to live my last days here. Too much of the world has passed within me. In prophecies and dreams we glimpse our fates. When the gods spoke within me, I had to answer. If you find me impious, I welcome your stones."

My father paused, his sinewy arms wrapped about the snake-headed staff. What longing and pain I felt for him. He lived beyond me. He had returned, but in his heart he wandered yet. How would I ever hold him to me? How could I speak for his life when death too would continue his god-given fate?

Odysseus lifted his head as if to speak again. Instead, he surveyed the men before him and extended the staff to the herald.

Peisenor came toward me with the staff. I rose and took it in my hand. Words rose in profusion from the innumerable speeches I had imagined for this moment. I felt the smooth grain of the wood. Wondering that generations of men had held this staff before me, I filled my lungs with the sea-scented air. I felt each detail, each waiting and watching face, would remain forever in my memory. In Pylos, King Nestor told me, "You speak as fine and truly as your father." Encouraged by the memory of his praise, I stepped forward with the staff.

"Like Polybos, I will not keep you long.

"Polybos says he lost a son. And I've lived twenty years without a father.

"Polybos speaks of impiety, but he presents no witnesses. Nor does he give us examples of pious and impious acts.

"The poets sing of the two statues of Athena in her temple at Troy.

"One statue, the Palladium, had to be taken from the city if we Greeks were to win the war. The Trojan seer Helenus admitted this when my father captured him. Athena herself fought beside my father and the Greeks. If a theft from her temple would win the war for the side she favored, it couldn't be impiety. So, my father and Diomedes stole the Palladium and carried it out of Troy.

"The other statue of Athena fell with the city. The lesser Aias found the priestess Cassandra clinging to the statue. With her streaming hair twisted about his hand, he tried to pull her free. But so desperately did she cling that the statue itself toppled and shattered.

"The Greeks wanted to stone him to death. Aias took refuge in this same temple of Athena where he had raped Cassandra. No Greek would violate the holy ground to drag him out. Not Agamemnon, Neoptolemus, Odysseus. So Aias lived.

"Athena punished all the Greeks. She cursed their fleets. No sacrifices could quiet her anger. She took horrid men like Nauplia as her agents. Could he have lured the Greek ships with his false lights unless Athena helped him? The winds blew Menelaos to Egypt and my father far beyond.

"What of Aias? When the gales wrecked his fleet, he swam to a reef and cursed the gods. Without any intervention by men like us, sea-maned Poseidon drowned him.

"I haven't recounted this oft-told tale to amuse you. First, no proof has been given against my father. Second, if the accusation against him were true, the acts complained of are nothing like those of Aias. Finally, the gods punish those who offend them. From time beyond reckoning they have done so. Poseidon drowned Aias for his impiety. We crossed the sea returning from Thesprotia. If Poseidon wished to kill my father, would he be alive today? Every man's destiny is god-given. We've seen no signs for the death of Odysseus. If the gods are content, do you dare harm Odysseus?"

I handed the snake-headed staff to Peisenor, who brought it to Lord Aigyptos. A turbulence rippled through the men crowded on the field. I saw one man bend and lift a rock. Odysseus looked unruffled. Could he be enjoying the warmth of the sun on his uplifted face? Were there no other thoughts in his mind?

To my surprise, Lord Aigyptos rose and readied himself to speak. By tradition, the master of the assembly only presided. But he took the staff with both his hands and leaned the weight of his bent trunk against it. When he spoke, his words flowed like a great river whose ever-changing source is seldom revealed to men.

"I presided over the assembly that sent Odysseus to Troy—and many assemblies before that one. I would not speak, except to serve the truth.

"I have no doubt Polybos loved his son. For myself, I had four sons, two of whom stand among you.

"How many of you remember my eldest boy, Antiphos? He joined our army for the Trojan campaign. I loved all my sons, but Antiphos was my firstborn and should have comforted me in my age. For twenty years I cherished the hope he might still live.

"Odysseus told me that Polyphemos—a Cyclops, a giant—devoured my son. How I raged against Odysseus and cursed him for a liar. Why couldn't Odysseus have returned after my death, after the deaths of all of us who fathered the sons given to Troy? If Antiphos had to die so far from me, why did I live to hear of it? What gratitude I would have felt to learn Antiphos lived as a pirate or even a slave. If he had simply been slaughtered, what return had I been given for my boy? Why did the gods allow me to father him? When Odysseus said this monster devoured my son last, I wished the gods had dulled

131

the monster's appetite. What made him eat another man—hunger, cruelty, or the boredom of that cave? Why hadn't he feasted on sheep or taken someone else's son in place of my Antiphos?

"As you know, my next eldest son was Eurynomos. There's little to his story. He courted Penelope, although she might have been his mother. He lacked the manliness of Antiphos, but I lavished on him the love Antiphos would never have. When Eurynomos spent day after day in the hall of Odysseus, I lightly imagined the master long dead. To myself I rebuked his widow for mourning more than seven years. I didn't tell my son to feast at my own hearth and not take the provisions belonging to Odysseus. Nor did I tell him to be civil and respectful in visiting the home of Penelope. I couldn't have told him not to plot with Antinoös and Eurymakhos to murder Telemachus, for I only learned of this later.

"I sat among the elders who hosted Agamemnon, Menelaos, and Palamedes. I listened to their songs of glory, those same songs that made us send Laertes against Nerikos. Have we learned so little? Must the gods always punish us with greater slaughter before we heed their warnings?

"How many times did Halitherses prophesy the deaths of our sons who courted Penelope? Men, you lived here on these islands. Should a traveler come from foreign lands to tell us of the troubles in our homes? Are we so blind, so lost to the truth of our failings?

"We sent our sons to Troy, not Odysseus. We let our sons plunder another man's home. This world has terrors far worse than spears and swords—terrors of the heart. If we kill the man who makes us see this, the man who suffered for our own desires, what will we accomplish? Are we beasts like the giant Odysseus blinded? Do we not want to see?

"I fought in battles before Laertes gained his glory and shame. Why should I care for the life of Odysseus? Why, when I dreamt of taking my old spear to strike Odysseus unaware, did I feel the spear would pierce my own heart?

"Death will take me soon enough. And in this world, the few years remaining to mortals pass quickly. You will not live this life again, nor have any other to remember.

"I thank Odysseus for leading my boy Antiphos to Troy. If any man could have saved Antiphos and brought him home, that man is Odysseus. As for my other son, Eurynomos, I thank Odysseus for letting him die like a man. If he couldn't live with courage, at least he died with a sword in his hand. Who will ever say a weakling killed him, when his slayer was Odysseus, plunderer of cities?"

The old man wept openly, the staff cradled to his chest like the lost sons of whom he spoke. Drying his face, he raised the staff overhead and flourished it.

"This carved staff can never give leaf or bough. It is lifeless, bereft of what made it grow. Only as we use it can it have life.

"If anyone in this assembly of men knows the will of the gods, let him hurl the first stone. I will not condemn pious Odysseus."

Lord Aigyptos cast down the staff. His youngest sons, one at each arm, supported him from the council.

For a long moment when he finished, each man stood still as if listening again to his words. If times before our own could have spoken, their voice might have been that of Aigyptos. Small groups silently detached themselves from the crowd on that field. In the moment they parted from Polybos and his followers, the raptness in their faces vanished. Rocks fell from fists. The crowd separated ever more quickly. At last, I stood with Odysseus, Laertes, Eumaios, and the others of our old friends.

Tears glistened on my father's beard, but I can't tell you why he wept. When he silently raised his arms like a supplicant, I assume he prayed to Athena, but I'm not certain.

I wished I could be alone. I wished the past could simply be the past. I wanted more than dead stories of Troy. I wanted to breathe the rushing air and embrace my future. But I feared for what my life would be among those men who had silently departed from the assembly.

Embracing Odysseus, I wept that this man to whom I clung could never give me all I wanted. In my pain, I felt I would always be Nobody's son.

CHAPTER 17

———

Why did I grieve when Odysseus lived?
I grieved for myself.

Why had I killed Amphinomos, my dearest friend? Why had I killed the other youths who shared with me their joys and revelries? Who had that fierce Telemachus been? What part of me concealed him? Or had I fallen under the influence of a wandering spirit, this Odysseus who claimed to have lit my mother's thighs with my life? If I followed another's spirit, even that of my father, how could I justify those bodies I had stacked like a cord of wood? How could I explain to myself the maidservants swinging from that thick sea rope? At moments I no longer believed I had fought beside Odysseus in our great hall. I couldn't have cast the long spear that embedded itself between the shoulders of Amphinomos. I couldn't have taken the body of my friend and rudely tried time and again to yank the spear from its gory sheath. What new Telemachus had been sired by Odysseus?

I wanted the love that had flowed from my mother to encircle me like the eternal river Oceanus. I missed that special pleasure of knowing she favored me over all the suitors. To be wealthy, handsome, or ardent meant nothing compared to the simple fact I was her son. Part of this love I enjoyed belonged to my father, but I realized this only after his return.

I longed for the Odysseus whom I had imagined as a boy. No hardship could lessen that unscarred man whose war cry made mighty Hector tremble. I spent so much of my youth dreaming of my father's return. He and I would hunt the tusked boars with our hounds sleek by our sides. If he missed his thrust, my spear would save him from that black bristling beast. If that father were a faceless man to me, I could yet believe in the love between us. If Odysseus had died at the assembly, I would have always remembered him in this way. I would have forgotten the beggar who attacked the unarmed suitors and ordered me to kill the maidservants. I missed the respect and friendship of our islanders. In the town no one looked in my eyes. I seemed a ghost and soon felt I lacked substance. Had I died with the suitors? If I had met Achilles or Agamemnon in the narrow streets, I would hardly have been surprised. What pain of the Underworld could be worse than this? Warriors died in the glory of battle, while I faced a life that seemed far too long.

I grieved for Amphinomos. He loved me as an older man loves a younger. If he found in me an image of what he had once been, I saw in him the man I might someday become. You remember how he hurled the discus, his long curls tumbling over that wide brow and blazing dark eyes. On Doulichion his family ranked with that of King Meges. In fact, Amphinomos told me that Meges frequently extolled the feats of Odysseus at Troy. What hopes Amphinomos had for the life ahead of me. He wanted me to marry his sister. If I could have chosen a suitor for my mother, he would have been Amphinomos. When his wit made my mother toss back her head and show her fine teeth in her amusement, I imagined I might share her love if it would gain me Amphinomos for my father. He alone tried to save me from the suitors plotting to kill me. Why should Athena have despised such a man? Odysseus warned him to flee before we trapped the suitors in our hall. If he had heeded my father, I might not have lived unmarried and childless. I might have married his sister as he desired and had Amphinomos for the uncle of my sons.

Should Amphinomos be blamed for imagining my father dead? What of a man like gentle Leodes, who prophesied of my future in the smoke rising from our holy hearth? Having aided my father, how easy it would be to imagine I had always hated the suitors. But I couldn't assuage my grief with that lie. Certainly, I lived among the suitors against my will. You sang against your will, Phemios, and my mother was courted against hers. But didn't we enjoy the appreciation these men showed for our qualities—youth, beauty, and song?

Odysseus and I could have freed the captive suitors one by one. What tribute Odysseus might have gained by peacefully retaking his home. Of course, the suitors died like warriors with weapons in their hands. But when I thought of the maidservants with their faces black and bloated, I felt I truly entered the Underworld on the day of their deaths. I wished I could blame Odysseus, but I listened to my own heart when I slew them.

I came to loathe the past. It shimmered behind me like the life of another man. My father had sacrificed far too much of our livestock for us to prosper. I lived a hard life as his overseer. Odysseus used all his craft to plan our plowing, seeding, and harvesting. The stars, the cries of the migrating cranes, and the gray-husked buds of spring all guided him. Each day I hiked the mountainsides to where our herders kept our sheep and, higher yet, to the pinnacles where only our goats could graze. Even in winter we rose before the dawn and labored into the nights. Then we increased the food for our slaves while giving half portions to our oxen. Other men might crowd around the roaring fires in the smithy, but we prepared for the next season of planting. With holm oak hewed when the leaves fell and the trees were free of worms, we carefully fit together our plows. My drudgery made me crave our cups of bitter wine. In finer weather I welcomed cutting the grape clusters, exposing them ten days to the sun and covering them five days. How I splashed my libations to Dionysus when the crushed grapes flowed into our empty jars. In this and so much more toil the years passed until the laughter of the noble suitors struck me as an impossible joy.

Odysseus spent much of his time at his stony shrine. What dreams invaded his meditations I can hardly tell you. Nor can I tell you how my mother and father lived together during these years. Over our dinners in the empty hall, the three of us talked about the events of each day. My mother managed the maidservants in their weaving and other chores. Could it have been our frugal life that made me feel an anguish growing in her?

I wondered if we had driven evil too forcefully from our home. The insolence of Melantho—that twisted pouting mouth and the invitation of her fawn eyes—struck me with its intensity. Even Antinoös had a beast-like vitality and a feeling of grandeur that Ithaca no longer permitted. Odysseus rarely spoke of Troy, as if that life of heroism and violence had been thrice plowed and buried beneath our stony fields. Hadn't Odysseus once been a suitor? Certainly, I had taken pleasure in such men. We had the right to defend our home against those who came uninvited. But when we denied we might be like the suitors, we earned the hatred that would otherwise have been theirs.

My mother and father shared their hewn bed night after night. Could this white-haired couple be lovers? They had each lost their glory from those days we shared with the suitors. I remember how Penelope swept into the hall with her maids in attendance. Head high and eyes flashing, she treated the suitors like hounds baying and snapping at her heels. She might have been Helen for these younger men. Would Antinoös or Eurymakhos have hesitated to sail to war to win her? She lived for those men like an image of their souls, the dream of every man to transcend himself and be godlike. The beggar Odysseus possessed this same splendor of life. If he looked repulsive and stank with his filth, yet he lived each challenge. Do you thrill to remember the way he drew that bowstring back to his grizzled cheek while the astonished suitors stared? How the arrow sang that poked its shaft through the throat of Antinoös. But this Penelope and Odysseus vanished in the exhausting routine of our days.

In the seventh year after the return of Odysseus, my mother took to walking up toward the lookout where she and I had spent so many hours in my childhood. Stopping short of the shrine where Odysseus prayed, she would stand and watch the sea. With the constant wind tossing her white hair like the foam, she studied the waters for a sign. Could it have been the sails of the returning fleet that she and I searched for so many years earlier? Could she relive those long years of waiting? Did she regret unweaving Laertes's shroud each night and delaying her wedding until Odysseus murdered the men who desired her? When I saw the pain in her eyes, I would turn away from her to continue my chores.

I lacked the courage to question her. My own life struck me as painful enough without seeking the pain of others. No doubt this caused me to avoid both my father and my mother. I didn't want to learn how their renewed marriage troubled their spirits. I knew so little of women. When I remembered how Penelope enchanted the suitors, I feared her power. How did Odysseus dare go to her arms or resist her desires? I felt an urging in both my parents, but it lacked form or name. Odysseus might have been Ithaca and Penelope the sea which rushed again and again against him. How could earth and sea find unison?

Why didn't I marry? Wouldn't other voices—those of my wife or my children—have lightened my inner burden? But where would I find a bride? When I trusted in Athena, I believed I would marry a woman of beauty and live that long and happy life of which you poets sing.

No woman on Ithaca or any of our islands would have me. Nor could I find some sparkling princess in a foreign court. We had no wealth. We owned only the shame of our violence. What wise father would marry his daughter into such a line? Laertes, Odysseus, and I had each slaughtered our countrymen. If we had done this for plunder or a throne, my life might have continued in feasts and revels. But we did it for Athena, who showed little care for the fates of men. I dwelt in the tasks that filled my days and expected no relief. I would never be that brash Telemachus who warned the suitors to leave our hall. I imagined little of yesterday and nothing of tomorrow. When my grandfather Laertes died, I went to live in his hovel on the mountainside. I preferred that poverty to quiet evenings in the hall of Odysseus.

One day, hiking to the upland pastures where our goats grazed, I saw my mother standing in the shade of an olive tree. The cliffs fell away beneath her to the jagged rocks where the surf sprayed in white geysers. Ten years had passed since Odysseus returned to his hall. How many months had it been since I had spoken with my mother? I spent my days in toil and my nights in the damp, low-ceiled shack where Laertes had lived out the miserable end of his life. Seeing my mother on that day—a sunny day, with a soft breeze blowing from the east—did I have a faint recollection of how she cradled me in her arms and covered my child's face with her kisses? Where was the woman who made the suitors turn their heads? Could that younger Penelope live within this white-headed woman who stared toward the restless sea? Did I crave the love that had always been mine before my father's return? I can hardly tell you what made me sit quietly beside her.

"Are you all right, Mother?" I asked.

She turned and studied me like a cipher. Did she see a man, a stranger, who bore no resemblance to the child whom she had loved? Or did she see in me a hint of the youthful Odysseus for whom perhaps she yearned?

"I was remembering my childhood in Sparta," she said, her dark eyes moist and gleaming. "I miss my father, Ikarios, and those days of joy before I married."

Seeing that I listened, she spoke more freely.

"My father was a man of craft, not unlike Odysseus. When my uncle, King Tyndareus, invited the suitors to court Helen, my father knew that many of those disappointed men would seek a bride elsewhere. Why should I marry a boy from Sparta, when the finest princes in all Greece might also want me?

"My father moved among the suitors, talking with each, learning the qualities that made them fine or indifferent men. He didn't want a hall full of princes competing for me, but only those few whom he felt would make the best match. Each evening he would come home and speak so colorfully about the different suitors that they appeared before my eyes. I almost felt they had assembled to marry me, not Helen.

"Of the suitors, Ikarios soon preferred Odysseus to any other. I believe there were finer athletes and men more skilled with weapons. Many men could drink and eat far more and at least some could tell a tale as well. But no man, according to my father, had the spirit of Odysseus. If I didn't like Odysseus, my father's next choice would be the prince of Euboea, Palamedes. In Palamedes he saw many of the qualities that he admired in Odysseus.

"I became impatient to meet these suitors. Would I admire the same men my father had chosen? If I instantly cared for another, would Ikarios relent and let me choose whoever might please me? I was seventeen, ten years younger than Odysseus and most of the suitors.

"In the blazing hall of Tyndareus I saw these men assembled. So many were handsome, clean of limb, and graceful. My cousins Helen and Klytaimnestra sat on thrones by their father Tyndareus. Agamemnon, a giant of a man, stood beside Klytaimnestra. While he poured a flagon of wine down his gullet, Klytaimnestra studied him with smiling lips and cool eyes. I never imagined what her look might mean until our heroes returned home from Troy.

"Helen captivated these men. She glowed with their attention. She had always been a beauty, but now she looked like an earthly Aphrodite. For these suitors, who came from all of Greece, she was the essence of woman. In her soul, Greece lived. United by their passion, the suitors forgot war and plunder to offer gifts to this near goddess. How I envied Helen's blazing hair that matched the flush forever dawning in her cheeks. Why had the gods gifted her with a form that launched men's hearts into the unknown? Compared to her, I was a plain girl—attractive enough by myself, nothing compared to the beauty of my red-headed cousin.

"How easily Helen moved among the men. Even the strongest and most awkward treated her with deference. Aias the giant and Menelaos with his great girth bowed at her approach. All the suitors' eyes followed her. Only one man might win this beauty, but the rest would carry the memory of her for the length of their lives.

"I knew I would never move among men with her grace. She looked like a magical woman who tamed the wild beasts about her. The whole hall might be in turbulence, men arguing, cups clattering to the floor, a scuffle here or there, but on her entrance these men rose as one. Imagine the impression this made on me, a girl of seventeen. How happy I felt I would be to have men treat me as they treated Helen. The storerooms of the castle filled with gifts brought by these princes. Every disagreement—with words, fists, or swords—centered on the love of Helen. She must have been gifted by Aphrodite. Could a mortal woman have made men so delirious? If she found Aias in his cups, a touch of her hand on his shaggy head would bring awareness to his eyes and make him hastily wipe the spittle from his lips. When Menelaos in his bearskin crashed into tables and beat the stony floor with frustration, she used the instep of her dainty foot to quiet him. She cured any madness, except the madness they felt for her.

"As a girl I had little interest in what men prize. Who cared which man was strongest? After all, they were all stronger than I was. Their endless games were boring. Their swiftness or agility impressed me very little. Nor did their wealth or the domains they ruled matter to me. I would bring a fine dowry to the man I wed. Of course, I could hardly have imagined how barren and stony Ithaca would be.

"Odysseus stirred me like no other man in that hall. Physically he frightened me. He looked enormous through the shoulders, and I could see the knotted muscles in his short legs. When I tried to imagine myself in the embrace of a man with such strength, I wondered how women ever married men. Nor did his face appeal to me. He looked like a man beaten mercilessly. The planes of his face seemed crude and ill-shaped. His eye sockets were thick and bony, and his nose broken from some accident or combat.

"But when he spoke, I heard a godlike voice. The others bragged of their feats and conquests, but Odysseus spoke of the longing of his spirit. He wanted a queen equal to her king, a wife to match her husband. Equal in love and toil, we would meet in the bed he would hew with his own hands on the site he had chosen for his hall.

"Palamedes spoke finely too. Certainly, he was more handsome than Odysseus. His father, King Nauplius, ruled a far richer kingdom.

"But Odysseus came to me first. He came before Helen had decided which suitor would be her husband. He left the other men, including Palamedes, in that spell of Helen's. Only Odysseus saw in me a woman as desirable as Helen. While the others courted my cousin, he came with gifts to my father's hall.

"I could hardly believe Helen chose Menelaos. The girth of the man disgusted me, not to mention his gluttony for meat and the way he guzzled wine. He had wealth, but Helen's father had a vaster fortune. If Helen loved a man from a poor kingdom, she could have married him anyway. I believe her sister, Klytaimnestra, convinced her to marry Menelaos. Who could have imagined the bloodshed that would follow this pairing of sisters and brothers?

"Once Palamedes knew he had lost Helen, he came to my father's hall. A slender man with close-cropped dark curls, he had a narrow, angular face. I listened patiently to him. He could name the thousands of oxen, bulls, sheep, and goats that would be mine if I followed him to Euboea. He knew the hectares of the royal family's crops and grazing lands. The fleet and army of his father's kingdom would impress any man.

"But I was a woman. In my heart, I knew Odysseus to be truer to me. He chose me ahead of Helen. Strong as he might be, I understood him for a gentle man. He had no elaborate notions of his place in the world. To rule stony Ithaca, or rich Sparta, hardly made a difference to him. He wanted to share with me the harmonious life of family and hearth.

"So, I asked my father to accept the proposal of Odysseus. I knew little of the love between a husband and wife, but I trusted Odysseus as I have trusted no man since. After Helen's fabulous nuptial feasts, Odysseus and I had a small wedding. From Ithaca, only Anticlea, Laertes, and Ktimene came to my father's hall. When we sailed from Sparta, I felt a sadness for the life I had known as a girl. But my life as a woman, a bride, opened ahead of me.

"How could I imagine, when soon I carried you inside me, that I would live so much of my life alone and grieving? Why should Odysseus have gone to Troy? I tried to hold him to me. But who can resist the fates? I cannot, nor could Odysseus."

CHAPTER 18

Listening to my mother, I couldn't help but recall how ten years earlier I had listened to Odysseus. We had sat much as I sat with her. The sea stretched away before us. He spoke of the past as she did. What could their lives have in common? He had fought at Troy and wandered across the world while she lived on Ithaca. Despite this, might some essence of their stories, their histories, connect their spirits?

"I was a child when Agamemnon and Menelaos sought refuge in Sparta." Her cheeks flushed as she spoke the names of these brothers. "If only my uncle had been less generous in welcoming them. After all, their father Atreus had boiled the children of his brother, Thyestes. Then Atreus carved the children's flesh and served this meal to his brother. They say the sun's chariot ran back across the sky and left the world in darkness the day of that horror."

Of course I knew the story of Atreus and Thyestes, but I had never heard her speak of it before.

"When Agamemnon sacrificed his daughter for a wind to Troy, he showed himself worthy of his father."

How angrily she spoke of the house of Atreus. These memories animated her. The shrouded woman who stood in the shadow of the olive tree vanished in the depth of her feeling.

"In my childhood Helen and Klytaimnestra were like older sisters to me. Nothing prepared me to believe Helen would run off with Paris or Klytaimnestra take the despicable Aegisthus for her lover.

"I wish my uncle had never given sanctuary to the sons of Atreus. Or, if he did this in honor of Zeus, why did he marry his daughters to such violent and vengeful men?

"Aegisthus, the last son of Thyestes, murdered Atreus while he offered sacrifices by the sea. Should I praise Aegisthus for the murder? Or condemn them all for being monsters?

"Those marriages entangled the fate of our family with the destinies of Agamemnon and Menelaos. How often I've wondered what might have happened if my cousins had married pious men like Philoctetes or Menestheus. I've prayed to Zeus to roll back time and unwed these monsters from their brides. I might as well pray that the thick walls of Troy tumble in a breeze. Fine men are given unhappy lives and brutes like Menelaos have prosperity. I can't measure what should have been for Odysseus and me.

"Of course, Agamemnon murdered Thyestes and took back the throne of Mycenae. When my uncle died, Menelaos became king of Sparta."

Tears welled in her eyes. She couldn't weep for Agamemnon or Menelaos, so she must have wept for herself. I wondered why she left out part of this history of brothers. She didn't say Atreus and Thyestes joined together to murder their stepbrother Chrysippus. When they were expelled from Elis for this, they came to Mycenae and inherited the throne of Perseus. Why wouldn't my mother have mentioned that Atreus banished Thyestes from Mycenae? Or that Thyestes stole the youngest son of Atreus and raised him to murder his father? That gave Atreus a reason to kill Thyestes's children and serve them as a stew. She seemed to forget this in her desire to make Atreus as evil as a man can be.

"I can understand the gods wanting to punish Agamemnon and Menelaos. Why shouldn't Helen have run off with a barbarian? Menelaos had to show his prowess at war by leading the Greek armies. At least this generation of brothers fought on the same side. But for what? If Helen wanted to live in Troy, why couldn't Menelaos have let her go?

"If he had pursued her from love, I might not feel so bitter. But he couldn't love her. He didn't know her. He loved her beauty. When he had her in his bed, he must have loved the way his body quivered above her. But did he speak with her? Did he know her feelings and fears?"

"She chose to marry him," I said.

My mother turned on me. "She wanted to live as a virgin of the goddess Aphrodite. Did men care for her wishes? Did her father Tyndareus shield her when he wanted a powerful son-in-law to strengthen his rule? She should never have married. Who asked Helen what she desired?"

Of course, I had no idea, but the coarse woman I had met in Sparta bore no resemblance to the memory my mother conjured. Nor could I connect this virginal Helen to the woman Odysseus courted and met again in the halls of Paris and Deiphobus. That Helen served Aphrodite, but hardly as a virgin.

"Did you want to marry?" I asked my mother.

She smiled like a bashful girl. No doubt she had smiled and bobbed her head like that when her father Ikarios asked her the same question so many years earlier.

"Someday you'll marry too," she said fervently. "I know you will."

She knew I would never find a woman on these islands to marry me. Odysseus shared her hope I would marry. Many mornings, when we met to plan our chores, he spoke of how sons ease a father's burdens. I knew his wish that I would have a son of my own to cherish.

"And what of Klytaimnestra?"

"She wanted children and a hearth. She despaired when Agamemnon sacrificed their girl. If Odysseus had done that to you, I'd have killed him with these hands." She raised her closed fists for emphasis. "No wonder Klytaimnestra took Aegisthus for her lover. She wanted revenge."

If it was wrong for Agamemnon to slay the girl, how could my mother ignore Odysseus's part in deceiving Klytaimnestra? But my mother straightened alertly, and I followed her gaze to where Odysseus picked his way down the stony path from his shrine. Observing him like a stranger, I thought how his appearance had changed in ten years. From the scarred chieftain who had looked a man made by the world, he had returned to his role of the beggar. He clothed himself in a mangy reindeer hide and cared for little beside his prayers. After commanding so many captains at Troy, now he commanded only me. Could it be the failed harvest and scraggy herds that made his eyes look into the distances? Even when we planned the work for our field hands and herders each morning, he hardly concealed his impatience to leave for his humble shrine.

He used his staff like an old man. Slowly he descended, walking around rocks he would have leapt over easily when he and I built his altar. He kept his eyes fixed on the path he followed. My mother watched until he vanished from our view.

She shook her head. The years fell away while her memories moved her.

150

"Your birth gave us joy beyond any we had known. We had finished building the hall. Our lives prospered.

"I loved Helen, but I loved my life with my Odysseus far more.

"Who were these princes to demand Odysseus fight? Agamemnon proved a coward at Troy. When the Trojans had the upper hand, he wanted to float the ships at night and sail for home. Later Odysseus used this idea of retreat as a ruse to trick the Trojans. After the victory, Menelaos insisted on sailing before offering sacrifices. Can you believe any man could be so foolhardy?

"But Palamedes proved worse than either of these brothers. I had so little experience of men. I never imagined Palamedes might despise me for rejecting him. He brought a message from my father ordering Odysseus to fight at Troy. I pled with Odysseus not to go.

"I remember how Palamedes sat in our hall. He lounged in his chair and twisted his dark curls of hair. His eyes followed you so intently. I wondered what could fascinate him about a child. He frightened me by his constant staring. I kept you in my arms to protect you from those eyes. Clever man, he used you to trick Odysseus.

"After that, everything fell apart. Odysseus failed in his embassies to Troy. The sentiment for the war carried him away from us. His absence shocked me. To a young woman, he seemed wise in so many ways. If I asked about the stars, the fields, or the sea, he always had a ready answer. He knew the secrets of the loom and which ores make the finest dyes. If our hall was humble compared to that of my father, I flourished in the love and nearness of Odysseus.

"After a few months, I wondered why I had lost my husband. What had I done to make the gods punish me and my suckling baby? I tortured myself with the idea that I had caused his departure. Each night I wept myself to sleep. Should I have been kinder to Palamedes? Had there been a better way to reject him, a way that a woman like Helen might have known? Eurykleia tried to help me. She told me how Laertes left your grandmother to besiege Nerikos. But Nerikos is so close. After a year or more, when you no longer nursed at my breasts, I began to lose the hope Odysseus would return. The supply ships returned with news of Troy's massive walls. Then I wondered if Odysseus deserted me because he wanted to live his life plundering the towns near Troy. Had I been worthy of him? When I worried over this, I felt myself a leper, an outcast. Looking in the polished bronze of my mirrors, I expected to see my secret illness that had driven him so far away.

"While these fantasies tormented me, you grew from a baby to a boy. You had so much of your father in you. I could see him in your face, your shoulders. When you built the Trojan walls of sticks and besieged them with your tiny soldiers, I saw the boy your father must once have been.

"Loving you cured me of my torment over Odysseus. My pain continued, but my blame vanished. He had gone to war as men do. He tried not to go. He withstood more than other men might. But when men gather, they become less and more than men. Agamemnon called our assembly to war. Some great voice spoke in reply, but not the voice of any single of our heroes. It was the voice of an ancient heart. How their voices chorused in reply. Even great Odysseus, resourceful as a man can be, lost his own voice in the cries of that crowd. He demanded a mission of peace when the others cared only for war. Nonetheless, in the end, it came to war. If only he could have been stronger and had even greater vision. But then he'd have been a god, instead of godlike, and even the gods love war."

For a moment, I thought as my mother must have for so many years. Why had Odysseus left me? Had I caused him to go? If he hadn't loved me, he might have plowed me under the earth when Palamedes tossed me down. Should I, a baby in my swaddling-cloth, have wished the plow had ripped open my flesh? Might my blood have saved my father from his journey? But what had I done to Odysseus? How can a baby be blamed for his father's fate? It couldn't be, but I remembered how Odysseus wept while he eulogized his own father.

We had stood in front of the funeral pyre for Laertes, the small corpse neatly wrapped in the shroud my mother had woven. Rain misted about us, the sunlight diffuse and silvery. Odysseus wore his purple cape that day and spoke as if our islanders listened in assembly. He opened his arms to encompass the living and the dead.

"Here lies Laertes, king and father to me. He came like all men from his father's fire and his mother's blood."

I felt the incongruity of his words. He sounded like an Achilles speaking to a field of troops over a slain comrade. But Laertes died of old age and only Mentor, Halitherses, and a few others joined us to mourn for him. If Odysseus spoke too long, I worried the wood in the pyre would be sodden with the rain.

"My father cursed me for failing to learn from his bitter lesson at Nerikos. He rejoiced to have me home from Troy again, but he never forgave me for our long separation. He spoke often of my mother's death while I fought far from Ithaca. He remembered that in my absence the suitors drove him from my hall."

Odysseus turned to implore the shrouded corpse on the pyre.

"Father, you lived the quiet and pious life the gods favor for men. But you also served when others commanded. The assembly elected you king, so you gave up your fields and herds to lead our army. If men despised you for razing the walls of Nerikos, I can say you did your duty. Did I differ from you? You taught me the skills to undermine and breach fortress walls. But had you come with me to Troy, you'd have seen an impregnable city."

Odysseus bowed his head. Looking at the pyre, I imagined my grandfather like the seed from which Odysseus grew. In so many ways, Laertes contained the potential of Odysseus. If Laertes had journeyed like his son, he might have returned a hero or a beggar. But he had chosen not to journey. He had stayed on Ithaca and tried his best to father me until the suitors drove him out. If he cuffed me for not obeying him, he also gave me the love of his presence. I would have wept for his death, except that his unhappiness had finally ended. All my life he had grieved for Odysseus. In a family of single sons, I can understand the sorrow that made him wear his goatskin cap. But why couldn't he forget once Odysseus returned? Why did he continue to live in that hovel and seldom visit the great hall? In truth, since I went to live in Laertes's home, I might have asked those questions of myself.

At last Odysseus spoke again.

"If only I could accompany you into the Underworld. I know the dark descent. I've seen the flickering multitudes who draw their airless breaths. There, blood is worth more than gold. Sunlight is like the memory of those once loved. Nonetheless I would take your hand in mine to meet Arkeisios and his fathers.

"We are born of gods to the glory of life. Yet my spirit feels the blindness of this world of kings. In the Underworld might we gain the vision of divine Teiresias? Or storm the impregnable cities of our hearts?

"All I could have done as your son, Laertes, I have done. Here I add my sacrifices, my love, and the flames that carry you to heaven and return you to earth."

Odysseus gestured for the brand. Despite my fears, the pyre quickly caught fire. I watched Odysseus stare at the shimmering flames and the black smoke rising heavenward. He had never spoken before of men being descended from the gods. What else had he imagined in his hours at his shrine? Absurdly, I wondered if he imagined himself the son of a god and not the son of Laertes. Of course, Odysseus believed that generations before Laertes's father, Arkeisios, all men had been fathered by Zeus. I looked from face to face as the pyre crumbled. How soon these few mourners might follow Laertes. I didn't fear the misery of living alone. But when I eulogized Odysseus, who would share my grief?

CHAPTER 19

The years that followed brought me many dreams. I believe my conversations with my mother caused me to think more often of the wedding gown Helen had given me. I imagined the woman who might give form and life to that garment. Despite the impossibility of finding a bride, I began to hope that Laertes's farmhouse might be the home to which I would someday return with a wife. I lost much of my pain over the islanders' hatred of me. After all, they acted as if I were a ghost. Perhaps they shunned me out of habit. I seldom imagined or cared what they thought.

Instead of worrying over such unchangeable facts, I began to rebuild Laertes's house. It had been constructed many years earlier as a shelter for shepherds in the upland ranges. I had simply accepted the rain dripping from the ceiling beams and the ease with which the winds whistled through the cracks in the log walls. The oppressive lowness of the roof and the narrow slits for windows gave the feeling of a cave, especially in winter. I planned how best to raise the roof and chink the log walls to hold out the sea-flung winds. I wanted large windows with shutters to close in bad weather. Most importantly, I wanted a hearth where I might cook my meals and offer sacrifices to Zeus and Athena. From time to time, Odysseus visited and listened to my plans for these improvements. He advised me how Epeios with his infinite craft might have solved one problem or another.

Slowly the house transformed. The high roof gave a feeling of space. On a bright day, light flowed through the windows. The hearth offered a center for my meals and prayers. New rooms added to the fullness of my home. I slept on a bed in a bedroom instead of that rough pallet in the main room. My mother brought bright-dyed blankets. She gave me plates and bowls glazed by Arnaios before he went to Troy. On the wall she hung her weaving of the goddess Hestia, whose face gazed with loving warmth on my home and hearth. In the evenings, when I sat by the fire with my hounds beside me, I felt I belonged in this place. Stroking the silky ears of one of my retrievers, I might recollect Argos bounding by me while I climbed the steep path to the lookout. Or, glancing at one of the new ceiling beams, I might recall how my adze slipped and gashed my wrist beside that old scar from the battle with the suitors. I felt an ancient calm as if the spirit of Laertes remained close by me. Bitter as he may have been, he gave me what he could.

In the tranquility of remembered pain and pleasure, I might have imagined I would always live this same way. Certainly, I had accustomed myself to the miseries of my life. I found comfort in my pain. The islanders couldn't take that from me or deny me any more than they already had. I might have lived in this changeless state to a very great age. Laertes and Arkeisios lived far beyond the span of most men. But I came to feel my future unknown and vaster than my past. Early in my thirty-fifth year, my dreams became like visions. As Odysseus had wandered at sea, I found myself in other realms.

Apollo is the god of light. Yet he also sent me these dreams that rose from the darkness of the night. I don't claim my dreams offered a vision of events like those of Teiresias or Halitherses. But as the dreams succeeded one another, I felt an unexplored reality of my own life. If my journey were only in my bed beneath my mother's bright blankets, nonetheless I suffered terrors much like those of Odysseus on his return from Troy.

In the first dream I stood beside a boiling sea. The whole surface heaved as if some creature sought to rise. At last, the boiling waves peeled apart, and the head of an immense sea serpent appeared. A gray, slender neck followed the head and then a vast body shelled like a turtle. Gradually it rose until it hung like a moon barely free of the waves. I had seen many strange creatures fishing in the waters off Ithaca, but nothing like this monster. It might have been the dragon Apollo destroyed when he seized the shrine of Delphi. Or the ghastly snake that came from the sea to crush the Trojan priest Laocoon and silence his entreaties to burn the wooden horse. When the serpent opened its jaws, I knew its desire to speak to me. Its jaws opened and closed, opened and closed again. Why didn't it speak? Suddenly I imagined it had existed far earlier than language or mankind. Its truths, whether ghastly or transfiguring, were ineffable. As slowly as it had risen from water to air, the serpent descended again into the boiling sea.

Later my dreams returned me to this unknown island of black and gray. Its volcanic beaches showed some vast eruption had devastated the island and blackened its sands. Black cliffs like coral towered above the sea. I saw nothing alive, not even birds in flight. The ocean looked a shroud and this bleak island a marker.

Once I found myself in the island's interior, a world of stone. The sun rode gray and distant in the sky. A cool breeze blew through me like a phantom. What island could this be? Another time I imagined I faintly heard voices singing. They must have come from the sea or within the thrusting pinnacles of stone. Or could the voices be moving, encircling the island? I strained to hear the words or learn if the voices were those of men or women. Soon I realized the inhuman power of the waves and wind gave lung and throat to these sighing songs.

The lifelessness of these dreams made me relieved to wake. No child had been born on this island, no family worshipped here and later searched elsewhere for better lands for grazing and cultivation. The flotsam of a storm-wrecked ship, the skeletons of its crew, any hint that men had come here before me would have relieved me.

I had been lonely as a child, but here I lacked the mother who made me and the father of whom I had dreamt. The wild dolphins forgot the shoreline and submerged far out in the dark roll of the waves. Nothing lessened the terror of the death I had seen for myself when the suitors circled me with their spears.

After such dreams, I would lie stunned. The island remained with me as if I had surely been there. My bedroom, my hall with its holy hearth, my crops and herds—the waking world could hardly be as real as this island. My dreams tormented me. What could I imagine this island to be but myself, barren and lost to other men? Or Ithaca? The bolder of the townspeople hawked or spit to the side when I passed; the timid gestured to protect themselves from evil as if a ghost had passed by them unseen. Like a figure in a dream, I became for them an embodiment of the violence about them. If I had to choose between the island of the dream and Ithaca, I might well have chosen the eternal loneliness of my dream. After all, Aigyptos, Laertes, and Halitherses had all died. Soon Ithaca would be without any of the men who had supported us and remained our allies. When my father died, I would be an outcast despised as much for the fears of men's nightmares as for the slaughter of the suitors.

Of course, I forgot many of my dreams and remembered only fragments of others. Often, I dreamt of my father's hall and the round tower where I spent my childhood. Sometimes Argos ran springing by my side. I returned to the court of Menelaos and even saw the high walls of Troy. In that dream red-haired Helen walked smiling on the ramparts and urged both armies to greater slaughter. I hid while the giant Polyphemos grew ever larger in the darkness of his cave. Strangely, he had two eyes the way most men do, and yet another larger eye in the center of his forehead. So, my dreams embellished adventures too fantastic to believe in any case.

The magical quality of the dreams let me imagine a magical bride for myself. I felt she would have to be divine like the women Odysseus had been forced to love in his wanderings. I needed a woman unmoved by the calumnies men might speak against one another. Why not Circe, forever as young and languorous as when my father spent his rapturous year with her? She would fit Helen's gown. Or would she remember Odysseus and lack desire for me? I might have sailed to her distant island, if only my father remembered the route. Nor could I reconcile these restless urgings with my pleasure in the changes I had made in Laertes's farmhouse. If I could feel tranquil by the fireside each evening, why should my dreams propel me toward unknown worlds?

I remember a palace of smooth stone. It stood in a landscape of amorphous rocks like strange men-beasts slumbering until some future call. I reached the marble walls of this white temple. The cut rock glistened, smooth and cold to my touch. Endlessly I walked around the rectangle of the walls in search of an entrance. Neither doors nor windows opened inward. No sound came from within, although I hoped to hear a song carried by the wind or the hum of a loom in flickering motion. If this were a temple, to which god or goddess had it been raised? By whom? Would I walk forever outside its shining walls?

When my dreams returned me to this temple, I found the rocks transformed as if these men-beasts had struggled to rise from a spell. A sculpted portal revealed the dark interior of a palace. Alert for dangers, I entered to find a large room with its walls and floors of the finest marble. The empty banquet tables looked the length and width of those in the great hall of Odysseus. The suitors might have feasted here in comfort. I walked through other rooms with ample beds like the one shared by my father and mother.

What temple would lack an altar and a statue of its god or goddess? Yet I imagined a wedding celebration might be performed in this hall. The emptiness had a presence, the air shaped like an eternal bride and groom struggling to be visible. If words fail me, you understand how the meanings of dreams can be wordless.

I woke with a child's fear, like those nights when my mother took me to her bed and enfolded me to calm my crying over a nightmare. In the darkness of Laertes's home, I trembled at phantoms. Should I have sacrificed my sleep and kept a vigil by my hearth to avoid these fleeting images? As Odysseus needed light in the cave of Polyphemos, so I faced the darkness of my sleep.

After many dreams, I returned to find this marble palace changed. It had risen skyward, peaked and upward sweeping. The shifting stones had risen too, like men nearly standing. Light flowed from the interior. Inside I found an altar, beside which rose the most beautiful statue I have ever seen. It glowed with a golden ambiance. Nothing in the court of Menelaos matched this exquisite craft.

I imagined the statue portrayed Hermaphroditus. It offered the finest of both the male and the female forms. In fact, while I studied the graceful curves and articulations, I realized I couldn't tell whether this nude figure was male or female. That is, one moment I saw the breasts of a woman and the next moment the sex of a man. It shimmered before me like a vision in stone. The youthful Teiresias might have appeared like this when he changed from man to woman and back again to man. Could he have been so beautifully handsome? Who had imagined such a being and possessed the artistry to perfect this portrayal? I walked closer, studying every aspect of the statue. Did I see the tones of skin instead of marble? Did the chest flutter imperceptibly? The delicate fingers tremble? If I touched the marble, would it have the warmth and pulse of life? I reached to caress the chest. Would I feel a woman's rounded breasts or the nippled plain of a man? My hands moved over the polished marble. As happens in a dream, I forgot my concern for the sex of this inanimate form. Instead, I felt the chaos within this statue. It blended the perfection women and men might attain, but it contained the demonic genius of giants. If this statue could move, its very motion would unleash the horrors petrified in its volumes of stone. A rhythm seized me, a waking fear as endless as the encompassment of the rolling waves.

I couldn't sleep again that night. I wrapped myself in a worn reindeer hide and walked to the orchards that Laertes had seeded, mulched, pruned, and harvested. My hounds ran like lean shadows by my side. If only I struggled with a living enemy instead of these imponderable images. In the darkness of my orchard, I saw the statue as clearly as in my dream. I cried out and pressed my skull to free myself from that vision. I heard my hounds leap away. When I sat and wept in my own embrace, they returned to nestle close and comfort me with their warmth and their caressing gentle tongues. I felt such loneliness. I the dreamer had built this statue of stone. I had been father and mother to that beautiful form with its inner demons and chaos. My lands, my herds, my fine-built house, my father and mother, Ithaca—nothing sustained me.

I embraced the earth. Its stones repelled me. My cries to the vacant fields brought no more response than when the Cyclops raged against the crimes of Nobody. I imagined fleeing from Ithaca. If I had remained the Telemachus who sailed to Pylos and Sparta, I might have taken ship again. My friend Peisistratos ruled in Pylos since King Nestor's death. Peisistratos had been captain of the palace guard, worthy of his elder brother Antilochus who perished at Troy. Again, I recalled his gentle sister, Polykaste, who bathed and attended me during my visit. But if I fled to Pylos, would my dreams vanish? What foreign land would remove me from myself? Would the broken walls of Troy or the deserts of Egypt make me other than I had become? If only Amphinomos lived, what his love would have meant to me that night. In utter exhaustion, I finally curled among my hounds to wait for dawn.

In my next dream, I wore that same shiny hide of reindeer. I waited in a dark room or cave. I could hear the sea beating close by, far closer than I would have imagined the waves to come. I pulled the tattered hide tighter about myself, remembering Odysseus had worn such a hide when I first saw him. Slowly, fearfully, I felt myself drawn into the daylight.

What a strange landscape I found! About the doorway from which I emerged the white-foaming waves crashed with a deafening roar. The salt scent burned my nostrils. A mist off the sea billowed above me. Looking from side to side, I found the ruins of the marble temple where my dreams had so often brought me. An army might have laid siege to this palace, for it had been razed beyond any hope of resurrection. I realized the waves had covered the rocks that once threatened to rise and walk like men.

In the sea the statue rose among the rushing passes of the waves. Glistening, it stood on the water like a son of Poseidon. If dolphins had carried it toward the shore, I would have been no more struck by the fearful magic of its prowess. Golden armor covered it from head to feet. Across that face moved the sublime beauty of male and female, transforming constantly in a flux like that of the sea. Its limbs danced in ceaseless change. I shielded my eyes from the brightness of this being. Could the sun glow within that shining armor? It stood with the waves boiling about its knees.

"Who are you?" I cried at last.

"A child born far from its homeland." Its answer echoed with the voices of both woman and man.

Compelled, I asked again, "Who are you?"

"Death from the sea," it answered, its sword sweeping aloft.

Feeling bound, I asked once more, "Who are you?"

"Telegonus," it answered, "child of Odysseus and the sea-born Circe. Deserted by my father before my birth, I come for vengeance."

The waves rolled back to the sea and vanished. The fearful rocks transformed to men. Glistening in this new birth, I saw the unruly mob of suitors. Antinoös stood crouched with sword in hand. Eurymakhos carried his long-shafted spear. Who had given blood to spirits such as these? In vain I sought a glimpse of Amphinomos.

The hide of reindeer became my skin. My arms were long tapering legs, great antlers weighted my brow. With fear and a divine energy, I leapt upland from Telegonus and the hundred suitors. How clearly I recognized this island as Ithaca. I bounded past the spring of Arethusa and the cliffs where the black ravens roost. Like jagged lightning, I fled across the forested mountainsides toward the great hall of my father. A spear grazed my flank. Shouts resounded in my ears, my own breath singing and trembling in my deep-slung chest. If I reached my father, would he too slay me for a beast? Or, if I escaped the arrows from his bow, would he die at the hands of this demon Telegonus and the shades flown up from the Underworld?

I woke in terror. For years I had shunted aside Halitherses's prophecy of my father's death at my hands. If Halitherses were alive, I would have asked him to explain the mysteries of these dreams. Had Telegonus been some slaughtering part of myself, like the Telemachus who surprised the suitors in the great hall?

I rose and dressed quickly in a chiton and cloak. Without thinking, I reached up on the wall and unhooked the sword I had used to kill Eurynomos and others of the suitors. I ran its sash around my waist as if to fight any phantoms I might meet in the darkness. Striding toward my father's hall, I saw how I continued the action of the dream. Like Telegonus, or the stag, I rushed to Odysseus.

What emptiness I felt in my father's courtyard. Standing before the altar for Zeus, I stared at the round tower glimmering in the moonlight. I had spent so many nights sleeping peacefully within the circle of those walls. But in this courtyard, Eumaios, Philoitios, and I had stacked the bodies of the suitors and butchered Melanthios. Beside the tower we hanged the maidservants who joined their lovers in the Underworld. I could recall none of the joyous sounds of my childhood, only the cries of anguished men. Soundlessly, I crossed the threshold where Odysseus and I had stood against so many. How insubstantial our great hall looked to me. The empty tables wavered in the faint glow from the hearth. Shades might easily dine in this darkness. If Telegonus and his hundred men pursued me here, they might feast on fresh blood to give them substance in this hall.

My hand curled about the hilt of my sword. What phantoms waited to rush from behind the pillars? For a moment, I imagined I should lock the arms room door. But who would I lock it against? The phantoms of my dreams? Odysseus sleeping in my mother's arms?

I didn't call to wake my parents. Instead, hand on sword hilt, I slipped like air into the chamber where they slept.

The embers glowed in the banked fire by their bedside. Within that great trunk Odysseus had carved to build their bed, I saw my mother and father sleeping. He lay on his back, his head and shoulders propped on his pillows and his arms flung out to the sides. Whatever the night might bring, he looked ready to give it his embrace. My mother curled on her side, her face beside his scarred massive chest. I don't believe they touched, yet they dreamt within inches of one another.

I realized the ease with which I might murder Odysseus. By slipping my sword quietly from its sheath, I could strike home to his unsuspecting heart. Would men remember Aegisthus if he hadn't killed Agamemnon? So I might be famed among future men. This captain who had survived the valors of Troy might die by my hands as Halitherses predicted. My striking sword could cloud the eyes that watched Hector, Paris, and Priam die. Might this quiet the suitors who raged within me? Might it turn the demonic son of Odysseus back to stone?

Phemios, I had no desire to kill my father. Desire is in the blood, in the pounding of the heart. My thoughts were like the figures of my dreams, images that never were or are no more. I took my father's hand in mine. He woke alert and studied me. I felt he might have been waiting for me to return as Laertes had waited so many years for him. Moving gently so as not to disturb Penelope, he rose nude and quickly slipped on a chiton. I marveled to think of the great cities he had seen and the many men among whom he had striven. I couldn't imagine his response to the story of my dreams, but I wanted to speak my heart to him.

CHAPTER 20

I followed Odysseus to our hearth in the great hall. He knelt and stoked the embers until flames leapt to the blackened spit. Turning to the side, he piled the split logs on the flames. He rose and, with a speed so graceful as to seem slow, he lifted my sword from its sheath. The blade flowed in his hand as he forgot his age and danced before the rising flames. I remembered that night when he nearly drowned me in the baths. Would he turn his flickering blade from unseen foes to the son who caroused with the suitors? How easily he made the sword arc, lift, and dive. He advanced across the floor as when he slew the suitors; he advanced as he must have when he faced his Trojan foes. I couldn't see that age had dulled his force, his quickness, his desire.

At last, he lay the sword aside and sat at the head of the long table nearest the hearth.

"Laertes took that sword to Nerikos. I remember it as a boy."

He might have said more, but instead he studied me as if to learn what had brought me there. Without waiting for him to ask, I began my story of the dreams that rose within the walls of Laertes's farm-house. I paced and gestured and spoke like a singer. For me and per-haps Odysseus, that island with its phantoms lived as vividly as our own Ithaca. Odysseus listened intently, his eyes gleaming in the firelight. As I moved before our hearth, I felt the light of its flames within me while all else stretched away in darkness. My words carried me to beautiful Telegonus and the suitors who died in that very hall. Odysseus nodded like a dreamer lost in these visions of other realms. When I finished, he rose and embraced me, the thick sinews of his arms tight about my slender height.

I embraced him in return. In our firelit hall, Odysseus offered wine to Athena and Zeus and the other gods. He splashed a good por-tion to the floor before cutting it with water and filling our cups. Its warmth ran in me like courage. Then my father spoke.

"When I sit at my shrine, the sea spreading beneath me to the horizons of our world, I think of everything—gods, men, Ithaca and Troy, my wife and son, my life. I wonder why I was given such a por-tion of war and wandering. I returned too old to enjoy the tranquil life of harvests and hearth so many men prize above all else. When you speak of Telegonus and the suitors, I think of the godlike and pitiable strivings of men.

"Like Telegonus, Teiresias lived as both man and woman. The goddess Hera blinded him for admitting the sexual pleasures of women are nine times greater than those of men. Zeus gave Teiresias inner vision to compensate for that loss. But isn't this the pattern with all men? If we receive inner vision, we sacrifice part of what we admire in the world around us. If we hold to our halls, our victories, and our wives, we never follow the inward spiral that gives us the vision of Teiresias. It is the completion of a man's life, the vision of two realities to be lived as one.

"I had to leave off hoping for an Ithaca I abandoned in the prime of my manhood. I had to sacrifice the part within me that believes, like Telegonus, that violence can win any reward. I had to prepare myself for journeys ahead. I abandoned the hundred suitors, each of whom promised me some destiny other than the one I lived. I accepted the portion given me by the gods.

"Many nights I longed to lie beside your mother in our bed. Often, I called myself the father of Telemachus and longed to touch the only boy I would father with my beloved Penelope. I cared far more for my son and his sons than for my father and his fathers. Who can live the past again? But you could be the possibility of me. My valor and shame at Troy would always be mine. I would never become a youth. But had I fathered another who might learn from my life and be a better man? I dreamt that for you, battling on the Trojan plains and weeping by the sterile sea on the island of immortal Calypso.

"I knew a baby who wept in my arms. How to face the full-grown man who would greet me after my twenty years of exile? Would you be a Telegonus, raging over my absence or greedy for my wealth? Would I find in my boy a memory of what once I had been, that magical root to heal the suffering of my loneliness and contending? Nor did I harbor nostalgia for the day I boarded the ship for Troy. Life is change. Once I embraced my fate, I lived as I had to live. Why should I have imagined a girlish wife with her baby in arms, when I had aged and suffered countless scars? I knew you grew, became a bearded man unknown to me. I loved you nonetheless. I loved you unknown, a seed of my own heart. I learned how painful love can be. If I hadn't loved you, your mother, and stony Ithaca, I might have lived uncaring in a foreign land. But had I done that, I would not have been Odysseus. If I feared how

171

difficult it might be to meet a full-grown son, nonetheless I strove ceaselessly homeward.

"When I returned and met you in Eumaios's hut, I looked a beggar. Athena had disguised me. How you cursed when I wrapped my arms around you and claimed to be Odysseus. You expected a finer man, a father of renown. But I saw in you a boy to match my dreams—pious and sturdy.

"Athena had cursed us all—Agamemnon, Menelaos, myself. After we sacrificed Polyxena, Menelaos and Agamemnon quarreled. Should they offer sacrifices to the gods by the walls of Troy? Or make their offerings on the island of Tenedos where the fleet had waited while the Trojans dragged the wooden horse within the city? Eager to start home, I joined the half of the army that followed Menelaos. But when we anchored off Tenedos, I no longer felt Athena beside me. Heavy-hearted, I helped Menelaos offer his hecatombs to the gods. But the fat dripping from the thighbones of slaughtered oxen and our curling smoke rising to the heavens couldn't change our god-given fates. I imagined I should have stayed with Agamemnon. Splitting our forces again, many of us returned to the mainland to offer sacrifices with Agamemnon. But gray-eyed Athena no longer gave me her voice.

"In my meditations at my shrine, my desertion by Athena chafed me more than any other part of my fate. She deserted all the Greeks. That's why Agamemnon sailed home to death, while I wandered and Menelaos merchanted the plunder of pirates to the Egyptians.

"I could have escaped from Troy. When Agamemnon ordered our armies to flee, I didn't have to turn the men back to war. I could have boarded my men on their ships and sailed to Ithaca with our spoils. Athena implored me to stand against that stampede of men. So, I put my thoughts of you and Penelope aside and called for wisdom and courage. Later, when the Trojans breached our fortifications,

Agamemnon would have launched our ships at night for home. I hadn't fought so long to let him forsake our cause while our armies remained on the field.

"But if we fought so long, sacrificing so many men and years, why should Athena have turned against us? She sought to restore lawful order by returning Helen to her true husband. Ten years Athena fought beside the Greeks. First, I imagined I angered her by taking Troy with a ruse. The horse-taming Trojans had long worshipped her as the deity of their city. After Hector's death, I told Achilles of my plan to build the wooden horse. How he scorned pretending this horse would be an offering to Athena to trick the Trojans. He had killed noble Hector. Why not take the city by force of arms? If we warred another ten years, at least we would have honor. But when he decided to risk the marriage to Polyxena, he called me back. He trusted my devious wit to bring me inside Troy and arrange that ill-fated marriage of Greek to Trojan.

"After Achilles's death, my hollow horse seemed our only hope. I drew elaborate plans. Epeios helped me and supervised the construction. But I gave little thought to what would happen to Troy after we captured the city. Would we slaughter the men? The children? The women? Would we burn the palace? The temples? Would the high walls be razed?

"The years of war made me think only of war. I could devise a ploy to open the city, but I thought nothing of the consequences. We became demons that night—not soldiers. I shouldn't have made the horse a false offering to Athena, but worse followed. If I had planned wisely for our victory, the lesser Aias would never have violated Athena's temple. He wouldn't have damaged her statue and raped her priestess, Cassandra. After the sack of Troy, I believe Athena punished me for aspiring to her brilliance. Having seen my pride, she chose as well to punish the failure of my genius. If I could devise the horse, why couldn't I devise a victory to please both gods and men? If I truly had the genius of the gods, I might have done this. So I—and the Greeks—suffered her wrath."

Listening to my father speak, I wondered why I hadn't come years before to listen to his wisdom. Or had my phantoms made him trust that I could hear of the questing of his mind? I realized he had become another man in the years since his return. He struggled to understand his vaporous deeds. His adventures continued, but on plains far different from those of Troy. His voice made me forget the phantoms that brought me to him. He piled logs on the fire, renewing its trembling flames. Returning to his seat, he spoke of other goddesses.

"If Circe and I had a son, no doubt he would have been like the Telegonus of your dream. Circe spent her eternity in pleasures of the flesh. She beguiled me, it's true, but only for a year. In her palace of smooth stone, she revealed to men the beast in them. When my men pled with me to continue our voyage, I left her without a tear. Nor did she weep for my departure. We shared nothing outside the paradise of her bed. She had that gifted beauty of the immortals, but I despised her. What had brought us to Troy except the careless pleasures of Helen and Paris? How much suffering would be caused by bestiality like hers? A man grows beyond such pleasures, or he perishes in his spirit. When I ordered you to kill the maidservants, I remembered those nights with Circe.

"The goddess Calypso tempted me in a different way. I remember her cave as a place of beauty, calm and hidden from the turmoil of the world. After the terrors of my voyage, what man wouldn't have greeted such a landfall with joy? I had seen my ship destroyed and the last of my shipmates and friends lost to the sea. Nine days I clung to the broken keel and drifted with the currents. On this island, a goddess more beautiful than Circe greeted me and nursed me to health.

"If I imagined my genius equal to that of the gods when I built the wooden horse, Calypso loved me as if I were a god. She offered me immortality. I could live forever with her in that beautiful cave. No cares of the world would ever touch us. Our love would be youthful to eternity, our passion ever at white heat, our tenderness softer than mortals dare imagine. I listened, but never consented to what she offered. I knew myself to be a man, nothing more. When my wounds healed, I walked the boundaries of her island and searched for a ship to carry me toward Ithaca. No sails appeared on her horizons; nothing broke the empty face of all that surrounded me.

"I tried to accustom myself to the pleasures of ambrosia and nectar. I spoke to the goddess of my quiet beginnings on Ithaca, my courtship of Helen, my wife and son, and my adventures at Troy. But what had Calypso experienced in the endless years of her life? She knew the pleasures of her cave. With all experience and striving in her grasp, she cared only for the easy beauty of her own island. She knew of nothing beyond, nor did she want to know. She had heard of Troy, but the affairs of men bored her. She loved me like a child loves a toy. Not wanting to lose such a delightful plaything that groaned and throbbed between her thighs, she offered me immortality—not once, but again and again.

"If I had stayed with her, she would have loved me endlessly. Penelope might hunch with age, but I would be the dark-headed hero forever. I tried to convince myself to stay with Calypso. I knew the world and could hardly blame her for shunning it. I had seen the monster Scylla devour six of my finest men, her gaping mouth filled with arms, blood, and shrieking heads. Hadn't I learned enough of dying—all my crew, my loyal comrades-at-arms, slaughtered on Trojan fields or on this journey homeward?

"Why, I wondered, should I prefer Penelope to this goddess? The wife I left had changed, perhaps beyond my knowing. I lived with an inner image, my own Penelope created from my soul and my yearning for a peaceful life. But if I ever reached Ithaca, the Penelope who greeted me would be herself—not some image plucked from a wanderer's heart.

"I wish I could say that courage and love for this inner woman drove me homeward. In fact, I tried to love Calypso and her island. I had been abandoned by Athena and cursed by Poseidon. I had hoped to return with the wealth of Troy to make Ithaca a center of learning and commerce. That I failed in this made me hesitate to come home. In any case, I doubted I would ever reach Ithaca. Years passed. I hungered for so much. I would have kissed the stones and earth of Ithaca. I formed a thousand images of Penelope. Who had she become? Had she kept her beauty? Become more blessed with age? Of you, Telemachus, I hardly knew what to imagine. Had you become a man of strength like Aias? Or of wrathful honor like Achilles? Did you show the wisdom of a youthful Nestor? Would your hands possess craft like those of Epeios? Or might you have the ingenuity of noble Diomedes? So I speculated with my hours and my days.

"At last, I missed Troy. Yes, I wished I could return to the war, the cries of charging men and the shrieks of the dying. Our plans, the shifting fortunes of battle, the moment of the hero, the fear of the Underworld—I would have given my endless life for a glimpse of the high walls we fought to breach. To be challenged, to face danger, to be a man—I would have given everything for that.

"Each day I wept by the surging sea. True, I wept for myself and the desolate life I lived. But I wept for Calypso too. She cared for me, and I cared for her. In her cave, she faced the terror of forever. She needed a companion, a comfort against her immutable fate. If only she could have eaten the grain of mortals and risked dying.

"She made me think of Achilles. If he chose to live in obscurity, he would have a long life. But he chose to die in the glory of battle and have his fame live for future men. At Troy he seemed a god, handsome and fearless. How death changed him. When I met him in the Underworld, he told me that he would rather live as a slave than be king of all the dead. He only cared to hear of Neoptolemus. In his son he sought his true fame.

"If Achilles found death so dreadful, why didn't I accept Calypso's offer of life? Her life seemed deathlike to me. She feared so much of what we imagine life to be. She clung to the form of life, its appearance. But ambrosia and nectar left her forever the same. What gift is it never to gain the wisdom of age? What gift is it to live forever like a shade? Heroes shiver to imagine death, but are the gods wiser for knowing only life? And must the phantom afterlife always be loathsome? Why can't there be more than life and death, flesh and phantom? If death is always near in life, shouldn't life be near in death as well? Who can say that phantoms are phantoms forever? Who can know what my death would have been—or will be?

"I am Odysseus. I have a face, a name, a past. My blood leaps, my limbs dance, the world flows into my eyes, my heart and head live with visions. But I claim nothing for my own. I am a faceless, unnamed man, living a gift. My accomplishments, my heroic deeds, truly these belong to Nobody."

CHAPTER 21

"Why did Athena forgive you?" I asked my father as the embers offered a soft oval of orange light.

"Night after night I refused Calypso's gift of immortality," he replied. "In my sorrow, I humbled my spirit. I wished those high walls of Troy could stand again. I would have raised young Astanyax from where I crushed his skull and tossed him down the ramparts. Brought Andromache back from her slavery and returned life to great-plumed Hector. Why did I test my ingenuity against Athena's city? Why offer that deadly horse as a gift to the goddess? If only I could have gone again to Troy and pled for peace.

"By refusing immortality, I showed myself a man. The epithet godlike no longer described me. Then Athena came again to counsel and protect me.

"I remember how you tried to convince me to let the suitors live. Did you see one hundred men as an insurmountable force? Or were you simply more merciful than a man hardened to violence? I feared a death like Agamemnon's. Killed by his wife's lover, his young son unknowing and unable to save him. What passion I felt to imagine a man like the suitors had killed Agamemnon. I liked Amphinomos and some of the others, but Athena demanded I kill them all. They had flouted her laws as Paris had. Trusting Athena, I spared no one and made no plans for what might happen after the massacre. Would we survive the blood feuds? Live our lives on Ithaca? When the goddess took my treasure—for it was she, disguised as Mentor—to buy off the suitors' vengeful families, I accepted that sacrifice too."

My father hadn't killed the suitors for revenge, pride, or the lessening of his stores. But if his merciless killings had been for Athena, I wondered at the goddess herself. She must have seen Odysseus build the hollow horse and dedicate it to her. If she objected to this deception, why didn't she warn him? Why let him play out his fate and incur her wrath? If she protected the pious Trojans, why did she battle ten years on the side of the Greeks who besieged the city walls? Could it have been because a Trojan youth, Paris, said Aphrodite had a greater beauty than Athena? Or because the Trojans loved the pleasures of Aphrodite more than the lawful wisdom of Athena? Surely so many lives lost must rest on more than the vanity of goddesses. In any case, my father no longer spoke of his deeds alone. Changed by his years of meditation at his shrine, he sought the meanings of these deeds.

"So much of life seems a forgetting," Odysseus said. "It is as if we shed our own lives, the facts of ourselves.

"Calypso gave me provisions and a breeze to carry me toward Ithaca. If I could have been one hundred Odysseuses, I might have given her one life of mine to have forever.

"How quickly Poseidon tested me when I left her enchanted island. His storms drove me to the extremity of life and cast me unconscious on the island of a godlike people.

"Their king, Alkinoös, gave me more wealth than I could ever have plundered from Troy. If I had brought such riches to Ithaca as a young man, I might have transformed our island. He invited me to marry the princess Nausikaa, who had clothed me when I approached her naked and wild from my struggle with the sea. But Nausikaa reminded me of the girlish Penelope I had left on Ithaca. No doubt this princess would be a queenly woman, but I had already married, loved, and had a son.

"Alkinoös lent a ship to bring me home with my treasure. When I woke on the shore, I couldn't recognize this island as Ithaca. Did another Cyclops live here? Would I find Circe among her beasts? Or some new danger? Athena came to reassure me and guide me to meet you at the hut of Eumaios."

Phemios, my father spoke of life as a forgetting. I remembered that later when it became far more important. Listening to him, I wondered what made him my father. The sperm that ignited my mother's womb? My resemblance to him or our shared love of words? The thoughts he had of me during his exile? The stories he told me, some repeatedly, on his return? His love for me, unknown boy that I was?

I asked if he had fathered children with Circe or Calypso.

"How could life come from their sterility?" he questioned in reply. "They bore me neither sons nor daughters, and certainly not the Telegonus of your dream."

"But they were goddesses," I said, wondering how such magical women might exist in this world. "Don't you ever miss their beauty? The promise of immortality?"

"On Calypso's island," Odysseus answered, "I wondered if Penelope would truly be different from Calypso. Every woman is a

181

weaver—Penelope, Helen, Circe. Would I find myself on Ithaca and wish that I might return to Calypso's cave, to her charms and the long life she promised?

"I hardly feel I live on Ithaca. I know the islanders despise me. Our life might have been far easier if I hadn't sacrificed our herds so lavishly. But my shrine looks out to a world far greater than a sea-swept stony island. Circe demanded men see the world as beasts. Calypso forced her lovers to see a changeless world. Only Penelope has left me free to see what is. She made no bargains with my restless spirit. If she had tried to hold me by promises, I would have traveled onward. We eke our living from Ithaca. Every man concedes those long hours of labor to the earth. Beyond that, I live in myself, in my visions of the world. If I stayed with Circe or Calypso, I would have lived life as they imagined it to be. But I have my own life, my own god-given spirit that rises in my meditations.

"I remember my marriage night with Penelope. She seemed a child, fresh from the care of her father. But she joined with me innocently, eager to become whatever a wife might be. How differently she greeted me after the death of the suitors. Twenty years her desire had been denied. Although she believed me to be Odysseus, she couldn't change that long habit. In our great bed, I told her of my life. We wept together, grieving for those years we would never share. Our tears spoke of the hardships we faced, each yearning for what our fates might never give us. No wonder she wove a shroud for Laertes. Death had been constantly in her thoughts. Had I survived? If I hadn't, which terror had ended my life? Would she ever hear of me again? Or feed a thousand beggars and hear only the lies of hungry men? As that endless first night culminated and we gently reunited our bodies as husband and wife, could anyone know better than we two how fragile and momentary our love might be? So we clung together, a mist of flesh and spirit.

"I've never regretted my journey home. Nor wished I stayed with Circe or Calypso."

He rose and piled logs on the fire. When he turned back toward me, a double flame leapt to the spit behind him.

"Odysseus."

My mother stood in her long white robe in the doorway to their chamber. Tears poured from her eyes, her white hair disheveled and her face red with her tears.

"I saw the mist," she said, her voice faltering. She took a step toward him. "My sister Iphthime stood by our bed. She seemed so real. I might have touched her. She spoke of the mist rising from the sea. I saw it on the waves, rolling toward the land. Is it the mist that saved you by the walls of Troy?"

Odysseus rushed to her. Arms encircling her, he supported her to sit between us at the table. He poured a cup of water and raised it to her lips. His hands held hers while she drank. He cradled her head to his chest and stroked her hair. His eyes glistened. I knew she spoke of the mist Teiresias prophesied would bring Odysseus his peaceful death. I felt the closeness between my parents that once gave life to me.

"How much there is to say in the farewell of a dream," my mother said when she stopped her weeping. "Our marriage vows you honored and yet transcended. I imagined us side by side. But you remained the free man, lawless Nobody, adrift in the world. Home at last, in your endless meditations you explore your own soul. What of the souls of others? My soul? What leads you so far away and within? What is the universe but the human heart, filled with desires?"

Odysseus didn't answer her. He held her hands, his eyes downcast. Why had my mother and I dreamt that death faced Odysseus? I studied him. Behind his chiton, I imagined the white scar where Sokos's lance had pierced his breast. How easily he might have died that day, his shape flowing back to the earth. Why survive so much to die on Ithaca? But if he had never returned, wouldn't I have always imagined him as a young man changeless as the immortal who might have lived with Calypso in her lovely cave?

My mother touched my shoulder, then my cheek and chin. How tenderly her eyes beheld me, her grown child.

"I want you to be a different man," she said to me, "Your father found worlds to explore. War and magic weren't equal to his cunning. Nor could any challenge stop him from his return. Now he lives in the imagery he carries within, father and mother to himself. Each day, at his altar high above the sea, he sails again to unimaginable islands. This world"—here she gestured to our hall and beyond—"he cares little for. I wonder, if he had never left Ithaca, would he have become such a man?"

My father lifted his eyes to my mother as she spoke. He gazed intently, showing no need to speak in reply. I had heard all my father's stories, but that night I learned so much more of his feelings. Had my mother known why he refused to stay with Circe and Calypso? Was she pleased he had quested for her like a spirit in himself? Or did she wish he had only loved her, the real Penelope who suffered in his absence?

"I've saved Helen's gift for you, the wedding robe as fine as the one she wore to marry Menelaos. I might have discarded it, but Helen can't be blamed for her beauty. She can't be blamed because men saw Aphrodite in her. She was a child, a lovely friend. Iphthime and I played with her and Klytaimnestra. What she became, men made her.

"Your father escaped that enchantment. He saw the girl in Helen where others saw their own passion. When he came to me, why shouldn't we have lived long and happily? Yet he left me. Not for other women, but other realms. I want you to have a bride and children for us to name. Be uxorious. Enjoy warm meals and the warmth of your bed. Men age so quickly with hardship. Forget goddesses, barbarous men, and beasts of the spirit. A woman is no trifling thing. Explore her. Live the life denied your father and me. Live the life men crave, pious and hard-working."

She may have felt I would protest, and she continued, "What life will you have as a man like Odysseus? On Ithaca, you're condemned to hatred and ridicule. If you ride the seas, you'll be the Nobody of your father's cunning. I want more for you."

Odysseus watched her with an unbroken gaze. His shaggy beard flowed about the broken planes of his face. He looked a man made by his trials. My mother faced him and spoke again to her husband.

"If happiness were all I wanted, I might have taken one of the suitors. So many perished in this hall for admiring me. I made the horizons of their world and the seas rising and subsiding between.

"I feel your unquiet spirit always. Nobody possesses you. Nobody cleaves to you. I learned to live in my own heart. As best you were able, you gave me what you could.

"You never asked that I live in the past. Again and again Helen hears the adventures of Menelaos. But I want more than the pain we've shared. We could have wept for our years apart, the pleasure lost to us. Each evening by our hearth, you might have sung of battles and triumphs. In that way, you'd remain forever on your journeys. I would never have lived for you. Stony Ithaca would have been your shroud and all your vision gone to glories of the past. I longed for you," she said, speaking warmly, "but I don't want to cling to that pain. I don't want to be Penelope who waited. I want each moment for what it is. You have tried to live with me as I am. That gift you gave me."

She paused, tears glistening again in her eyes. She touched him, her hands holding his as she spoke.

185

"I feel such pain to imagine the world without your spirit. Each of us someday becomes that other we carry within us, that spirit of which we know only shadows in this daylit world. But in the darkness of the Underworld, those shadows are white flames of spirit. So I believe you shall be. Never extinguished but burning with a new vision in another world than ours."

Odysseus rose and lifted her to his embrace. In my mind, I saw them like the double flame—separate, but nourished by the same source from which their different lives arose. Arm about her waist, Odysseus gently walked with my mother to their bedchamber.

Alone in the hall, I realized my own nightmare had dissipated. Had it been the breathing strength of my father that vanquished Telegonus? Or my mother's hope that one day I would marry and live a life more joyous than theirs? I looked from weapon to weapon on the wall. I remembered how we had used these spears, swords, and the great bow. I wished Laertes could be with us again. I remembered the exultation in his voice when he saw his spear strike Eupeithes through the eye. No doubt Odysseus gave the same shout of triumph when he and his Ithacan men probed the eye of that Cyclops, Polyphemos. But no matter how many men or monsters Odysseus might vanquish, wasn't death his inevitable end?

He returned from the bedchamber and sat quietly beside me. The fire guttered, but we no longer heaped up the logs.

"When I returned to Ithaca," he said, "Athena obscured the island in a mist. She kept me from recognizing my homeland, just as she disguised me so I would be unrecognizable. But sometimes I feel I never returned to Ithaca, as if these islands and seas changed since I sailed for Troy. When I first took the kingship from my father, men argued furiously over whether to join the expedition to Troy. But men who live today see a different world from those men who quarreled over the rescue of Helen. Troy is rubble and Helen reigns in Sparta.

So, farmers worry over their harvests and livestock, while traders fear the storms and pirates sell their spoils.

"For many years at Troy and in my wandering, I fancied myself the king of Ithaca. It made my hardships and fears easier to bear. That title served me like a shield against the terrors of the world. I knew myself as a hero. I don't think I saw the monsters and witches as they truly were. Kingly, I faced them as their equal or superior. If I felt fear, I cursed my own weakness. What kind of man had I become? Why tremble at death or slaughter? So, I entered the cave of Poseidon's son, monstrous Polyphemos, believing all men owed me my place in the world. When we fled, I yelled to the monster that I, Odysseus, had blinded him. I couldn't see myself as Nobody, buffeted by chance.

"Only when I returned to Ithaca did I realize how meaningless my kingship had become. Without war, men have no need for kings. I had longed to make you king to follow me, but strangers feasted in my hall. The islanders despised me for losing the army sent to Troy. You and your mother lived half-lives dreaming of my return."

Odysseus paused.

"Sometimes I think Polyphemos wasn't Poseidon's son at all. If he had a divine father, why did he lose his eye to me? No, I think Polyphemos had a heathen giant for a father and that I was the son of Poseidon."

I couldn't believe he said this. For years, he had told us how Poseidon refused to let him return from Troy. He sat before me, his eyes fixed on some realm of inner imaginings. Where had he traveled in his meditations? What strange connections had he made between the gods and men?

"What about Laertes?" I asked.

"Of course, he'd be my father too." Odysseus spoke in an off-handed way, as if I should have seen the obvious. "How could I have journeyed so long at sea and survived?" he asked. "Why would the sea nymphs have been so kind to me? Circe preferred me to her beasts and Calypso wanted me for her cave. Even Ino sought to wrap me in her magical cape and save me from the wild sea-storm. Poseidon punished me like a father. His strength showed me my own limits, the outer boundary separating man and god. On that night when Laertes and Anticlea conceived me, who can say the spirit of Poseidon was absent?"

Nobody could say that, of course, nor could anyone say Poseidon had been present. I marveled at how Odysseus constantly sought new meanings, fathering himself again and again in his own imagery. Could he make me king in such realms as he had known? At dawn we parted with a long embrace. Knowing how my frame and face resembled his, I imagined myself like a young Odysseus. But if this were true, would I ever be heir to the meditations and passions of my father?

CHAPTER 22

I don't want to speak at length of the funeral of Odysseus. Remembering his anger that Agamemnon buried the greater Aias, I decided to burn Odysseus's corpse on a pyre. If I buried it or built a tomb, how would I protect it from desecration by the islanders? That fear had made Odysseus burn the remains of Laertes. But I could hardly believe the procession of dark-clad mourners climbing with me toward the heights of Mount Neriton. Men and women from Kephallenia, Doulichion, and even the Thesprotian mainland joined our Ithacans. Tears poured from eyes. Arms beseeched the tranquil blue skies for some grief-easing sign.

I saw the sister whom Amphinomos had wanted me to marry. I would have spoken with her, but what could I say? That her long-dead brother had hoped she might be my bride? That I had sometimes thought of the life she and I might have shared, whether on

Ithaca or her own island of Doulichion? She wept and stumbled, her grief absorbing her. When the line halted for a moment, she pitched herself among the rocks and shrieked and pulled her graying hair.

But why did she, and the others, grieve as if their loved ones had just died? Twenty years had passed since we killed the suitors; forty years since the first man died at Troy. By the time we reached the windy peak where I had ordered the pyre raised, I understood their presence. Odysseus had outlived so many men. To these relatives, he became like a memory, a symbol of their loved ones. His existence affirmed that once there had been an Amphinomos, Elpenor, or Polites. In despising him, the islanders affirmed their love for those whom he had lost in his command or vanquished on his return. For the islanders, I felt that Odysseus the man had died long before. How could a man return from Troy and the monstrous trials of his wandering? How could a man slay one hundred suitors? This Odysseus who had walked among them seemed more a mystery, a timeless spirit cast up to prove that once their husbands, sons, and brothers had gloried in life.

In the last years of my father's life, his mind often ranged far from us. Perhaps I heard the first hint of this on the night he claimed to be the son of Poseidon. Certainly, he looked much the man he had been. The wisdom of his eyes governed his face, blunting the harshness of his other features. His hair and beard grew white, and his body shrank with age, but he kept his bullish chest. You would have recognized him as the man who spared your life so many years ago, Phemios. Carrying a heavy and weathered staff, he walked ceaselessly on the paths intertwining across the island. During these restless years, even his shrine no longer had the power to calm him. In the evenings, I would often have to seek him out and bring him home to my mother.

From moment to moment, no one could know his mind. He seldom remembered me as his son. At noon he might stare at me like

190

a stranger and an hour later imagine me one of his shepherds. He cursed Poseidon for hiding the entrance to the cave where Odysseus hid the treasure given him by King Alkinoös. I believe he searched for this treasure in his wandering, as if the stones of Ithaca might miraculously transform to a finer substance. If I reminded him that he had given that treasure to the families of the suitors, he would stare closely into my face.

At last, he might say, "You look so much like my son, Telemachus. Did you know him?"

If I replied, "I am your son," he would smile faintly and shake his head to hear an apparition claim such kinship with him. A few minutes later, he might curse Poseidon again or ask me once more if I had known his son Telemachus.

I believe this to be the mist that Teiresias prophesied. It rose from the seas within Odysseus himself and obscured the keenness of his mind. Constantly, he transformed the shape of his life. If a story appealed to him, he would repeat it again and again to anyone who might listen. He spoke freely to the islanders, forgetting they despised him. He told his stories to our shepherds and to me, hardly caring whether we had heard the same story innumerable times before. I can't count the number of times he cursed Polyphemos for violating the hospitality that Zeus decrees all men honor. One episode might obsess him, while the rest of his life would be forgotten. He became less and more than Odysseus. As he forgot the truths of his own life, his cunning invented other lives that only he might have lived.

At my mother's request, I returned to help her when my father became feverish and bedridden. I resumed sleeping in the round tower of my boyhood and sat long hours beside him. Often, I remembered how as a child I imagined my own histories for this godlike man. His eyes brightened with his constant fever. Since he ate only soups and gruel, he thinned until his body looked a fragile sheath for his spirit. Once, when his labored breathing made me prop him on his pillows, he woke from his dreaming and seized my hand. He seemed awake, but the story he told me belonged to a dreamer. He imagined me to be a Trojan, his keeper or jailer. He didn't speak as a father to a son, but rather as a man might tell of his life to aid his own contemplations.

"Many years ago, I lived on Crete, the birthplace of Zeus. I was a young man, handsome and strong as you are. Nine times I led our ships to plunder in strange lands. With my newfound wealth, I built my hall and brought home my bride."

His eyes watered with his recollections, although he no longer knew his own room, or the bed carved by his own hands.

"I married Penelope, the daughter of Ikarios of Sparta. I labored and made nature abundant. In my hall I wore the robes of a prince. Kings as great as Agamemnon and Nestor feasted with me. Many slaves worked my fields and tended my herds. In sacrifices no man was more generous than I. Each feast day I observed. I traveled to Dodona and gave bronze tripods to Zeus. At temples of Athena, I worshipped the gray-eyed goddess. I hoped for children to offer me even greater joys.

"One day I saw black smoke billowing skyward. Seized by a pre-monition, I rushed homeward to discover my hall in flames, servants strewn dying or dead across the courtyard with its altar holy to Zeus.

"I ran through the burning hall. On my hearth I found a wounded stranger in strange war garb. The fire swirled around us while I held my sword to his throat. He told me how a raiding party from a foreign city had landed on Crete. Choosing my house by chance, they slaugh-tered my servants and stole the bronze, weapons, wine, and food that I had stored in my deep cellars. Penelope lived, but as a captive of these marauders. In that moment, I saw the life she would lead, a slave in an unknown land. Our love would be unrealized, our hopes for sons and daughters forgotten. I knew I would follow these men to the Underworld itself to bring home my bride and have my vengeance.

"What city spawned raiders such as these? He answered with a strange name—Troy, the city of horse-tamers, whose high towers peaked in the heavens. Paris, a prince of that city, had led their expedition. The balcony tumbled in flames and the great beams of the roof leapt with fire. I slit the man's throat and crawled on my belly like a snake toward the door.

"I salvaged nothing. That night I drank and raved. The next morning, I left the smoking ruins where I had built my life. Before our assembly, I stirred my fellow islanders to launch an expedition of vengeance. These brave men wept to imagine the loss of their own hearths, halls, and loved ones. I had my pick of men, too many for the twelve ships ready to sail. Soon beloved Crete, with its snow-capped mountains and numberless cities, vanished to the stern. The wind carried us on the wine-dark seas. The near islands fell quickly away. What fine heroes rode with me in those scarlet hulls! We told each other of our feats as youths. Eagerly we dreamt of the sight of Troy. What plunder we'd wrest from these Trojans. We had seventy-five men on each ship, nine hundred soldiers determined to leave this foreign city in ashes and bring Penelope home."

My father fell silent. His hands opened and closed, but words no longer fit his story. Those far-seeing eyes searched inward. What could he see, remembering battles that were never fought? What world, what Troy could this be? Did he imagine himself Aithon, the youthful brother of Idomeneus of Crete? Why not choose that shining name for himself again as he had while deceiving his wife into imagining him a beggar?

"I've seen terrors, no doubt of that. If only a goddess had sailed with us. I had imagined us heroes like Herakles who could face innumerable perils. What danger might daunt us?

"How quickly the first peril overcame us. The bow slid through the clapping waves. In the distance we heard a singing and strained to hear the words. Soon the voices rose everywhere about us. The waves might have sung, such was the unimaginable beauty of these voices. The song sounded within me like the voice of my own heart, my own thoughts. It called me a hero, ablaze with greatness. The others must have heard this or their own enthralling song. We forgot our tasks and listened dumbstruck. The voices were neither women's nor men's, but some exquisite melding of both. The helmsmen leaned on the rudders. I hardly noticed the yawing of our ships.

"When this trance overcame us, the singing changed ever so subtly. From the beauty of heroes gleaming in this world, the singers of the waves presented an even greater beauty. We might never have lived. We might never have been men or known the island of Crete. Saved from our mothers' wombs, we might have remained in the chaos of darkness—unbeings, not-souls, nothings. In this immaterial night, we would be as the cosmos—elemental, pervasive, greater than the Olympian gods themselves. We would become the is-not beyond language to describe.

"Listening, you probably imagine I speak of death. I can only say these voices promised far more than death. The temptations of women, even goddesses, couldn't tempt as these singers of the waves tempted.

"Chance, or my bitter heart, saved me. For an instant, I recollected the face of Penelope. My self-pity made me feel the anguish of my own quest. 'Helmsman, hold firm the rudder!' I cried. My own islanders turned on me. No voice should interrupt this singing that stirred their spirits. A dozen men seized me and stripped me naked. Holding me to the mast, they coiled strand after strand of sea rope around me until I could barely breathe. Finished, they returned to the singing.

"One after another, my beloved friends, my brave companions on my quest to Troy, leapt from the deck to the welcoming waves. They drowned with blissful smiles, tumbling into the bottomless dark of the ocean. Nine hundred soldiers, the finest heroes of Crete, died without ever giving battle. They are now the air, fire, water, or earth. But they are no longer men.

"My ship sailed before the wind. No hand guided the rudder. Helpless, I gave up my struggle against the ropes. What man could endure this? My wife lost in a barbarian city, my men and ships lost within a few days of our departure. We had triumphed over nothing; the first of the world's terrors had vanquished us. If I could have freed myself from the ropes, I believe I might have leapt to my death as well. What hope did I have? If I grieved to lose my wife, nine hundred families grieved for husbands, fathers, and sons whom I had lost. I would die slowly by thirst or starvation. Or the merciful seas might break apart my ship and give me a quicker end. If I freed myself and survived, what could life offer me? I would be a wanderer in foreign lands. If by a miracle I rescued Penelope, she would wander with me. In my shame, I could never return to Crete.

"Finally, I lost my sight. Nor did I hear the waves and feel the sea breezes on my skin. From this fainting, why shouldn't death have been the next easy step? But Poseidon must have stirred the sea and split apart my ship. Perhaps a sea nymph guarded me while the mast rose and fell in mountainous seas. Had I clung with my own strength, no doubt I would have slipped into the depths. But I had been bound inseparably to the mast. Whatever shore it reached, I too would be carried there."

CHAPTER 23

"I woke on a straw pallet with the scent of cooking filling the room," my father continued, seeming to draw his strength from the flow of his story. "A young and slender woman stirred a stew above a humble hearth. Seeing me wake, she moved furtively to the far side of the fire. Goats and chickens lived here with this woman. The room itself had no windows. Later I found it had been built into the mountainside like a cave.

"This girl had rescued me when I washed up on the shore. She had cut the ropes lashed about me and placed my naked body on a litter to drag it to her hovel. She proved a simple soul, living alone on this barren island.

"As a child, soldiers had murdered her parents, raped her, and sold her into slavery. But a storm wrecked the slaver's ship and carried her—along with sheep and goats and fowl—to this unknown island where she grew to womanhood. She remembered little of the world beyond. In fact, she spoke a broken tongue that at first I hardly understood. She had lived as best she could. Her herds thrived, but she knew little of treating skins and smelled rank. To rid herself of lice, she washed her hair in the urine of the goats. She tended a fire for warmth, but rarely cooked meat. Instead, she lived on milk, cheese, and the eggs of the hens.

"All around this nameless island the great seas swelled. I dreamt of my Penelope captive in a strange land, but I had lost my heart to see the towers of Troy. I had imagined myself a hero, a prosperous man blessed by the gods. On the wine-dark seas I had learned the pitiless terror of what is. No flight of my imagination could bring back my comrades or relieve me of the sight of this stony island. I learned each rise and hollow. It had fields for grazing the livestock and I collected driftwood on the beaches for our fire. Soon, this strange girl joined me on my pallet of straw. I wouldn't call us lovers, although our bodies certainly connected. We were joined by the terror of our fates, by our frailties before the violence of nature, gods, and men. Seven years passed. I had a son by her. The barren island yielded us a modest life. I built a finer hearth and enlarged the hovel with stones and a crude mortar. I can't say I felt content, but I hardly dared imagine I had lived any other life. I would have stayed forever on that island if the choice had been mine.

"I soon lost my desire to signal a passing ship to rescue me. If I happened to see a sail on the horizon, I would hide with this child-like woman and our baby in the rocky depths of a cave where vapors rose from far below. But one day a warship moored near our coast and sent a longboat leaping through the waves. Fearing for my family, I hid them and went docilely to greet these strangers. I offered to share our humble provisions, but these raiders cared nothing for the laws of hospitality that Zeus decrees. They took me prisoner and chained me to their oars. Two homes I had lost, two wives and my son.

"Seven years I spent in the dark belly of their ship. The great-girthed captain sometimes swaggered among us. He had fought in a war and lost his homeward course. Slaver and trader, he plied the coasts as far as Egypt. I believe he searched for treasure, an elusive magic that might transform his wandering life. But I gave no thought to transformations. Living among bold rats and exhausted men, I knew I had reached the Underworld. I would never see the dawn glowing back of the snow-peaked mountains of my homeland. I would never walk like a youth in the pine-scented forests and dream of future joys.

"My only rebirth from that wooden hull would be a drowning in the sweeping clutch of the ocean's belly. As the dark years passed, I no longer felt myself in this suffering body. A man pulled the oar, chafed with his chains, fought for the food begrudged to slaves. But I saw great Poseidon twist the sea storms with his blazing trident. I knew the golden thunderbolt of Zeus, the voices beyond imagining. Light leapt within me; my soul floated free. I hardly worried that I would cross the sea again and again until my life flowed out through my arms and into the waves. I imagined that in death I would join my soldiers of Crete. I regretted I had waited so long to follow those voices singing of oblivion.

"I proved wrong as always. Our greedy captain violated the hospitality of one host too many. I heard weapons clashing and the cries of wounded men. Soldiers in strange uniforms dragged us into the sunlight. I later learned we had reached wine-rich Ismaros. My plundering master and his men had been slaughtered by the army of the Kikones. So, I entered a new slavery. Now I worked in the vineyards, mulching the saplings, harvesting the laden limbs, and treading the fermented grapes.

"I soon learned that a man could easily walk from Ismaros to Troy. I watched with a third eye and learned all a slave could know of Ismaros. How skillful I would have to be to elude the guards. Nor could I trust the men who labored with me. They'd have turned me in for a scrap of food or a skin of Apollo's burning wine.

"I seldom thought of Penelope. She and I had spent a single year together. So many years had passed since then. How could I imagine who she had become? What she might have suffered? Would she despise me for failing to rescue her or no longer care to recognize me—scarred and worn by so many hardships? To escape had become my own life's urge, my own instinct.

"One night, in my seventh year of slavery in Ismaros, I killed Maron, the priest of Apollo, with this hand." He raised a loose-fleshed, veiny hand from his covers. "I wore the priest's robes on the road toward Troy. Even the robbers treated me respectfully and asked for my blessings. Finally, twenty years after sailing from Crete, I saw the soaring towers and high walls of Troy.

"Two vast armies encircled the city. On the plains stood tens of thousands of men, supported by a high barricade where the number-less ships of their fleet lay beached in the sands. At the foot of the Trojan walls, I saw an army of women, their faces painted in wild masks. From my lookout above the road winding down toward the plain, I could see the invisible zone that separated these immense forces. I could sense the violent attraction between them. Like a principle of life, tomorrow would join these opposites in some terrible slaughter.

"In the twilight I puzzled how to move through the ranks of these armies. When I slept, I dreamt I had returned to Crete. For the deaths of my comrades, I had been condemned to enter the labyrinth of the minotaur, that dread man-bull beast in fact killed by the hero Theseus when my father was a boy. I walked trembling in its dark maze. The sunlit world vanished to strange subterranean sounds. Was the monster ahead or behind me? Would I ever find it or would I wander until I died of thirst or starvation? If I faced this beast my own failures and losses forced me to confront, would I triumph? In the dream Penelope appeared, luminous and calm in the darkness. She gave me a ball of thread to lead me from the labyrinth. So, I might follow this path she offered me or remain to battle the minotaur. Before I could make my choice, the dawn light woke me—a slave and a murderer in the robes of Apollo's priest.

"On the plain the armies stirred. This would be no ordinary day of sallies and hard fighting. From each army a delegation came forward under a flag of truce. I had learned from a straggler that the besieging army came from the cities of Greece, but I knew none of the captains he named. Ten years the Greeks had battled on this field. The army of women had arrived recently to aid the Trojans. These women lived in Cappadocia on the banks of the Thermodon River. No men lived with them but, if the stories I heard were true, they visited each year with the men in a neighboring city. Of the children born from these annual visits, they kept only the girls and returned the boys to their neighbors. I don't know how this strange state of affairs developed, but the ferocity of these women—known as Amazons—had already become legendary.

"I made my way into the rear guard of the Greeks. Soon I moved among the captains near the delegations from each of the armies. My priestly robes made me invisible. The men who saluted me saw only a priest, aged in his years of service to the archer Apollo.

"Each army had chosen a champion. From the Greeks, the captain named Achilles. From the Amazons, the queen called Pentilesia. When the delegations withdrew, I sized up each of these champions. I believe no more godlike man could have lived than Achilles. He had a fineness of form that only his face betrayed. Beautiful as he might be, grief filled his eyes. Did he grieve for the long war, or his beloved Patroklus lost on the field? That I can hardly say. I saw too the heat of anger in the flush of his cheeks and the knobbiness of his brow. An immortal craftsman had forged his armor. I've never seen such an extraordinary shield. Around the silver rim flowed an image of the eternal river Oceanus. The starry heavens, the sun and moon, rode above the earth and seas. In what exquisite detail I saw two cities, one at peace and one at war. In the peaceful city, families gathered to celebrate a joyous wedding feast. Could this be the scene of heroic Achilles's own wedding? In the warring city, an army besieged the high walls that looked much like Troy's. The gods had taken sides, far larger than the warriors who fought beside them. I saw Apollo with his bow high above the city walls. At that moment I glanced up to the ramparts of the real city of Troy. Crowds from the city watched this duel. One man, handsome beyond all others, struck me. He wore the skins of a leopard and leaned on his longbow. If the Trojans needed a hero, why not this savage-skinned man instead of Pentilesia?

"Seeing Achilles, I wondered how anyone dared face him. But in Pentilesia I saw a woman far beyond the mastery of any man. Painted slashes of red, white, and black transfigured her face to that of a demon. Her blue eyes flashed. Her blond hair curled about her shoulders. In a festive hall, she would have drawn the attention of innumerable suitors. But she chose to wear a heavy-breasted cuirass and carry a Gorgon-faced shield. When her eyes met those of Achilles, I imagined each admired the ferocity of the other.

"Nothing I have seen compared with this battle of man and woman. The gods must have taken the field that day. If Pentilesia fought like Athena, Achilles fought like Zeus himself. Hours they danced forward and back while everyone watched in awe. Their blurring sword strokes and swift parries slowed until each thrust took its own measure of strength and will. Blood glistened from countless wounds and left brown crusts on armor that had gleamed.

"Why did they battle? If Pentilesia won, I imagined the Greek armies would lift their siege and float their ships for home. If the Greeks triumphed, the coffers of Troy would be surrendered to ransom the safety of the city. But I can't swear to the true reasons for this combat. Watching these dancing forms, I could believe Pentilesia guarded the earth itself. Nature lived in her and her Amazons. Whatever the world brought forth, she affirmed it and guarded what the hands of men need never touch. Achilles showed the prowess of men, builders and conquerors of cities, owners of land and herds and slaves, dreamers of empires yet unknown. But could Achilles compel the earth to yield? Could the dazzling strength of a godlike man make the vastness of nature obedient?

"Finally, the swords and shields fell from the weary arms of the combatants. Over and over, they tumbled in the dust, shrieking in the violence of their embraces. What ages had made women such as these? Pentilesia wrestled evenly with this powerful man. For a moment I saw them as lovers passionate with youth. Soon they'd join their bodies as man and woman. In the rocking of that connection, the cries and exquisite silent pauses, would come a completion achieved by neither alone. When I looked again, Achilles had mounted Pentilesia from behind and wrapped his forearms around her neck. Tighter and tighter he throttled her until I saw the urine flow down her legs and her body hang limp. Achilles held her a moment longer before he dropped her corpse in the dust. The Greeks gave a great cheer, while the Amazons keened and wept and embraced one another for comfort. Wearily Achilles turned his back to the walls of Troy and started toward the ranks of the Greeks.

"On the ramparts the leopard-skinned man nocked an arrow in his longbow. While everyone watched Achilles leaving the body of

Pentilesia, this archer gracefully drew his bowstring and sent a dark shaft hurtling high in the air. This poisoned arrow struck Achilles on the heel. Like a man in the terror of a dream, Achilles turned with arms lifted to the sky. His eyes searched the ramparts to where the leopard-skinned man raised his bow exultantly. Achilles tumbled lifeless beside Pentilesia.

"What a slaughter followed, as each army battled for the bodies and armor of these champions. In the confusion I slipped through the opposing lines. Who would challenge me, a priest of Apollo? At the high gates, the guards hardly looked away from the struggle on the plain. I found myself on the terraced streets of Troy, home of Paris and his plunder—my own Penelope.

"How difficult I imagined it would be to find her, a slave girl brought here twenty years before. With my cup, I pled for bits of twisted bronze and promised Apollo's rewards to each giver. When I asked for Penelope, these givers looked at me like a madman. In perplexity, I wandered in the labyrinth of small streets crisscrossing the city. Suddenly I emerged into a crowded larger street where soldiers roughly cleared a passage. Six powerful slaves carried a divan surrounded by princely-looking men in resplendent robes. When I saw the woman within the divan to whom they devoted their attention, I doubted my sight. Penelope, like a queen, sat amidst gold-threaded cushions. She no longer looked the bride of my youth. She glowed with the surpassing beauty that lets men imagine themselves heroes. Her thick hair had a scarlet hue. I followed the pleading voices of the princes who walked beside her, until the entire procession vanished into a splendid palace.

"Soon I learned Penelope's tale. She had given leopard-skinned Paris a son and he rewarded her with her freedom. When she declared herself ready to marry, a hundred princes gathered from the east to win her. Each day she promised herself to one prince, only to repent that

204

evening. On the next day she would promise herself to another and repent again. Twenty years she had woven and unwoven the dreams of these men who hoped to marry her. Some of the suitors died battling the Greeks, while others lost heart and married the Trojan women. I believe Paris and his wily father, King Priam, used Penelope to bring these princes with their armies to the defense of Troy.

"I should have left Troy after that first encounter, but where would I go? Where would I find a hearth and a home? I remembered the strange woman who had rescued me from the sea. If only I could find my way back to that island. I thought often of my son, a youth reaching manhood. Would he be heroic and guard his fragile mother from the desires of men?

"At last, I slipped within the great halls where the hearty suitors feasted at their laden tables. A common beggar, I went to each suitor to plead for scraps from his plate or bits of bronze from his purse. One prince or another might make some rough joke and laughter would fill the hall. Some gave me food and others cuffed my head or tossed a stool to silence me. I reached the throne where Penelope watched these men, her eyes moving easily from one to another. What qualities she valued or despised, I can hardly say. I wondered at her scarlet hair, the radiance of her presence. If I hadn't eaten the bitter root of my hardships, I might have feasted there like a beast at its trough. She looked in the midst of some decision, alert, preoccupied, and wary. Seeing her, I knew her indecision genuine and no ploy to aid King Priam. How the besieged Trojans must have valued her to squander such foodstuffs on her guests.

"I could never kill so many suitors in combat. I had aged and my vigor flowed back to the earth. Any one of these youths would have outmatched me.

"Then I faced Penelope. She started ever so slightly. Her roving eyes fixed on me. I, for my part, opened my filthy robe and let her see the ugly scar above my knee. Certainly, she knew I had been her husband long before on the beautiful island of Crete, but I felt she no longer recognized me. She lived in that high-beamed hall with her hundred suitors. She dreamt to be a queen in an eastern kingdom. If she chose innumerable times, it was not for loving me. She had her own doubts, her own life I no longer shared or knew—if I had ever known it.

"So, my quest ended. Hangdog, I prowled the corridors and slunk past the doorways in the palace. A priest's robes can make a man invisible. Days passed and weeks while I planned a deed that future men might remember. I believe a god or goddess inspired me in this. I crafted wood and stockpiled my supplies, possessed by a strength and ingenuity greater than my own.

"One night, when all the suitors feasted at their tables under Penelope's watchful eyes, I closed the heavy door to that hall and blocked it with an immovable wedge of my own construction. Hurrying to the side corridor, I arranged my faggots of wood and struck the sparks to kindle them. What must the Greek sentries have imagined seeing the burning hall of Prince Paris? In the darkness, I watched this conflagration rise skyward like a flame from the earth's heart.

"The Greeks soon learned of Penelope's death. By the surging sea they held a vast assembly and offered sacrifices to each of the gods. On the following dawn, they launched their dark-hulled ships and sailed for home. Soon afterward, the allies of the Trojans left as well. On the days your guards march me from one cell to another, crowds of Trojans cheer me in the streets.

"You say you are the son of Paris and Penelope and this city is Troy. But I've seen how you look at me. Would you feel such tenderness and pain for a stranger, a beggar? Sometimes I imagine you my son and this island my home of Crete. In my illness, how many times have I told you this same story? Will you remember it to sing of me, if you are a singer and men care to listen?"

He watched me, his head sinking more deeply into his pillows. I had heard his story innumerable times. Not only this story, but so many others. He had told me of joyous campaigns on the plains before Troy. While the Trojans stayed within the city walls, he and his men plundered the countryside. He feasted like a god and owned beautiful slave women for his pleasures. He hunted stag, boar, and bear. If he thought of Ithaca, it was only to compare its stony poverty to the richness of fertile Troy. How cogently he spoke of visions, dreams, and fantasies. Lives he had never led became as believable as his own.

Sitting by his bedside, I wondered what to make of his life. He abandoned me for the war. When he returned, he made me an outcast among my people. He gave my patrimony to the gods and the islanders. When he prayed long hours at his shrine, he abandoned me again for his inner visions. In his last illness, his mind wandered far from me while he voyaged on the wine-dark seas of himself. What do I truly know of him but the wonder of his journeys?

My father often called himself Nobody. As Nobody, he scorned those heroes who yearn for immortality on a poet's lips. I believe he wanted future men to hear far more of Nobody than Odysseus the sacker of cities.

Phemios, I have little left to tell you. I count you a true friend for your patience. Odysseus praised you. He compared you to Demodocus, who sang in the court of godlike King Alkinoös. My father wanted his story sung by a poet of love and war. You saw my mother greet him as a beggar in the great hall. You witnessed his slaying of the suitors, four men against one hundred. Who better than you might sing of famed Odysseus?

CHAPTER 24

I kept my vigil at the pyre until even my mother and her maid-servants returned to the hall. Carefully I searched through the warm ashes for the bones of my father. When I finished my gathering, the gray ash covered me. I must have looked a ghost, a servant of the Underworld, as I carried the remains of my father down to the sea he had watched from his shrine. I had grieved when he no longer recognized me and told me tales of lives he never lived. Walking to the sea I felt an exultation that Odysseus had made his passage. I imagined I too stepped through a door. At the far end of this great hall I entered, I saw my father open yet another door and vanish ahead of me. Only his going forward made possible my own entrance to this unknowable place.

By the water's edge I left my clothes and walked naked toward the depths. The chill waves coiled about my waist. Alone, I stood surrounded by the sea. I extended my arms with the linen-wrapped remains of Odysseus.

"Poseidon, hear my prayer for my father Odysseus.

"Men called him a godfighter. I know he cursed you in Thesprotia. No doubt he blinded your son Polyphemos. He even told me Olympus itself would one day perish. Gods, heroes, and men—he saw them all pass away.

"My father fought for the knowledge which you gods so easily possess. He glimpsed the cosmos, the greater shapes that will surpass and be surpassed.

"His flesh floated in the smoke toward heaven. What remains, carry on your great currents. Let him plumb the depths above which he once journeyed as a man.

"If nothing more, remember that I, Telemachus, stood in your awesome flux and offered these prayers for Odysseus and godlike Nobody."

I let my linen open, let the bones slip into the sea. A great force, like an undertow, swept about my ankles, legs, and waist. When I returned to the shore, I wept for my father. Pondering his death, my thoughts turn often to Polykaste. Nearly twenty years have passed since I traveled to Pylos, but last night I dreamt of her. She cradled two babies in her arms, a boy and a girl who suckled at her breasts. Lovingly she wept, looking at once a girl and a woman. Did she weep for the beauty of this life she created and sustained? In the last moments of the dream, I had the strangest thought. I imagined I had become Polykaste or had always been Polykaste. These children nursed from my nipples. I gave them life and the fluids of nourishment. If I have children, might they live beyond the hatred these islanders hold against Odysseus and me? Might my son be a singer such as you are and travel far-seeing through the world?

Only a fragment remains to be told of my father's story. At the very end, he roused himself. My mother held his left hand. I held his right. He lacked the strength to lift his head from his pillows, but he spoke quietly to us.

"I saw the woman who brought me to this world . . ."

"Anticlea," I whispered, seeing the tears rise in his eyes when her name eluded him.

"Yes, Anticlea." He spoke her name like a treasure. "She gave me this illusion of flesh and loved me for it. So, I thrived in the world for her—son, soldier, farmer, a god-fearing man. But in the end this shape vanishes before what is truer."

His eyes closed. I believed him dead, but I felt him try three times to raise his hand. Had he embraced the phantom mother who three times eluded his yearning arms? Did he salute Achilles, Agamemnon, and Aias? And what guide to the Underworld did my father greet with his final words?

"Whatever hounds of hell or chaos wait," he whispered, "lead on."

GLOSSARY OF NAMES
AND PLACES

Achilles—Son of Peleus and the goddess Thetis, he chose fame and early death over long life and obscurity. Foremost in fighting prowess among all the Greek heroes at Troy, he refused to fight because of his anger over Agamemnon taking a woman, Briseis, awarded to Achilles as a spoil of war. After the death of his close friend, Patroklus, he returned to battle and killed Hector. Later he was slain by an arrow shot by Paris.

Aegisthus—The lover of Klytaimnestra who helped her murder Agamemnon when the king returned from Troy.

Aeneas—Son of Anchises and the goddess Aphrodite, he led the Dardanians in the defense of Troy and escaped to found Rome.

Agamemnon—Son of Atreus, brother of Menelaos, and husband of Klytaimnestra, he led the Greek forces in the siege of Troy.

Agelaos—A suitor of Penelope.

Aiaia—The island of Circe.

Aias—(1) Son of Telamon, a Greek hero from the island of Salamis; (2) Son of Oileus, a Greek leader from Lokris.

Aigialeia—The wife of Diomedes.

Aigyptos—Leader of the Ithacan assembly, whose name implies a reverence for his age by its reference to the ancient culture of Egypt.

Aithon—A name assumed by Odysseus in several fabrications in which he claimed to be a prince from Crete.

Alkinoös—King of the Phaiakians and father of Nausikaa.

Allwoes—When first meeting his father after his long absence, Odysseus pretends to be someone named Strife or Quarrelman whose father was King Allwoes.

Amazons—A tribe of warlike women who chose to live without men. They were allies of the Trojans against the Greeks.

Amphimedon—A suitor of Penelope.

Amphinomos—The finest suitor of Penelope.

Amymone—Her union with Poseidon produced Nauplius, founder of the city of Nauplia.

Andromache—The wife of the Trojan hero Hector, she is taken captive as a spoil of war by Neoptolemus, the son of Achilles.

Anticlea—The wife of Laertes and mother of Odysseus, she dies while her son is gone, and he meets her in the Underworld.

Antinoös—Son of Eupeithes, a leader of the suitors of Penelope.

Antiklos—One of the Greeks in the wooden horse.

Antilochus—Son of Nestor, killed at Troy.

Antiphos—(1) Son of Priam killed in battle by Agamemnon; (2) Son of Aigyptos killed by Polyphemos on the homeward journey with Odysseus from Troy.

Aphrodite—Goddess of life energy, who gives the sensuality and passion that leads to love between couples and fertility or, if misdirected, to jealousy and bestiality. She supported the Trojans against the Greeks.

Apollo—One of the twelve major divinities of Olympus, Apollo's arrows bring a quick and painless death. He is also associated with healing, prophecy, and the arts. He sided with the Trojans against the Greeks.

Ares—The god of war.

Arethusa—A nymph who attended Artemis and was changed into a spring on the island of Ortygia to avoid the amorous advances of the river god Alpheus.

Argos—(1) Hound loved by both Odysseus and Telemachus; (2) Region of the eastern Peloponnese.

Arkeisios—The father of Laertes and grandfather of Odysseus.

Arnaios—The father of Iros, who fought with Odysseus at Troy.

Artemis—Daughter of Zeus and Leto, she is the protector of virginity in man and nature. Twin of Apollo, she preferred the Trojans against the Greeks.

Astanyax—Child of Hector and Andromache, he is tossed down the walls of Troy by either Odysseus or Neoptolemus.

Asteris—An islet in the channel between Ithaca and Kephallenia where the suitors kept watch to ambush Telemachus on his return from Pylos.

Athena—One of the twelve major divinities of Olympus, she is wise, chaste, and powerful. Protectress of many of the Greek heroes, she abandoned Odysseus after the fall of Troy. She was also worshipped by the Trojans and the wooden horse was dedicated to her by the Greeks as a subterfuge. Her rage against the Greeks for the way in which Troy was sacked may relate to her role as protectress of cities. Her sacred image in Troy was the Palladium, a wooden statue of her which had to be taken from the city before it could be captured. Athena appeared in many different forms, including taking the appearance of Mentor and perhaps Callidice. The owl and the olive tree are sacred to Athena.

Atreus—Father of Agamemnon and Menelaos.

Autolykos—Father of Anticlea and grandfather of Odysseus, he was renowned for his lying, cynicism, and sharp practices. Given the opportunity to name his daughter's son, he chose a name suggestive of odium and anger.

Briseis—Woman captured as a spoil of war by Achilles, whose wrath is aroused when Agamemnon takes her from him.

Callidice—Queen of Thesprotia, a part of the mainland northeast of Ithaca.

Calypso—A goddess and nymph who offers Odysseus immortality if he will remain forever on her island of Ogygia.

Cappadocia—Homeland of the Amazons.

Carthage—Kingdom in northern Africa.

Cassandra—A Trojan princess to whom Apollo gave both the power to prophesy and the curse of never being believed (due to her refusal to consummate her bond with the god).

Centaurs—(1) A race in Thessaly with the head, chest, and arms of men but the body and legs of horses; (2) A tribe in Thessaly renowned for their equestrian skills.

Charops—A Trojan killed by Odysseus.

Chersidamas—A Trojan killed by Odysseus.

Chrysippus—Stepbrother of Atreus and Thyestes, one or both of whom murdered him.

Circe—Goddess and enchantress who lived on the island of Aiaia. She had the power to change men into beasts. In some versions of the myth, she and Odysseus have a son, Telegonus, who seeks his father and unwittingly kills Odysseus before realizing who he is.

Crete—Large island ruled by the Greek hero Idomeneus. Odysseus pretended several times to be Aithon, the brother of Idomeneus.

Cretan—Of or from the island of Crete.

Creusa—Wife of Aeneas. In *The Aeneid* Creusa is separated from Aeneas and killed on the night Troy falls, but her killer is not named.

Cyclopes—A race of giants encountered by Odysseus.

Cyclops—The giant named Polyphemos who trapped Odysseus and devoured a number of his men.

Cygnus—Son of Poseidon, he fought for the Trojans. He was invulnerable to the sword or spear, but Achilles strangled him. His father transformed him to a swan, which is the meaning of his name.

Deiopites—A Trojan killed by Odysseus.

Deïphobos—A younger son of King Priam of Troy, he became Helen's lover after the death of Paris.

Delphi—Oracle frequently consulted by the Greeks.

Demeter—Daughter of Cronus and Rhea, she is the goddess of the harvest.

Demodocus—A blind bard in the court of King Alkinoös on the island of Phaiakia. His song of Troy makes Odysseus weep and, finally, tell the story of his wanderings.

Demokoon—A son of Priam killed by Odysseus.

Dido—Queen of Carthage who committed suicide when Aeneas deserted her to continue his journey.

Diomedes—Son of Tydeus, this Greek hero often accompanied Odysseus on daring raids against the Trojans.

Dionysus—A god born of Zeus and a mortal woman, Semele, Dionysus partakes of the joy and terror of nature (symbolized in man by the intoxicating force of wine).

Dodona—An oracular shrine located in Thesprotia in northwestern Greece. Sacred to Zeus, the priests interpreted his prophecies from the rustling branches of an oak tree.

Dolios—A loyal supporter of Odysseus who fights against the suitors' relatives despite the fact Odysseus has killed a son and daughter of his who aided the suitors.

Dolon—A Trojan who is caught trying to spy by Odysseus and Diomedes. He is killed by Diomedes.

Doulichion—An island near Ithaca but not positively identified. It is ruled by King Meges in *The Iliad* but appears to be part of Odysseus's kingdom in *The Odyssey*.

Egypt—A wealthy kingdom which took no part in the Trojan war.

Ekhetos—A king of Epirus renowned for his cruelty.

Elis—District in the northwestern Peloponnese, at one time ruled by King Augeas. Here Pelops founded the Olympic games.

Elpenor—A member of Odysseus's crew who loses his life by falling from Circe's roof.

Ennomos—A Trojan killed by Odysseus.

Epeios—The builder of the Trojan horse, he had more skill as a boxer than as a warrior.

Epirus—A region in northwestern Greece to the north of Thesprotia.

Euboea—Large island north of Athens, ruled by King Nauplius, whose son was Palamedes.

Eumaios—A shepherd who remained loyal during the twenty years of Odysseus's absence and fought beside him against the suitors.

Eupeithes—Father of the suitor Antinoös, he seeks vengeance for his son's death and is killed by Laertes.

Euryades—A suitor of Penelope.

Eurybates—Odysseus's herald who is killed on the homeward journey from Troy.

Eurydamas—A suitor of Penelope.

Eurykleia—Odysseus's nurse who recognizes her master by his scarred thigh and acts to help him against the suitors.

Eurylokos—A kinsman of Odysseus killed on the homeward journey from Troy.

Eurymakhos—A leader among the suitors for Penelope.

Eurynomos—Son of Aigyptos and a suitor of Penelope.

Greece—Greece, of course, did not exist as a nation until modern times, but the term is used to refer roughly to the geographic area from which the besiegers of Troy came.

Greeks—This is the Roman term for a group of peoples connected through language and customs but divided into many subdivisions based on tribe and township.

Hades—Son of Cronus and Rhea, this god ruled in the Underworld.

Halitherses—Gifted with sight, this elderly Ithacan sought to aid Odysseus.

Hector—Son of King Priam and leading hero of the Trojans, he was killed by Achilles.

Hecuba—Queen of the Trojans.

Helen—Daughter of Zeus and Leda, her mortal father was King Tyndareus of Sparta, and her sister was Klytaimnestra. After her marriage to Menelaos, Helen eloped with Paris to Troy (or, in some versions, went to Egypt to a shrine of Aphrodite).

Helenus—Son of Priam and Hecuba, twin brother of Cassandra who taught him to be a seer, he was captured by Odysseus and revealed to the Greeks the conditions to be fulfilled before Troy would fall. Taken by Neoptolemus as an adviser, he married Andromache after the death of Neoptolemus. They ruled in Epirus.

Hephaistos—The god of fire and metallurgy, whose lameness and ugliness disgusted his mother Hera.

Hera—This goddess is the wife of Zeus, whose dominion she bitterly resents. Supporter of the Greeks against the Trojans, she protects legitimate marriages, fertility, and women in childbirth.

Herakles—Son of Zeus and Alcmene, Herakles's (or Hercules as the Romans called him) great strength made him one of the most famous heroes of Greek mythology. The pillars of Herakles are the two promontories on either side of the Strait of Gibraltar.

Hermaphroditus—The handsome son of Hermes and Aphrodite, he was melded with a nymph and became an androgyne.

Hermes—The god who brought messages from Olympus to Earth and conducted the souls of the dead to Hades. He is the guide for travelers, patron of thieves and merchants, and god of sleep and dreams.

Hermione—Daughter of Menelaos and Helen, she married Neoptolemus. Orestes murdered Neoptolemus in Delphi and took Hermione for himself.

Hestia—Goddess of the hearth and the household.

Hypeirochos—A Trojan killed by Odysseus.

Idomeneus—King of Crete and a hero for the Greeks at Troy, he vowed to sacrifice the first thing to meet him on his return after the war. His son met him and was sacrificed, after which a plague caused Idomeneus to be driven into exile. He founded a city in Italy.

Ikarios—Brother of King Tyndareus of Sparta, father of Penelope, and uncle of Helen and Klytaimnestra.

Ikmalios—Highly skilled artisan who made Penelope's chair.

Ilion—Another name for Troy.

Ino—Daughter of the mortal Cadmos, she was changed into a sea goddess.

Iphigenia—Daughter of Agamemnon, sacrificed by him at Aulis for a wind to take the Greek fleet to Troy.

Iphthime—The sister of Penelope.

Iris—Minor goddess who served as a messenger from Olympus to Earth.

Iros—An overweight beggar who picks a fight with Odysseus (when Odysseus is disguised as a beggar to move freely among the suitors) and is quickly beaten.

Ismaros—A city in Thrace.

Ithaca—Home island of Odysseus, located to the west of mainland Greece. This small island (apparently somewhat larger in antiquity) served as the center for Odysseus to rule over a larger group of nearby islands.

Kephallenia—The largest of the islands ruled by Odysseus.

Kikones—A people living in Thrace, whose city of Ismaros is stormed by Odysseus on his return from Troy. His men refuse his orders to cease their plundering, and many are killed by the main army of the Kikones.

Klytaimnestra—Sister of Helen and wife of Agamemnon, she and Aegisthus murdered both her husband and Cassandra.

Ktimene—The sister of Odysseus.

Ktesippos—A suitor of Penelope. He tossed a cow's hoof at the beggarly Odysseus and later was killed by the herdsman Philoitios.

Laertes—Father of Odysseus and husband of Anticlea.

Laocoon—Trojan priest of Apollo who opposed bringing the wooden horse within the city. Two monstrous serpents came from the sea and killed Laocoon and his two sons.

Lemnos—A large Aegean island on which Prince Philoctetes was abandoned by the Greeks after being struck by a poisonous snake on the island of Tenedos. His wound was unhealable, painful, and foul-smelling.

Leodes—A suitor of Penelope, he was weak-willed and fancied himself a seer.

Leokritos—A suitor of Penelope.

Leucas—Part of the mainland due north of Ithaca. Nerikos, sacked by Laertes, is on Leucas. Odysseus sailed past its white cliffs (where Sappho later leapt to her death) on the way to Thesprotia.

Leukos—An Ithacan soldier killed at Troy.

Maron—A priest of Apollo at Ismaros who gave Odysseus the wine that was later used to inebriate Polyphemos.

Medon—The herald in Odysseus's home, whom Odysseus spares because he was coerced by the suitors and not complicit with them.

Meges—King of Doulichion, a separate realm in *The Iliad* but ruled by Odysseus in *The Odyssey*.

Melaneus—Father of Amphimedon and friend of Agamemnon.

Melanthios—Son of Dolios who aided the suitors.

Melantho—Daughter of Dolios, she served Penelope but was insolent and took the suitor Eurymakhos as her lover.

Menelaos—King of Sparta, husband of Helen, and brother of Agamemnon, he took seven years to return from Troy but then reigned with Helen.

Menestheus—King of Athens and commander of the Athenians at Troy.

Mentor—Older man whom Odysseus trusted to oversee his home while away at Troy. Mentor was often impersonated by Athena.

Mount Neriton—See Neriton.

Mycenae—Agamemnon's city.

Nausikaa—Daughter of King Alkinoös and Queen Arete of the Phaiakians. She helped Odysseus when he was washed ashore on her island.

Nauplia—A port city on the Gulf of Argos.

Nauplius—(1) King of Euboea, father of Palamedes; (2) Founder of Nauplia.

Neoptolemus—Son of Achilles and Deidameia, he was raised on the island of Scyros and brought to Troy by Odysseus to fulfill an oracular prophecy that a son of Achilles would be needed for the Greeks to triumph at Troy.

Nerikos—Walled city sacked by Laertes on Leucas.

Neriton—Highest mountain on Ithaca from which Penelope and Telemachus kept their watch for Odysseus and the returning fleet.

Nestor—King of Pylos, he was the eldest of the Greek heroes at Troy. When Telemachus came to Pylos for word of his father, Nestor welcomed him.

Nobody—Imprisoned in the cave of Polyphemos, Odysseus claimed his name was Nobody. None of the Cyclopes would help Polyphemos after his blinding because he said Nobody had blinded him.

Noëmon—An Ithacan youth who lends Telemachus a boat.

Oceanus—Son of Uranus and Gaia, he personifies water and surrounds the earth like a vast river.

Odysseus—Son of Laertes and Anticlea, husband of Penelope, and father of Telemachus, he ruled in Ithaca prior to fighting ten years in Troy and wandering ten years on his return home.

Oedipus—Son of Laius and Jocasta, he unknowingly murdered his father and married his mother, who bore him children. Learning what he had done, he blinded himself.

Oileus—Father of the lesser Aias.

Olympus—Mountain situated between Macedonia and Thessaly. It is the home of the Greek gods presided over by Zeus.

Palamedes—Son of Nauplius, King of Euboea. He was a suitor of Penelope and a wily adversary of Odysseus.

Palladium—Sacred wooden statue of Athena that had to be taken from Troy if the city were to be captured by the Greeks. Odysseus and Diomedes stole this statue.

Paris—Son of Priam and Hecuba, his mother had a vision of destruction for Troy at his birth. Left to die by exposure on Mount Ida, he was rescued and raised by a shepherd. When grown, he judged Aphrodite more beautiful than Athena or Hera. This won him Helen, whom Paris seduced away from her husband and in so doing caused the Trojan war. He is also called Alexander.

Patroklus—Close friend of Achilles who fights in Achilles's armor and is killed by Hector.

Peisandros—A suitor of Penelope.

Peisenor—Herald for the Ithacan assembly.

Peisistratos—Son of Nestor who befriends Telemachus on his visit to Pylos.

Peleus—King of the Myrmidons in Thessaly, he marries the goddess Thetis and has Achilles as his son.

Penelope—Daughter of Ikarios of Sparta and the nymph Periboea, cousin of Helen and Klytaimnestra, wife of Odysseus, and mother of Telemachus. In most versions of the story, she remained faithful to Odysseus and resisted the suitors' demands that she marry or take lovers.

Pentilesia—Queen of the Amazons.

Perimedes—An Ithacan soldier lost on the return from Troy.

Perseus—Famous Greek hero who lived before the time of Odysseus.

Phemios—The bard whom the suitors forced to play for them.

Philoctetes—Wounded by a snake as he prayed on the island of Tenedos, he was abandoned by the Greeks on the island of Lemnos because his wound was unhealable, painful, and foul-smelling. An oracle said Philoctetes and his bow of Herakles would be necessary for the Greeks to capture Troy, so Odysseus and Neoptolemus returned to Lemnos and convinced him to come to Troy.

Philoitios—An oxherd who remained loyal to Odysseus and fought beside him against the suitors.

Pidytes—A Trojan killed by Odysseus.

Pirithoös—King of the Lapiths in Thessaly, he was educated by the Centaurs and had many adventures in the company of Theseus.

Poias—Father of Philoctetes.

Poliporthis—(1) Sacker of cities, a name derisively given Telemachus; (2) In some versions Odysseus and Penelope have a son by this name after Odysseus returns to Ithaca.

Polites—A popular Ithacan soldier lost on the return from Troy.

Polybos—(1) A suitor of Penelope; (2) Father of Eurymakhos.

Polykaste—Daughter of Nestor.

Polyphemos—(1) See Cyclops; (2) A captain of King Pirithoös of Thessaly.

Polyxena—Trojan princess sacrificed by Neoptolemus on the grave of his father, Achilles.

Poseidon—God of water and earthquakes, this powerful Olympian deity mated with many mortal women, and his offspring included the one-eyed giant Polyphemos.

Priam—King of Troy.

Priapus—An ithyphallic divinity of fertility.

Protesilaus—A prophecy said that the first Greek to land on Trojan soil would die immediately. Protesilaus showed his courage by being the first and was slain by Hector.

Pylos—Domain ruled by King Nestor in the southwest Peloponnese.

Pythoness—Priestess who served as a channel through whom the prophecies were received at Delphi.

Quarrelman—The name used by Odysseus when he first met his father after returning to Ithaca and slaying the suitors.

Rhesos—King of Thrace, who came to fight for the Trojans and was killed by Diomedes in the company of Odysseus. An oracle had predicted that if Rhesos's white horses drank from the River Scamander, Troy would never be conquered.

Salamis—The island from which Aias and Teucer came to fight for the Greeks at Troy.

Same—Name used by Homer for the island now called Kephallenia.

Sarpedon—A Trojan and son of Zeus, slain by Patroklus.

Scylla—A monster that devoured a number of Odysseus's men on the homeward voyage.

Scyros—An island in the Aegean where Achilles, at his mother's urging, lived at court in disguise as a woman so he would not have to fight at Troy. Odysseus fooled him into showing himself a warrior. Later Odysseus came to this island to bring Neoptolemus to Troy.

Sirens—Monsters who devoured sailors tempted by their beautiful singing. Odysseus plugged the ears of his crew with wax and had himself tied to the mast so he could hear the Sirens' singing.

Sisyphus—A King of Corinth whom some claim was the father of Odysseus. His punishment for many misdeeds, including defiance of death itself, was continually to roll a rock up a mountain only to have it roll down again and have to start over.

Skaean Gate—One of the gates to the city of Troy.

Sokos—Trojan who wounded Odysseus before being killed by him.

Sparta—Domain ruled by Menelaos and Helen.

Strife—See Quarrelman.

Teiresias—A seer whom Odysseus sought out in the Underworld to direct him homeward to Ithaca. Teiresias foresaw the death of the suitors. He advised Odysseus to go inland to sacrifice to Poseidon and then to make additional sacrifices on Ithaca. If Odysseus did this, Teiresias said he would live in peace on Ithaca and die a painless death in old age.

Telegonus—In some versions, the son of Odysseus and Circe.

Telemachus—Son of Odysseus and Penelope.

Telemon—King of Salamis, father of the greater Aias. He refused to allow his younger son, Teucer, to return to Salamis after the Trojan war because Teucer had not prevented the suicide of Aias.

Tenedos—Close to the shores of Troy, this island hid the Greek fleet while the Trojans brought the wooden horse into the city.

Terkias—Father of Phemios.

Thermodon River—A river in Cappadocia, the homeland of the Amazons.

Theseus—Famous Greek hero of the generation before Odysseus.

Thesprotia—A part of the mainland to the northeast of Ithaca.

Thesprotians—The people of Thesprotia.

Thessaly—Region in which Peleus ruled Phthia.

Thetis—Goddess who was desired by Zeus, but was married to the mortal, Peleus, because of the prophecy that her son would be more powerful than his father. Her son was Achilles.

Thoas—A Greek noble who served with Odysseus at Troy.

Thyestes—Brother of Atreus, father of Aegisthus, and uncle of Agamemnon and Menelaos.

Troilius—A Trojan prince killed by Achilles.

Trojans—The people living in and around Troy, whose allies came from a wide surrounding area.

Troy—Capital of the Troad, a region located at the entrance to the Hellespont on the coast of Asia Minor.

Tyndareus—King of Sparta, husband of Leda, and father of Helen, Klytaimnestra, and the Dioscuri—the twins Castor and Pollux. Helen and Pollux also had Zeus as their divine father.

Underworld—The fearsome domain of the dead.

Zeus—Son of Cronus and Rhea, he reigned over all the Olympian gods and established order with its possibilities both for abuse of power and for justice.

On Wine-Dark Seas:
Sources and Reflections

The author, moved by the energy of an archetype, steals fictions from what is primordial. To claim personal accomplishment is to ignore Jung's dictum: "It is not Goethe that creates *Faust*, but *Faust* that creates Goethe."[1] From an image in a dream, I found myself immersed in imagining the complex relationship between Telemachus and Odysseus after the end of *The Odyssey*. As I worked with *The Iliad*, *The Odyssey*, and the summaries and fragments of the other poems in the Trojan Cycle, I compiled innumerable notes for the novel that became *On Wine-Dark Seas*. Archetypal energy initiated me into a mediumistic creativity. It also brought me a far deeper understanding of the tradition behind the Trojan Cycle.

The Tradition Revealed

Returning to *The Iliad* many years after first reading it, the epic struck me as incomplete. Of course, Hector's death foreshadows the fall of Troy, but I felt how vivid the details of Troy's calamitous end must have been. Nor did *The Odyssey* provide more than the scantiest of background. This is truly curious, when one considers that the plight of Odysseus on his return home stems from Athena's wrath for the way the Greeks pillaged Troy. I sensed a far larger tradition from which Homer (whether male or female, one author or two) had crystallized only two parts. And, particularly in *The Odyssey*, the choice of the episodes to present might easily have been varied without impeding the overall story of the return of Odysseus.

Stanford, in his excellent study of the post-Homeric literature dealing with the character of Odysseus, confirmed my sense of a larger body of stories around the fall of Troy and the return of Odysseus.[2] After Homer had created *The Iliad* and *The Odyssey*, other authors fashioned six more epics (which survive only as fragments) to complete the Trojan Cycle. The creation of the myths composing this Cycle must have taken innumerable generations of refinement as folktales became oral epics and at last were reduced to written form.[3] *The Cypria* tells how Zeus and Themis plan to bring about the Trojan war. At the marriage of Peleus and Thetis, the golden apple of discord leads to Paris's judgment favoring Aphrodite as more beautiful than Hera or Athena. After *The Cypria*, the Trojan Cycle continues with *The Iliad* and then the story of the death of Achilles and the fall of the city of Troy as narrated in *The Aethiopis*, *The Little Iliad*, and *The Sack of Ilium*. Next are *The Returns*, stories dealing with the return home of the Greek heroes other than Odysseus. This is followed by *The Odyssey*. Finally, the Trojan Cycle is completed by *The Telegony*, which tells the story of the life and death of Odysseus after the peace decreed by Athena at the conclusion of *The Odyssey*.

Certainly, Homer worked from a well-developed tradition.[4] Selectivity—not invention—would have been the important test of Homer's genius with respect to action and plot. Vestiges of folktales and variant stories within the tradition remain in *The Odyssey*. Odysseus is a sophisticated example of the Trickster archetype, so familiar in folktales from many cultures.

The Trojan Cycle presents a fascinating question: Did the poems of the Cycle faithfully render the tradition as Homer knew it? To what extent did the later authors who composed the other six epics conform to the body of myth used by Homer for *The Iliad* and *The Odyssey*? I believe that all of the poems except for *The Telegony* did closely follow this received tradition. *The Iliad* organically develops from the story contained in *The Cypria*. The enmity between the Greeks and Trojans is reflected in the presence of Athena and Hera on the side of the Greeks and Aphrodite on the side of the Trojans. This warring of goddesses in *The Iliad* flows from the judgment of Paris in *The Cypria*. Aphrodite rewarded Paris for his judgment with Helen, an earthly Aphrodite. However, his choice also reflects the human struggle in choosing between the warring principles represented by Athena, Hera, and Aphrodite. The consciousness of men—and of gods, since the struggle reverberates on Olympus—is at issue. The goddesses seek to assert their place in a psyche dominated by masculine gods drawn to the transformation of external reality. The judgment of Paris and his subsequent elopement with Helen are necessary precursors to the story of *The Iliad*. This is one proof supporting the conclusion that the action of *The Cypria* arose from the same tradition used by Homer to form *The Iliad*.

The Odyssey similarly offers guides to affirm the poems whose actions precede it. For example, *The Aethiopis* includes the contest between Odysseus and the greater Aias, son of Telamon, for the armor of Achilles and concludes with the suicide of Aias. These events are confirmed in *The Odyssey* by the speech of Odysseus to Aias in the Underworld (Book XI, lines 541–66). *The Little Iliad* includes such events as Odysseus's bringing of Achilles's son Neoptolemus to Troy, Neoptolemus's killing of Eurypylus, Odysseus's mission into Troy disguised as a beggar and his recognition by Helen, and the ploy of the wooden horse. All these events are referred to in *The Odyssey* (Book IV, lines 235–64; Book XI, lines 505–37).

The Sack of Ilium portrays the desecration of the statue of Athena by the lesser Aias, the son of Oileus. This is followed by Athena's anger, which causes her to try to destroy the Greek fleet on its homeward journey. These events are a concrete expression of what Nestor alludes to in *The Odyssey* with some ambiguity as Athena's anger over men who act and think wrongly. He speaks of her determination to punish the Greeks on their homeward journey (Book III, lines 130–85), and Hermes confirms this (Book V, lines 103–11). Odysseus uses great delicacy when he first meets Athena on his return to Ithaca and tells her of his suffering after she abandoned him (Book XIII, lines 311–328). In fact, *The Odyssey* begins at the point when Athena has a change of heart with respect to Odysseus. She pleads with Zeus to allow Odysseus to leave Calypso's island, as if it was only Poseidon who had kept Odysseus from Ithaca (Book I, lines 44–79). But his return has also been prevented by Athena's own wrath, motivated in part by the shameful acts accompanying the Greek victory as described in *The Sack of Ilium*.[5]

In *The Returns*, Athena causes a quarrel between Agamemnon and Menelaos over the homeward voyage, which is also narrated by Nestor in *The Odyssey* (Book III, lines 130–85). Diomedes and Nestor arrive safely home in *The Returns*, while Menelaos reaches Egypt with five ships after losing the rest of his fleet in a storm. *The Odyssey* confirms this in speeches of Nestor regarding who returned safely (Book III, lines 165–85) and of Menelaos regarding his wandering (Book IV, lines 76–93).

It could be argued that the later poems are consistent because they were carefully fit to the relevant facts presented in Homer's poems but did not conform to any other preexisting tradition. However, *The Cypria* is far more specific than *The Iliad* regarding the causes of the war, just as *The Sack of Ilium* is more specific than *The Odyssey* in exploring the wrath of Athena. Also, the events that appear in the other poems but do not appear in *The Iliad* or *The Odyssey* are coherent and organically connected with the events that are confirmed by Homer's poems. While the authors may have added personal variants to parts of these other poems, the overall impact is of a tradition revealed.

The Tradition Defended

In "Tradition and the Individual Talent," T. S. Eliot distinguishes between poets who write from tradition and those who write from personality. The mature poet must possess the historical sense, which is "a feeling that the whole of the literature of Europe from Homer and within it the whole of the literature of his own country has a simultaneous existence and composes a simultaneous order."[6] In part through this awareness of tradition, "the poet has, not a 'personality' to express, but a particular medium . . ."

Why does *The Telegony* feel poorly—or "personally"—grafted to the myths of the Trojan Cycle? Chronologically, *The Telegony* is the last epic to be composed in the Trojan Cycle. Written in two books by Eugammon of Cyrene (fl. 568 BC), it comes nearly three hundred years after Homer. This is hardly a fatal problem, however, since Sophocles, Euripides, and Aeschylus came still later and we find the tradition alive in their work.

The Telegony begins with the burial of the suitors by their kinsmen. These kinsmen then bring a legal action against Odysseus, who consents to be judged by Neoptolemus, the King of the Epirot Islands. The verdict is that Odysseus should be banished for ten years from Ithaca, during which time the kinsmen will make restitution for the acts of the suitors. These payments are to be made to Telemachus, who will be king in Odysseus's absence.

Odysseus then travels to Thesprotia, part of the Greek mainland close to Ithaca, and offers the sacrifices to Poseidon that Teiresias had warned him to give. Marrying Queen Callidice of Thesprotia, Odysseus leads her armies to war. When his period of banishment has ended, he makes his son by Callidice, Polypoetes, king in Thesprotia and returns to Ithaca. Telemachus has been exiled because of a prophecy that Odysseus will die at the hands of his own son. Penelope rules Ithaca on behalf of her second son by Odysseus, whose name is Poliporthis. But the son who kills Odysseus is Telegonus, his son by Circe. Telegonus has come searching for Odysseus and, like Oedipus, kills while unaware this older man is his father. The Greeks believed the spine of the stingray inflicted an unhealable wound. It is with a spear tipped by such a spine that Telegonus fells his father, thus bearing out the prophecy of Teiresias that the death of Odysseus would come off the sea.[7] Telegonus then marries Penelope while Telemachus marries Circe.

The Telegony is not only improbable, but quite ill-fitted to what we know of the tradition from *The Iliad* and *The Odyssey*. At the end of *The Odyssey*, it is Athena who sets the terms of the peace between Odysseus and the kinsmen of the slain suitors. Assuming Athena used a human form to do this, Mentor would be the obvious arbiter. She is in his form as *The Odyssey* ends. It is unimaginable that she would allow any judge, whether Mentor or Neoptolemus, to banish Odysseus for another ten years. Zeus has just advised her to conclude a pact of peace in which Odysseus shall be king forever. Earlier Athena pled with Zeus to allow Odysseus to return home to Ithaca from his captivity on the island of Calypso. Restored to the favor of Athena, Odysseus is scrupulous in following her guidance once he returns to Ithaca. If Athena brought him home to allow him to be sentenced to ten more years of banishment, she would be unlike the Athena found in either *The Iliad* or *The Odyssey*.

Reviewing the assemblies in both epics, such a choice of judge and subsequent trial appears an anachronism more suited to the times of Eugammon than of either Odysseus or Homer. Finley writes:

Historically there is an inverse relationship between the extension of the notion of crime as an act of public malfeasance and the authority of the kinship group. Primitive societies are known in which it is not possible to find any "public" responsibility to punish an offender. Either the victim and his relations take vengeance or there is none whatsoever. The growth of the idea of crime, and of criminal law, could almost be written as the history of the chipping away of that early state of family omnipotence. The crumbling process had not advanced very far by the time of Orestes and Telemachus . . . Had Athena not intervened to close the poem, as she opened it, no human force in Ithaca could have prevented still more bloodshed.[8]

Moreover, the manner of Odysseus's death contradicts the prophecy of Teiresias in *The Odyssey* that Odysseus would have a gentle death. The banishment certainly contradicts the spirit of Teiresias's prophecy which implies death will come after Odysseus has lived a long life among his countrymen (Book XI, lines 90–137).

The marriages that conclude *The Telegony* are striking mismatches. Telegonus would be about seventeen when he kills his father and marries Penelope, who is probably three decades his senior and beyond the age of childbearing. Nor, in view of the struggle between the forces embodied by Athena and Aphrodite in *The Iliad*, would Telemachus forsake Athena to marry Circe. In this predatory goddess capable of transforming men to beasts, we find the aspect of Aphrodite which most opposes her to the virginal Athena.

Of course, *The Telegony* survives only in the form of a summary of its two books, but these observations persuade me that its plot is largely outside the tradition from which the Trojan Cycle arose. Eugammon created his poem from his ego, his will, and his personal ideation.

The Tradition and the Archetype

Yet is all of Eugammon's poem personal? What sources inspired him? Did he perhaps touch some small part of the tradition, despite the personal flourishes that make the poem false? In distinguishing the personal unconscious from the collective unconscious, Jung states that the collective unconscious holds the archetypal imagery, "a potentiality handed down to us from primordial times." Thus, Jung continues, "The primordial image, or archetype, is a figure— be it a demon, a human being, or a process—that constantly recurs in the course of history and appears wherever creative fantasy is freely expressed. Essentially, therefore, it is a mythological figure." This is the power of myth to enthrall us. So, the Trojan Cycle offers a mythic tradition enriched by thematic content that transcends the personal, a content that is impersonal and archetypal. On this level, it has been argued that *The Telegony* reflects a tradition in which the king serves his appointed time and is then sacrificed so new cycles may commence. In much the same way Odysseus allegedly refused at first to journey to Troy, so he refused to sur-render his kingship and his life when the time arrived for him to be the generative offering. This mythologem finds as its psychological correlative the inability of the son to be the father until the father has died.

Goldberg writes of the father's fears as shown in the relationship between Laius and Oedipus:

> This is the story concerning the threat of the next generation which is so familiar in tales about the gods. In man, of course, it is not a question of a threat; sooner or later one genera-tion does overthrow the other. That is why Laius' scheme to remain childless is doomed and Oedipus is born; that is also why in the prophecy about the mortal danger that the child

240

represents, there is actually concealed the desire not to have the child.[9]

But even Graves, who sees Odysseus as the king who refuses to die and let the new reign begin, finds the plot of *The Telegony* perplexing.[10]

Returning to *The Odyssey*, we find this archetypal pattern reflected in Telemachus's state of mind. He feels the suitors are feasting on his patrimony (Book I, lines 230–51; Book IV, lines 315–31). He goes to the courts of Nestor and Menelaos without any expectation that Odysseus is alive, but rather with the belief that his father's death will be confirmed (Book I, lines 354–55; Book III, lines 75–101 and 240–42; Book IV, lines 290–93). Of all the young men who crowd his father's hall, his mother loves him best. So, he naturally takes the bow to attempt to string it and compete with the other suitors to win his mother as a bride (Book XXI, lines 120–35). Only a look from his still-living father prevents him from challenging his father for the throne and hand of Penelope. He is readying himself for a life passage, for that day when his father and his father's generation have vanished from the earth. Then he will be the father and, for the first time, confront the unabated fear of his own inevitable passing.

Odysseus faces a different archetypal struggle. He has identified himself as king and father. Often in *The Iliad* he speaks of himself as the father of Telemachus. As the father, he must prepare himself for the sacrifice of his own life. Resourceful beyond the measure of other men, he struggles against the life passages that will require the death of his ego and finally the death of his body. It is interesting that Odysseus's own father, Laertes, is still alive. Laertes surrendered the kingship for reasons that are not clarified, but instead of dying he lives a life of grieving. He no longer contends for the throne or the queen since he deserts the hall of Odysseus after the arrival of the suitors. In refusing to surrender his life, Odysseus reveals his kinship to Laertes.

The Iliad presents the masculine world of heroic acts and externalized triumphs. But in his triumph in this heroic world, Odysseus commits such violence against his own spirit that he is deserted by the Athena alive within him. Without this connection to his own spirit, his ego is buffeted by fantastical and nightmarish disasters. At last, in the cave of Polyphemos, he discovers that his ego is inadequate to combat the giant monsters of the unconscious (Book IX, lines 105–555).

In that cave Odysseus must not only see his men sacrificed, but also must offer holy wine to celebrate this sacrament. To emerge unscathed, he must change his name and admit to a new identity.[11] His *metis*, his own wisdom and resourcefulness apart from that of his inner spirit Athena, has proven inadequate. He must truly become Nobody, the antithesis of the egoist Odysseus who believed all men owed him hospitality under the laws of Zeus. As Nobody, he must shed the vestiges of his old ego, symbolized by his male comrades who fought beside him at Troy. If he fails to accept himself as Nobody, his unconsciousness, portrayed by the image of the blinded and enraged Polyphemos, will destroy him.

So Polyphemos prays to his violent father Poseidon for the destruction of Odysseus. Nor does Odysseus readily accept the transformation implied by the death of the egoist-Odysseus in the cave and the rebirth of the self-Nobody brought into the light beneath the belly of a ram. On his ship again, the egoist-Odysseus risks all by goading Polyphemos to cast his great rocks. In this assertion Odysseus seeks to resist the ego-death that must come. But eventually, having lost all his men and his connection to the masculine world, he finds himself in another cave—the paradisical cave of Calypso (Book V, lines 201–24). If he chooses, he can remain here forever as an immortal and feast on ambrosia and nectar. At last, he embraces both his death and his rebirth. He refuses this immortality and accepts that he is no god. His inflation has ended. His spirit Athena intervenes to have him brought to Ithaca and disguises him as Nobody for his long-desired homecoming to his hall and his true self (Book XIV, lines 429–38).

Odysseus's slaughter of all the suitors startled me. Why not merely kill Antinoös or a few of the worst among them and receive restitution or even ransom from the rest? As Odysseus entered Troy disguised as a beggar, so he enters his own hall. In both episodes, this duplicity is later followed by a terrible slaughter. But, in contrast to the deaths at Troy, the slaughter of the suitors is sanctioned by Athena. She will not even spare Amphinomos, the finest man among the suitors (Book XVIII, lines 119–157). Graves sees the slaughter of the suitors as another refusal of the sacred king to die at the end of his reign.[12] But, recalling that Odysseus's journey to Troy was the result of his having been a suitor to Helen, I feel this slaughter is the refusal of Odysseus to continue to be a suitor. He slaughters that element in himself that made him crave to be king and marry the earthly Aphrodite known as Helen. In his individuation, he has passed from the outer to the inner life. In the suitors he slaughters the possibilities of what he might have been, the vestiges of the masculine ego that attach him to the world of external triumphs. Now he can seek inwardly for the spirit with which to meet the death prophesied by Teiresias.

Graves points out that twelve men entered the cave of Polyphemos with Odysseus and relates this to the primitive king's reign of thirteen months.[13] Thus, Polyphemos promises that Odysseus shall be the last—thirteenth—to die (Book IX, lines 368–70). After Odysseus strings his great bow, his arrow must be targeted through twelve axe-head sockets if he is to better the suitors in their contest to marry Penelope. Once he passes this test, he begins his killing of the suitors. Likewise, Odysseus gives Telemachus twelve maidservants to slay (Book XXII, 435–45). Twelve months must die by the hand of

Telemachus, and in the thirteenth month Odysseus shall yield his throne at last.

The Odyssey transcends any single interpretation, but the archetypal issues of the succession as both sacred king and father are present. In a literal way, Eugammon engages these issues in *The Telegony*. Our earliest source, Proclus, indicates that in *The Telegony* Odysseus journeyed to Elis to inspect his livestock and then either narrated or heard the story of Augeas. This story portrays a king killed by the king's son in alliance with Herakles. The King's son then ascends to the throne.

Queen Callidice is a new figure in the Cycle. As Queen of Thesprotia, it is quite likely that Odysseus might have encountered her. To meet the tasks imposed by the prophecy of Teiresias, Odysseus had to find a land where men ate unsalted food and knew nothing of the sea. Since no part of Greece is very distant from the sea, this may have been a more formidable task than it first appeared. It would have been sensible for Odysseus to go to Thesprotia, where he had apparently established friendships. In the Pindus Mountains, he might have hoped to find a pastoral people who used no salt and never journeyed seaward.

But what kind of woman would Callidice have been? Her name suggests beautiful righteousness, a combination worthy of Athena herself. Once Odysseus has reentered the favor of Athena, there is nothing in *The Odyssey* to suggest she would again desert him. In fact, wouldn't she certainly be present on his journey to make the sacrifices commanded by Teiresias? From this viewpoint, Callidice is a mortal Athena, just as Helen became a mortal Aphrodite. So Callidice by her name implies that Athena accompanied Odysseus on his journey, whether the ever-near goddess took the form of Mentes, Mentor, a sea hawk, or Callidice.

Next, we have a prophecy that Odysseus will die by the hand of his son, so Telemachus leaves Ithaca. But Odysseus now has three other sons—Telegonus by Circe, Poliporthis by Penelope, and Polypoetes by Callidice. This triad of sons inherits the experience of Odysseus. Poliporthis means the sacker of cities, Odysseus's own epithet. Polypoetes suggests the maker of many things, a name—like all names with *poly*—well-suited for Odysseus. Telegonus means far from the fatherland, an experience drawn from Odysseus's twenty years of war and wandering. These names represent the inheritance Odysseus will confer on Telemachus, whom Athena believes worthy of and able to integrate what his father offers him (Book II, lines 267–95).

Admitting that we voyage here on wine-dark seas, how do we imagine the tradition treating the period of Odysseus's life that *The Telegony* attempts to portray? Certainly, Odysseus journeyed to fulfill the prophecy of Teiresias. Probably he traveled to Thesprotia where the ever-near Athena aided him in the guise of Callidice. Once he had made his sacrifices to Poseidon, he returned to Ithaca to sacrifice to all the gods the pure hecatombs commanded by Teiresias. Living once again with Penelope, he imparted to Telemachus the triad within his own psyche—destroyer (sacker of many cities), creator (maker of many things), and explorer (far from the fatherland). Since having a son brings a man closer to the certainty that his own generation will die and be succeeded by this new generation of his own creating, all fathers die at the hands of their sons. The fact Telemachus lives means Odysseus must die. The sacred king must allow his own sacrifice so the new cycle may begin. If the longevity of Laertes speaks against this, it is because the sacrifice has become ritualized and the death symbolic. So, Odysseus need hardly die from the penetration of a spear barbed by the spine of a stingray. The violence of this unhealable wound is incompatible with the long life and peaceful death prophesied by Teiresias. Nor is this impalement a metaphor for the unhealable

245

wound of consciousness, since Odysseus's death appears to follow quickly after the wounding in *The Telegony*. Then what is the mist-like death that comes so peacefully from the sea (or occurs near the sea)? Could it be a far-seeing vision of other worlds, so absorbing that the struggles of heroes and beggars alike are dimmed as in a mist? With that speculation, I conclude my efforts to seize the tradition that opens beneath and overshadows what we know of *The Telegony* itself.

Or might Odysseus have refused to offer the sacrifices commanded by Teiresias? If he again dared to match his many-sided ingenuity against that of the gods, no doubt he would inspire future writers, such as Dante, Tennyson, and Kazantzakis, to dream of journeys far beyond the stony island of Ithaca.

The Energy of the Archetype

To carry Eliot a step farther, the mature poet becomes mediumistic when he or she contacts an energy that exceeds the personal. This energy comes not from the ego, but rather flows up from archetypal levels of the self. Eliot appears to acknowledge this when he writes, "The progress of an artist is a continual self-sacrifice, a continual extinction of personality." The shattered ego must reconstitute itself from this encounter with archetypal energies. Or, as Eliot writes in *The Waste Land*, "These fragments I have shored against my ruins . . ."

Jung writes, "The unborn work in the psyche of the artist is a force of nature that achieves its end either with tyrannical might or with the subtle cunning of nature herself, quite regardless of the personal fate of the man who is its vehicle." Describing the creative process as an autonomous complex, he continues, "It is a split-off portion of the psyche, which leads a life of its own outside the hierarchy of consciousness."

The author is often shocked and startled by the force and direction of this autonomous part of the psyche. A vivid example in my own experience involved the killing of Eupeithes, father of the suitor Antinoös, by Laertes at the end of *The Odyssey*. In the epic, Laertes glories to find himself giving battle with his son and grandson beside him (Book XXIV, lines 513–25). Athena encourages him to invoke her and Zeus before heaving his spear. He invokes Athena and his cast of the spear impales Eupeithes through the head. In this encounter neither Eupeithes nor Laertes speaks. At this point in my novel I heard Eupeithes curse Laertes, starting, "Goat-griever, isn't it enough that your son took a generation of men to die at Troy?" Laertes responds in kind, "Eupeithes, pirate and slaver, you saved your son from Troy while mine had ten years of war and ten years of wandering." These adversaries speak nearly three hundred words that I had never pre-imagined, but rather received or discovered in a finished form that required no editorial revisions.

This uncanny contact with a force exceeding the personal shows itself in other aspects of the archetypal energies. I found it curious that Eupeithes's epithet for Laertes should be "goat-griever." Why is this so insulting? In *The Odyssey* Laertes has worn a goatskin cowl to show his grieving (Book XXIV, lines 220–38). He may grieve for the death of his wife, Anticlea, or his enforced absence from the hall of Odysseus where the suitors feast, but most of all, one feels, he grieves for his absent son and the lost destiny of his own line. After Odysseus reveals his identity to his father, there is no indication in *The Odyssey* that Laertes will continue to grieve despite the return of Odysseus. But I had the strong impression that Laertes rids himself of this goatskin cowl when he discovers his son is alive. Thus, I wrote, "[H]e pulled the goatskin cowl from his head and cast it down. He spit on it and scuffed the dirt as if to bury it from sight." But I would have found it quite difficult to explain or justify why "goat-griever" should be a term of opprobrium and why Laertes should cast down and defile the cowl as soon as he finds his son is alive.

Later, reading Kerenyi's *Athene*, I found an original passage that explained to me why I had written as I had about the goat-skin cowl. Laertes, Odysseus, and Telemachus are all protected by the aegis of Athena. She is their patroness, their guardian and wisdom-giver. She cares for them far more than other mortals; in turn, they worship her and obey her voice. Given this background, I found a special significance in Kerenyi's Appendix titled "On the Goatskin and the Gorgoneion."[14] Kerenyi describes how the Gorgoneion was created by cutting the flayed skin of a goat, so the goat's head dangled on the wearer's breast. The goat's head would then be decorated and transformed into the horrible head of the Gorgon. Calling the goat by the name Gorgon created "a mythological fantasy-creature." Kerenyi continues: "This avoidance of the animal's name agrees with the strong 'taboo' . . . placed on the goat in the cult of Athene. . . . To Pallas Athene nothing of it at all was offered, since even the spittle of the goat is poison to the olive tree."

This passage reveals the irony of Laertes's goatskin cowl. He is grieving for more than the absence of his son, Odysseus. He grieves for his own desertion by the goddess. He recognizes his foulness in her sight by wearing the skin of an animal despised by her. No ritual rescues this garment from the odium felt toward the goat by Athena. It represents Laertes's admission that he had failed to maintain a proper relationship with the goddess. It brings parallel the story of Laertes with that of Odysseus who suffered an abandonment by Athena for allowing Troy to be ruthlessly pillaged. When Laertes believes himself restored to the grace of Athena, he casts down this symbol and again draws his strength from the goddess.

Kerenyi also observes the dualistic relationship between the goat and the goddess:

It is sufficient here as well, simply to refer to that *odium* behind which may also be concealed a positive relationship to this eagerly slaughtered and joyfully consumed creature. Through ritual, the animal is made *serviceable* to the God or Goddess. Could this not have been the case with the cult of Athene?

The Gorgoneion, the ritualized representation of the goat, presents the terror that is also part of the wonder of both divine and human nature. It is the goddess who initiated this transformation. If Odysseus never suffered the odium implied in the etymological derivation of his name, he would have lost the challenges of his journey with their possibilities for transformation. If Laertes never felt himself odious in his grief for Odysseus, he would never have humbled himself sufficiently to receive the wisdom and strength of the goddess. So, in the relationship of goddess to hero, or man to himself, the goatskin cowl suggests a vision that sees both the terror and wonder of what is.

The energy of the archetype can bring this experience of wonder and terror to the author. Whether male or female, the author working with archetypal energies must be feminine and receptive. Often the content that is to be received feels overwhelming. Faced with a material that is impersonal, the ego becomes acutely and increasingly aware of its own insignificance. The energy flowing from archetypal sources cares nothing for the form imposed on it or the audience that form may find in the world. Jung expresses this as follows: "The impact of an archetype, whether it takes the form of immediate experiences or is expressed through the spoken word, stirs us because it summons up a voice that is stronger than our own."

Art as a Vessel

Archetypal energy offers the dangers of its inhuman or transhuman power. In creating art from such energy, Jung observes, "The experience that furnishes the material for artistic expression is no longer familiar. . . . It is a primordial experience which surpasses man's understanding and to which in his weakness he may easily succumb. The very enormity of the experience gives it its value and its shattering impact." In a sense, the old ego does not survive. It is the lesser and it is destroyed by the greater. Thus, Odysseus is transformed to Nobody by primordial experience inflicted on and integrated into the ego. If Odysseus cannot become Nobody, then he must live a fearful madness in the blind giant's cave.

Art offers the forms for experiences too rapturous and terrifying to be nakedly confronted. The casual reader may form an incorrect impression from Eliot's observation that the artist's progress "is a continual self-sacrifice, a continual extinction of personality." Likewise, Jung writes that the artist seized by the impersonal creative process is "a vehicle and moulder of the unconscious psychic life of mankind. That is his office, and it is sometimes so heavy a burden that he is fated to sacrifice happiness and everything that makes life worth living for the ordinary human being."

The reader of these last two quotations might imagine that the fate of such an artist is hardly to be desired. This viewpoint implies the artist has a choice. But if the complex is autonomous in the psyche, how can the artist have a choice? Isn't it far more accurate to view this energy as irrepressible? If it is to be known, the desires of the individual experiencing this energy will matter for very little.

If no form can be given to this energy, the individual experiences direct contact with the impersonal and inhuman, the godlike and demonic. No doubt saints and madmen are born from such encounters. In this perspective, the sacrifices of the artist are gentled by the fact of the art. Gifted or branded to be medium to an archetype, the individual is without choice. Inflation and psychosis live in the primordial chaos. Our flesh, our thoughts, and our world may be insufficient to contain this elsewhere-originating energy. Faced with such danger, the medium is fortunate indeed to possess a form to temper, mold, and redirect this energy into the human community. To grieve for what the ego sacrifices is to ignore that the forms of the art may have saved the artist from the loss of all humanity. Thus, art becomes the vessel by which the primordial experience may leave the mediumistic artist with both sanity and a profound connection to the life and culture of the times.

Notes

1. The quotations from Jung are drawn from "On the Relation of Analytical Psychology to Poetry" and "Psychology and Literature," both of which appear in C. G. Jung, *The Spirit in Man, Art, and Literature*, trans. R. F. C. Hull, Vol.XX of Bollingen Series (Princeton, New Jersey: Princeton University Press 1966), pp. 63–105.
2   W. B. Stanford, *The Ulysses Theme: A Study in the Adaptability of a Traditional Hero* (2d ed.; Ann Arbor, Michigan: The University of Michigan Press, 1966), pp.81–89. For a discussion of the other poems in the Trojan Cycle and translations of the surviving summaries and fragments, *see* Hesiod, *The Homeric Hymms and Homerica*, trans. H. G. Evelyn-White, No. 57 of the Loeb Classical Library (Cambridge, Massachussetts: Harvard University Press, 1914), pp. xxviii–xxxiii, 489–531.
3   For a thorough discussion of this issue, *see* G. S. Kirk, *Homer and the Epic* (Cambridge: Cambridge University Press, 1965).
4   *See*, for example, "Postscript," *The Odyssey*, trans. Robert Fitzgerald (Garden City, New York: Anchor Books/Doubleday & Company, 1963), pp. 483–87.
5   For an interesting discussion of Athena's anger and forgiveness, *see* J.S. Clay, *The Wrath of Athena: Gods and Men in The Odyssey* (Princeton, New Jersey: Princeton University Press, 1983). Certainly, Odysseus' recognition that he is not a god is one reason for Athena to forgive him and plead on his behalf with Zeus to allow him to leave Calypso and continue home.
6   T. S. Eliot, "Tradition and the Individual Talent," *Selected Essays of T. S. Eliot* (New York: Harcourt, Brace & World, 1964), pp. 3–12. All the quotations from Eliot are drawn from "Tradition and the Individual Talent," which first appeared in *The Egoist* in 1919.

7 *Apollodorus*, trans. J. G. Frazer, No. 122 of the Loeb Classical Library (Cambridge, Massachussetts: Harvard University Press, 1921), II, pp. 303–5, footnote 2.

8 M. I. Finley, *The World of Odysseus* (2d ed. rev.; New York: Penguin Books, 1978), p. 77. This work provides an excellent background to *The Iliad* and *The Odyssey*.

9 Jonathan J. Goldberg, "Reflections on Oedipus," *Quadrant*, vol. 10, no. 2 (Winter 1977), p. 46.

10 Robert Graves, *The Greek Myths* (New York: Penguin Books, 1955), II, pp. 375–76.

11 *See, generally*, Edward Edinger, *Ego and Achetype* (New York: G.P. Putnam's Sons, 1972).

12 Graves, II, p. 374.

13 Ibid., pp. 366–67.

14 Karl Kerenyi, "On the Goatskin and the Gorgoneion," *Athene: Virgin and Mother in Greek Religion*, trans. Murray Stein (Zurich: Spring Publications, 1978), pp. 60–69.

MAPS

The map on pages 256–257 portrays the Mycenean world at the time of Odysseus's return to Ithaca. The map on page 258 presents the island of Ithaca as it is today, with the important sites from antiquity carefully marked. In the time of Odysseus, the island was probably larger, so that the suitors keeping watch from the islet of Asteris would have had an excellent view of Polis Bay.

THASOS

HELLESPONT • Troy (Hissarlik)

LEMNOS

TENEDOS

ANATOLIA

LESBOS

ROS

AEGEAN

CHIOS

LYDIA

SEA

SAMOS

• Miletos

DELOS

CYCLADES

KALYMNOS

KOS

OS

Ialysos

THERA

KARPATHOS

RHODES

CRETE

• Knossos

Phaistos

The Island of Ithaca

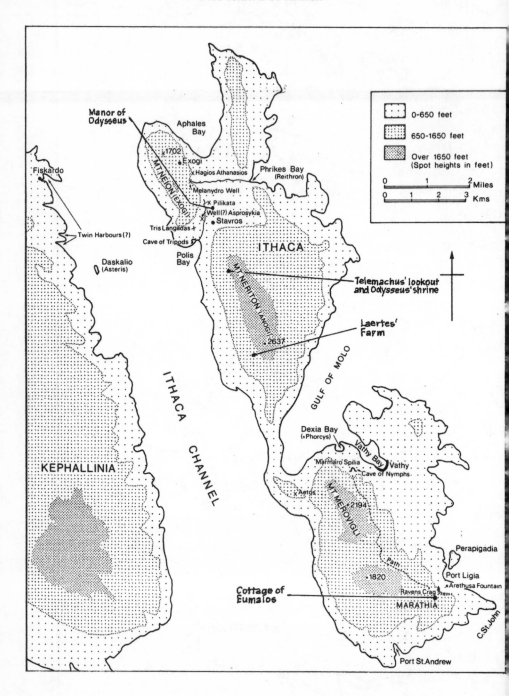

Manor of Odysseus

Aphales Bay

Fiskardo

·1702

MT NEION (EXOGI)

Exogi

x Hagios Athanasios

Phrikes Bay (Reithron)

Melanydro Well

x Pilikata

Well(?) Asprosykia

Twin Harbours(?)

Tris Langadas

Stavros

Cave of Tripods

Daskalio (Asteris)

Polis Bay

ITHACA

MT NERITON (ANOGI)

Telemachus' lookout and Odysseus' shrine

Laertes' Farm

·2637

GULF OF MOLO

ITHACA CHANNEL

Dexia Bay (·Phorcys)

Vathy Bay

KEPHALLINIA

·Marmaro Spilia

Vathy

Cave of Nymphs

x Aetos

MT MEROVIGLI

·2194

Perapigadia

Path

Port Ligia

Arethusa Fountain

·1820

Ravens Crag

Cottage of Eumaios

MARATHIA

C. St. John

Port St. Andrew

0 — 1 — 2 Miles
0 — 1 — 2 — 3 Kms

0-650 feet
650-1650 feet
Over 1650 feet
(Spot heights in feet)